Typewriter Pub, an imprint of Blvnp Incorporated
A Nevada Corporation
1887 Whitney Mesa DR #2002
Henderson, NV 89014
www.typewriterpub.com/info@typewriterpub.com

ISBN: **978-1-64434-076-9**

DISCLAIMER
This book is a work of fiction. The characters, incidents, and dialogue are drawn from the author's imagination and are not to be construed as real. While references might be made to actual historical events or existing locations, the names, characters, places, and incidents are either products of the author's imagination or are used fictitiously, and any resemblance to actual persons living or dead, business establishments, events or locales is entirely coincidental.

THE FIRST 30 DAYS

LORA POWELL

For Kaylyn.
Remember to always dream big.

Trigger Warning:
The following story contains profanities and violence.
Reader discretion is advised.

CHAPTER ONE
Day One

The trail of green slime worked its way down her face, moving steadily closer to her mouth. Like when you passed an accident on the highway and you knew you didn't really want to see any dead bodies, but you still found yourself looking anyhow. I couldn't pull my gaze from the horror unfolding in front of me.

The oblivious mother was at the other end of the cart, throwing groceries onto the belt as fast as her arms could move. Strapped into the seat, the blonde-haired toddler clutched a pink stuffed elephant that was missing an eye and watched me with equal fascination as I showed her. Big blue eyes lit up with curiosity when I shifted my overloaded shopping basket to my other hand.

The thick snot inched closer to her upper lip. I eyed it, not sure if I should say something to the mom. Moms didn't like unsolicited advice, right? Especially from twenty-year-olds who had never changed a diaper in their life.

My inner conflict was resolved when the girl's tongue swept out and the green streak disappeared.

Holding back the urge to gag, I looked anywhere but the kid.

The store was packed.

Why did I always manage to come do my shopping at the busiest times?

You would think I would learn not to shop on a Friday night. The lines were long, resulting in the painful wait behind the snot-nosed kid I was currently experiencing.

A large red sign hanging over the pharmacy advertised flu shots. Glancing back at the girl, I wondered if I should fork over the cash and get one. I never had before, but I really couldn't afford to miss any work, and the news stations were calling this year's flu an epidemic.

The line wrapping around the pharmacy counter was what finally convinced me to skip the vaccine for now. I had already suffered inside this grocery store long enough for one day and that line looked like there had to be dozens of people in it.

Finally, enough room appeared on the belt for me to put my groceries up. Flexing my shoulder, I tried to rid myself of the soreness that my heavy basket had caused. Thankfully, the mother was now blocking my view of her sick daughter.

After a few more minutes spent reading about the new president's policies—policies that had the country melting down—on the tabloids strategically placed at eye level, it was my turn.

"Thank you for shopping with us today. Did you find everything okay?" the bored cashier mumbled as she began scanning my things. She didn't even look up.

"Sure, I . . ." I trailed off. The woman didn't actually care and wasn't really listening. Not that I blamed her.

How many times a day was she forced to repeat that idiotic greeting?

I swiped my card and picked up my bags, stepping into the steady flow of shoppers leaving the store. Out in the packed parking lot, I found my ten-year-old Honda and jumped inside. All I really wanted to do was get home, put my food away, and curl up on the couch in my comfy pajamas. Netflix was calling me.

The house I shared with my roommate was only a few minutes away from the store, and in no time, I was parking my car.

The short driveway barely had enough room for both of our cars, so I parked carefully because I didn't want to bump her car again.

Once done, I lugged the bags up the sidewalk and through the unlocked front door.

"Evie!" I put one armload down long enough to twist the lock behind me. "You left the door unlocked again!"

My roommate was pretty good as far as roommates went, but she frequently forgot to lock the door behind herself, which was a pet peeve of mine.

"Sorry!" Evie's head of red curls appeared at the top of the steps. "I was thinking about what to wear tonight. I must have forgotten." She ducked back out of sight.

Sighing, I carried my bags to the kitchen and dumped them on the small table. Evie was never going to change, and I figured that out at some point during the nearly two years we had lived under the same roof. Restocking my shelf in the fridge with my purchases, I tossed the balled-up plastic bags in the trash and headed upstairs. An oversized pair of ugly flannel pj's, a bag of chips, and binge-watching my favorite pair of brothers were my only plans for the night.

Evie darted out of our shared bathroom, still putting an earring in her ear, and I jumped back to avoid a collision.

"Sorry!" She smiled brightly at me. "What do you think?"

Wearing a slinky black dress that barely covered her backside and sky-high heels that I would be guaranteed to break an ankle in, Evie was dressed for a good time.

"Going out with Austin?"

For once, she was dating a guy that I actually liked. Evie's usual type was jerk.

"Yeah. He's taking me out for our second-month anniversary." She flashed her dark lined eyes at me and grinned.

"You look great, Evie. Have fun." As I was talking, I noticed a Band-Aid in her upper arm. "What's that?"

3

Noticing the direction I was looking at, Evie gasped. "Oh! Thank goodness you noticed. I forgot." Reaching up, she pulled the Band-Aid off. "I went and got a flu shot today over my lunch break."

"I almost got one today too, but the line was too long."

"Yeah. I was almost late clocking back in. It took so long. At least, now I shouldn't get sick."

Three loud knocks on the door downstairs cut our conversation short. Waving goodbye, she rapidly bounced down the steps and I heard the door open. My room was the last door in the hall, and I walked there as I heard her happily greeting her boyfriend.

The next couple of hours were spent drooling over Dean and stuffing my face with junk food. I was sprawled out on our lumpy couch, almost asleep, when I heard the front door opening. Pulled from my food coma, I sat up far enough to see who was coming in over the back of the couch. Only three people had a key: Evie, me, and our landlord. But it never failed to make me nervous when someone came in the door. You could never be too careful.

Austin appeared, an arm around Evie's waist as if he was supporting her as they came into the room.

"Here you go." He helped her into the recliner.

Awake now, I sat up all the way. "What's wrong, guys?"

"Evie's not feeling so great."

"I'm fine. I'm just feeling a little dizzy." She swayed a bit as she attempted to smile at me.

Evie didn't actually look fine. Her normally pale skin looked even more washed out, except for her flushed cheeks.

"You don't look fine, Evie. Maybe we should take your temperature."

She waved my suggestion away. "No. Don't worry. I just need to sleep this off. Must be that danged flu shot. That'll be the last time I get one of those." She looked up to where her boyfriend was still hovering next to her chair. "Help me upstairs?"

4

The two of them slowly made their way up to Evie's room. I was awake now but no longer in a Netflix kind of mood. It wasn't like my friend to get sick.

I picked up the mess I had made in the living room and ran into Austin as he came back down the stairs. He left after soliciting a promise from me to keep an eye on Evie for the night. Not that he needed to ask; I planned to check in on her anyhow, but it was nice to finally see Evie with someone who was concerned about her.

Up in my room, I put away the basket of laundry that had been sitting by my closet for three days, then deciding to check on Evie before climbing into bed. I crept to her door and opened it as silently as I could. I didn't want to wake her up if she was asleep.

Covered with a pile of warm blankets, Evie shifted restlessly but appeared to be sleeping. After sneaking a glass of water and some Ibuprofen onto her nightstand, I quietly closed her door and went back to my own room.

CHAPTER TWO
Day Two

An ambulance siren sounding much closer than usual was what finally pulled me awake. Wiping the sleep from my eyes, I rolled out of bed and went to my window. I had to blink a few times to straighten out my blurred vision, but finally, the ambulance disappearing down the end of our street came into focus.

It was an odd sight.

While I didn't exactly live in a gated community, the neighborhood was quiet. I think the only other time I could remember emergency services on this street was the time Mr. Johnson had a heart attack after shoveling his sidewalk. I really hoped whoever was taking the ride to the hospital this time fared better than Mr. Johnson had.

I stretched my arms over my head, fully awake.

Sleep-deprived was never a good look on me, and I had gotten up a couple of times in the night to check on Evie. She had slept through the night though somewhat restlessly. On my last check, I noticed the fever meds and water I left by her bed were gone. I was happy to see that. I didn't risk actually touching her to know for sure, but the flushed color of her cheeks suggested that Evie was running a fever.

Remembering her state, I searched for the thermometer. I knew that we kept it around somewhere and rummaging in the bathroom cabinet finally produced the elusive object. Walking silently, I went to Evie's bedroom and placed the thermometer along with more water and Ibuprofen next to her, then I shut myself in our bathroom down the hall for my morning shower.

When I turned off the hair dryer, a mild thump from Evie's room told me that she was awake. Throwing on a pair of jeans and a sweatshirt, I opened the door, eager to talk to her and see how she was feeling. The news had been saying that this year's flu was a particularly nasty strain. I was hoping that wasn't what was wrong with my roommate.

Mentally kicking myself for not getting that flu shot the night before, I lightly knocked on her closed door. A groan answered me.

I guess Evie is still sick.

Frowning, I pushed her door open.

"Evie?"

Inside her room was dark. She must have pulled the curtains while I was in the shower.

I could make out her huddled form on the bed and stepped closer to her bedside. "How are you feeling?"

The form on the bed suddenly rolled over.

Flinging one arm over her eyes and the other waving in the air, she groaned again. "Check for yourself."

Her voice came out raspy and strained and, with her waving hand, she pointed toward her nightstand.

Realizing that she was pointing at the thermometer, I picked it up. My eyes practically bugged out of my skull.

105°F.

Was that even possible?

"Evie, I don't think this thermometer is working."

"Oh, it's working. You should feel how I feel."

Reaching down, I touched the back of my hand to Evie's arm. Jerking back in surprise, I just stared at my friend for a few seconds. She was burning up. I had never felt heat like that coming from a person's skin before.

7

"Hon, we need to take you to a doctor."

She weakly waved me off. "No doctor. I can't afford my deductible. I'll be okay. I just need to sleep."

"Evie, a fever this high is dangerous."

"Please let me sleep, Bri," she groaned. "Can you text Austin for me?"

I watched her for a minute, torn about what to do. Evie was really sick, but she was a grown woman too. She had the right to make her own decisions.

Reaching down, I pulled the comforter back over her huddled body. "Okay. I'll text him."

* * *

By midmorning, I was really worried about Evie. She hadn't moved from the position I left her in. I texted Austin, and within twenty minutes, he was knocking at our front door.

"Hey, she's asleep upstairs." I closed the door behind him.

Austin's worried brown eyes met mine before he turned to look up the steps. "Has she been awake at all?"

"Not since earlier this morning. Her fever was really high, but she didn't want to go to the hospital."

I crossed my arms in front of myself. I had been second guessing my decision to follow Evie's wishes all morning.

"Yeah. She's stubborn when she wants to be. I'm going to go check on her."

I watched as he bounded up the stairs, then I went back into the living room and decided to turn on the news. The news anchor was going over the same story that they had been running for a couple of days, urging everyone to get their flu shot. When she started reciting statistics on the number of children who had died already this year, I muted the TV. I already heard it yesterday and didn't really want to hear about dead kids again.

Austin's footsteps coming down the stairs alerted me to his return. "She's asleep." He sat in the chair. "She looks really bad, Bri."

"Yeah. I know. I don't know what to do. She said no doctor, but I've never seen anyone that sick."

Leaning forward, he rested his elbows on his knees. "I think she needs to go to the hospital. She's going to be mad, but I really think it's what needs to happen."

Austin was right, and I knew it. I had been thinking the same thing myself. Luckily, Evie and I went to the same doctor. Nodding, I pulled my phone from my pocket and dialed. She was just going to have to get over being mad because I was making her an appointment.

I sat, impatiently tapping a foot as I listened to the phone ring and ring. Suddenly, the line went dead. Frowning, I redialed. The phone rang for an uncommonly long time again before a stressed-sounding woman finally answered.

"Family Medical Group, this is Lisa. How can I help you?"

"Hi, Lisa. I need to make an appointment for Evie Edwards. She's a patient of Dr. Gordon and she needs to be seen today."

"Ma'am, I'm sorry. Our schedule is full for today." Lisa, the receptionist, didn't even hesitate to deliver the news.

"I know it's short notice, but she really needs to be seen."

Sudden loud talking in the background made it difficult to hear Lisa as she rushed on to say, "I'm sorry. We are already overbooked. This flu is brutal. If Ms. Edwards is really ill, my best suggestion for you is to take her to the ER."

Getting desperate, I tried again. "But I don't think you—" I was cut off by a shrill scream coming through the phone, then the line went dead again.

Who on earth was screaming in the doctor's office?

"She hung up on me," I told Austin incredulously.

9

The two of us just sat there, staring at each other. What were we supposed to do now? If Evie would have been mad over an unplanned trip to her doctor, she was going to go into orbit if we suggested a visit to the ER.

"I don't think we have a choice," I told Austin. "We're going to have to take her to the ER."

I had dialed 911 when a loud thump from upstairs rattled the whole house. Both of us were out of our seats, bolting up the stairs without any thought.

I reached the top of the stairs first and came face-to-face with Evie, who was struggling to walk down the hallway. Swaying on her feet, she trailed one hand along the wall to steady herself as she tried to make it back to her bedroom from the bathroom.

"Evie, are you okay?" I took another step closer to her.

Hearing my voice, she turned drunkenly around to face me, and what I saw made me stop in the middle of the hallway.

Her eyes were glazed over and unfocused. Her gaze was moving around wildly, not able to focus on one place. A thin trail of blood was leaking from the corner of her left eye, and more blood covered her lips and smeared across one cheek.

"I threw up." Her voice was raspy, nearly unrecognizable, and she sounded detached, as if she wasn't really able to comprehend our conversation.

CHAPTER THREE
Day Two

"Evie!" Alarmed, I stood rooted to the spot as I watched my friend sway sickeningly on her feet while her face was smeared with blood.

"What happened?" From behind me, Austin came forward and reached for his girlfriend. I had forgotten for a second that he was back there.

Just as Austin reached her side, Evie's eyes rolled back into her head, and she began to convulse violently.

"Evie!" he yelled as he dropped next to her, trying unsuccessfully to support her jerking limbs.

Still frozen, I watched a dark puddle grow under her twitching body.

"Call for help!"

The order jolted me back to awareness. I bolted back down to the living room where my phone lay when I dropped it just a minute ago. Fumbling with it, I punched the bottom button. My earlier aborted attempt to call for help lit up the screen, and I pushed the final number as I turned and ran for the stairs.

In my panic, I almost couldn't comprehend the drone of the busy signal.

"They're not answering!" I dropped to my knees next to my seizing friend.

Austin rolled her to her side and was doing his best to support her head. The pungent smell of urine hit my nose at the same time I noticed the warmth seeping into my jeans.

"Try again!"

My shaking hands botched the job. Too many nines.

Hyperventilating, I tried again.

The drone of the busy signal was loud in the sudden silence of the hall. Evie fell utterly still and her limbs all fell limply to the floor. The only sounds were my harsh breathing and the frustrating buzz from the phone.

"Evie?" Austin gently rolled her onto her back. "Evie, can you hear me?"

I looked at the chalky complexion of my friend. Her eyes were closed and the streak of blood that had come from her eye smeared all over her jaw line while red-tinged froth dribbled from her slack mouth.

"She's too still," I said the last observation out loud as I leaned in closer to her chest.

"Evie?" With his voice reduced to a near whisper, Austin leaned over her face, then turning his face toward me, he placed his ear close to her nose.

I watched as his already wide eyes filled with horror.

"I don't think she's breathing."

"What!" It came out as a shriek. Grabbing one of Evie's limp hands, I felt her wrist, looking for a pulse, but I couldn't find one. "No. No. No. No!" I chanted under my breath as I dialed the phone again.

Screaming in frustration, I threw the useless phone away from me, and even from the far end of the hall, the busy signal mocked me.

"We need to give her CPR."

Austin looked shell-shocked as he lightly patted Evie's bloodstained face, but hearing my suggestion, he nodded determinedly and tilted her head into what I hoped was the right position.

It had been a few years since my obligatory high school first aid class, and I prayed silently that I remembered it correctly as I clambered into position. I waited for Austin to pinch her nose and blow into her mouth before starting compressions.

Beneath my hands, her body still felt alarmingly hot.

Somewhere in my fourth set of compressions, I felt the sickening crack of a rib giving way under the force of my hands. Bile rose up the back of my throat, but I forced it back. I didn't have time for any of that now. Clinging to the faint memory of the first aid instructor telling the class that broken ribs were to be expected when giving CPR and hoping that it meant that I was doing this right, I kept going. I kept going until sweat dripped into my eyes and my arms burned with effort. I kept going even when sobs started to steal my breath.

My quivering arms were verging on collapse when I saw the glimmer of hope that I had been searching for. In my peripheral vision, I saw one of Evie's fingers twitch.

"There!" I gasped at Austin, who turned his grim gaze in the direction I was looking. I knew the moment he saw it too because an incredulous grin spread across his face.

"Evie, can you hear me?"

We watched as the finger twitched again, followed by the flexing of her whole hand.

"Evie?" Leaning down, Austin pressed his ear close to her nose again. "I still can't tell if she's breathing." He looked at me with a question in his brown eyes.

Any doubt that we had seen her hand move was erased when Evie's limbs all began to slowly come to life. She drew one leg up as her arms searched along the floor until her hand connected with Austin's.

Folding her hand in both of his, Austin stayed close to whisper, "Evie, it's okay. Bri and I are both here."

13

Evie's eyes suddenly snapped open, and I sucked back a gasp. They were completely bloodshot to the point that the whites had been taken over completely by bright red. She rolled her eyes before focusing on Austin, who was hovering over her. Struggling to sit upright, she tugged at the hand that was in his grasp while her eyes focused on his face with an intensity that sent a tendril of unease down my spine.

"Evie, maybe you shouldn't sit up yet. I think you might have a broken rib." I tried to convince her to stay down, but she gave no indication that she heard what I just said.

Her mouth worked but no sounds came out.

Straining to lean closer to Austin, she finally managed to lever herself higher on her arms that didn't quite want to work. Her lips moved again.

"What is it?" Austin leaned down to get his ear closer to her mouth.

Watching the exchange from less than two feet away, a flicker of unease bloomed inside me. The intensity of her gaze that was locked onto his face, plus the workings of her mouth that were starting to look less like an attempt at talking, reminded me of a dog eyeing a tasty bone.

"Austin." A warning tone escaped me. "Something is wrong."

He flicked his eyes in my direction, and at the moment he was focused on me, Evie made one final lunge. I watched in horror as she sank her teeth that were already stained with traces of her own blood into her boyfriend's face.

Yelping, I shot to my feet as Austin yelled out at the sudden pain, then he shoved Evie back to the floor and stood up.

"What are you doing?" He looked at the bloodstained hand that he used to swipe across his wound.

Still staring with that predatory look in her eyes, Evie scrambled to her feet with none of her usual grace, and without hesitation, she launched herself at Austin. In the confined space of

14

the hallway, he had nowhere to escape her attack. Evie crashed into Austin, biting into the arm that he had tried to hold up in front of him.

Growling an animalistic sound that should never have come from a human throat, she released her bite on his arm. She clung in front of him and dragged herself closer as he tried to shove her away from his body. Evie proved impossible to dislodge, and when Austin shoved her broken ribs, she didn't seem to notice what should have been extreme pain as she brought her teeth close to her goal.

Unable to react—either to help Austin or to run—I watched in shock as Evie bit deeply into her boyfriend's neck. In a trance, I watched the horrific amount of blood that immediately covered both of their fronts.

Austin sank to the floor under the ferocity of her attack, and before long, Evie was crouched over his unmoving body.

Guttural growls broke the silence.

Putting one foot behind the other, I started backing away from the scene at the end of the hall, but when my foot found the creaky floorboard, I froze. Hearing the noise, Evie stopped whatever she was doing and went still for a moment, then she slowly turned her body so she could see me standing frozen down the hall. She cocked her head slightly to the side and watched me with dead eyes.

Afraid to move for fear of provoking an attack, I stayed perfectly still.

Evie stared at me for the longest seconds of my life before opening her mouth and screaming a scream that raised every hair on my body.

Bolting toward the nearest door, I catapulted myself into the bathroom. The room was not all that large and offered no escape route, but at that point, all I wished for was a closed door in between myself and the creature that Evie had become.

Hitting the tiled floor, my feet slipped in something slick, and I crashed to my hands and knees. Flipping over, the red of Evie's eyes blazed at me from just a foot away. Her mouth was open wide in mid-scream and bloodstained spit flew out of it.

Reacting on instinct, I kicked the door shut just in time for Evie to crash headlong into it.

Scrambling around, I slammed up against the door, simultaneously reaching to turn the lock.

CHAPTER FOUR
Day Three

I was fairly certain that I had gone into shock at some point. Curled up in the bathtub in clothes stiff with dried blood, I had lost track of time.

When I slammed the door shut and closed Evie on the other side, the flash of relief had been brief when it registered that my hands were covered in a cool, thick liquid. I looked down and saw that I was covered in blood—a lot of it. The slick substance that caused me to fall turned out to be a huge pool of the stuff, which was now smeared around further when I slid and rolled in it.

When Evie said she threw up, she must have meant the pool of blood.

I tried wiping my hands on my jeans, but it didn't help much. They were already soaked in urine and spotted with blood while my shirt was also covered with it—front and back. The ends of my long brunette hair were clumped together and stained red.

I wanted to escape the filth on the floor, but Evie was just on the other side of the locked door, screaming and banging like a crazed animal. Luckily, the tub was clean, so I crawled in there and held my hands over my ears, trying to block out the sounds coming from the hallway.

The light that filtered in through the tiny window slowly changed. At some point, when the glow of the setting sun had lit the bathroom up in hues of orange, Evie stopped her assault on the bathroom door. Terrified to make any noise that would remind her that I was still there, I stayed curled up at the bottom of the bathtub all night.

In the dark of the night, sounds always seemed somehow louder. The muffled footsteps pacing the upstairs hall reached me through the closed door, then a crash came from her bedroom, sounding like the lamp on her nightstand meeting the floor. But the sounds Evie made as she wandered in our home weren't even the worst of it.

Inhuman screams echoed outside the house. The screams had the same animalistic quality that Evie had been making, and there were terrified screams of people under attack. Tires squealed on the pavement. Once, I was sure I even heard gunshots. My normally peaceful neighborhood sounded like a scene from a horror movie.

Through it all, I stayed pressed to the bottom of the tub.

By the time the sun drove the nightmare-inducing darkness back, I was stiff and sore all over. A day and night spent in a bathtub took its toll. I estimated that I had been crouched there for at least seventeen hours. While I was becoming increasingly glad that I was hiding in a bathroom, I also knew that I couldn't stay any longer.

When I pushed myself unsteadily upright, my bloodstained clothes peeled from the tub with a startling noise. I froze, waiting for any indication that Evie had heard. After a few seconds, during which the indistinguishable sounds coming from the far end of the hall stayed constant, I gratefully slid from the tub to the toilet.

My next order of business was getting my hands on some water.

Turning the sink on to barely more than a drip, the job of cleaning dried filth from my skin was torturous. Only once every trace of blood was clear from my hands did I use them to hold water to drink.

With stomach full of water and hands relatively clean, I began to feel slightly human again. Whatever Evie was doing at the end of the hall, she had been at it for some time.

Outside the house, the chaos from the night before continued, though I thought that the screaming was slightly less frequent.

Edging my way to the window slowly, careful to stay silent, I pulled the ruffled curtain aside. My first glimpse of what had been happening outside the house was horrifying.

A pair of bloodstained teens walked down the middle of the street with quick, almost birdlike movements. Their heads jerked this way and that. Down the street, almost out of my view, a house was engulfed in flames. No firefighters were battling the fire. Instead, at least a dozen more people who moved in jerks wandered dangerously near the flames.

A dark stain covered a significant portion of my neighbor's driveway, and a similar stain spread out over the sidewalk. Sticking out from in between a pair of parked cars were jean-clad legs and men's workbooks lying still on the ground.

Another of those haunting screams tore through the morning air, bringing my gaze back to the teenage duo. I watched as they poised perfectly still in the street. Their sudden lack of movement after their odd gaits from before somehow seemed to only add to the creep factor. I felt the hair rise along the back of my neck.

In a burst of flying white fur and furiously running legs, a small dog catapulted into view from the direction they were watching. The shorter teen screamed again as the pair took off with frightening speed in pursuit of the poor animal. With their attention drawn by the commotion, the others who had been circling the burning house also gave chase, and a chorus of screams filled the air.

An answering scream from the hallway made me jump. Pulled from God-only-knew-what she had been up to in the hall,

Evie began pacing again. Her excited, sounding steps passed the bathroom door, and I held my breath and begged silently for her to just keep going and to ignore my hiding place.

With my heart pounding in my chest, I listened to Evie pace the length of the hall several times. Now that she was riled up, she seemed inclined to stay that way. She bumped into things in the bedroom, skittered from one room to the next, and let out several short but hair-raising screams.

What had happened to my friend? I didn't understand the events of the past twenty-four hours at all.

Sinking to the edge of the tub, I tried to come up with a plan. I couldn't just open the door and walk out into the hall. Evie had attacked and, I was pretty sure, killed Austin by biting him. I shuddered at that thought. I did not want to experience that for myself, and if what I had witnessed outside was anything to go by, there were a whole lot more people out there who had been afflicted by whatever was making Evie sick.

I was going to have to wait until Evie left or find some way to convince her to go before I could escape from the bathroom.

I was trying to think over the thumps and screams and to come up with a way to get Evie out of the house without getting myself murdered in the process when an unexpected noise made my blood run cold.

A second voice joined Evie's as she screamed from the end of the hall.

CHAPTER FIVE
Day Four

There were two of them out there—two distinct sets of footsteps, two separate voices, and two people bumping and thumping their way through the upstairs of the house.

I had no idea how a second sick person had gotten in. I was positive that I had locked the door behind Austin when he came over, but a whisper of a voice in the back of my mind told me that I knew exactly who was out there with Evie. The same whisper that had been telling me for a day now that Evie had died. She had been dead and then, suddenly, she wasn't. And her first act upon getting up was to bite someone.

Evie had died and then came back as a bloodthirsty monster.

As much as my mind fought from making that leap, a part of me couldn't deny what was right in front of my face. And it wasn't just Evie. My frequent peeks outside the tiny bathroom window proved over and over again that my neighborhood had descended into madness, and I had no idea how to cope with the thoughts that were whispering through my mind.

An angry rumble from my stomach reminded me that it had been almost two days since I ate anything. At first, terror and drinking copious amounts of water kept my mind off thoughts of food, but nothing was stopping me from wishing for something remotely edible anymore. My stomach cramped painfully, and I had developed a headache that pounded mercilessly inside my skull. It brought into stark reality the fact that I wouldn't be able to wait in this bathroom forever. I was going to have to leave sometime or would slowly starve to death, but if I had been afraid to leave the dubious safety of the bathroom with Evie roaming the halls, I knew beyond any doubt that I couldn't leave with Evie and her plus one out there.

Caught in that conundrum, I waited out my second night in the bathtub. Exhaustion finally caught up with me, and I slept a few hours before jolting awake from nightmares. By the time the sun was fully up in the sky the next morning, I had come up with a plan. It wasn't a good plan, but it was the only one I could come up with.

I took a last look around the small room for anything that may be useful, but there wasn't much. All I had was a pair of scissors in one hand while I stuffed the small bottle of painkillers in one pocket. Other than those two items, the bathroom hadn't yielded anything that I thought would be worth carrying with me. I couldn't see how a bath poufy or nail clippers would help my situation.

I gripped the haircutting scissors in my hand but couldn't imagine actually using them on my roommate even if the whispers in my mind insisted that she was already dead.

Now that I was about to execute my plan, I felt my heart begin to pick up speed. Everything hinged on the first part going exactly right. If I miscalculated or if it just plainly didn't work, I didn't want to think too hard about the consequences.

Evie had always complained that the heating vents in her bedroom and the bathroom were somehow connected. She insisted that my occasional morning singing in the shower came through the vent like I was in the room with her. Now, I found myself hoping that she had not been exaggerating. If I could fool the two of them into going into the bedroom, it might buy me enough time to beat them downstairs and out of the house.

22

Outside, the street appeared abandoned at the moment. My plan actually working also rested on not getting cornered by a hoard as soon as I ran outside. The timing would have to be perfect.

With my heart racing like a thoroughbred, I decided that there wasn't going to be a better time than now. Climbing up onto the toilet so I could press my lips right up to the vent, I began to whisper. The trick would be to attract their attention to the noise in Evie's room without attracting them to the bathroom door.

After a few more seconds of my mumbling, I slightly increased the volume. The pacing footsteps in the hall suddenly stopped. Cringing and hoping that this would work, I kept going. A short yelp sounded right outside the bathroom door. I was just about to abandon the plan as idiotic when whoever was outside the door bolted into Evie's room.

A crash sounded directly on the other side of the wall from where I perched atop the toilet. A guttural growl came through the heat vent, followed by a scrabbling sound against the wall. I kept making noise, trying to decipher if they were both in there. It would do me no good if they weren't both in that room.

A scream blasted through the vent, followed closely by a second. It had sounded like two separate people. I hesitated, panic freezing my limbs, fearful about what I was about to do. More frantic clawing at the wall finally convinced me to climb off the toilet. This might be my only chance to escape the room.

With the scissors gripped tightly in my numbed hand, I crept to the door. I took one last look to the vented wall, and I clicked the lock. As expected, the sound of the lock disengaging was horrifyingly loud, and there was not much chance that they hadn't heard it.

Flinging the door open, I bolted into the hallway and raced for the stairs. Bounding down the stairs, I was nearly to the bottom when there was screaming from the hallway above me. They knew that I was down there. I hit the tile in the entryway, skidded toward

23

my keys that thankfully still lay on the small stand by the door, and hurled myself upon the lock.

My gasping breath started to sound a lot like strangled sobs as I fumbled with the locked door. There was a loud banging behind me, and it cost me precious seconds as I turned to see. Evie, eyes locked on me with frightening intensity, tumbled down the stairs and landed in a heap just a few feet away. Behind her came Austin and my breath caught in my throat at the sight of him.

Covered in blood, his shirt ripped practically all the way off, and he was stumbling over his own intestines as he landed on top of Evie, who was just getting to her feet.

Full on sobbing now, the lock finally gave in to my trembling hands, and I threw myself out the door, slamming it behind me just in time for one of my pursuers to crash into the other side. Spinning around, I clutched my keys and ran for my car. Furious screams rang from inside the house and I was sure they would attract unwanted attention before long.

With my sneakers pounding down the driveway, a movement I spotted from the corner of my eye spurred me on. I clicked the unlock button as I ran, then opened the door and bolted inside. Slamming my hand down on the door lock, I looked through the window as a potbellied man with grey hair and lifeless eyes raced across my lawn and slammed his gore-smeared face against my window.

CHAPTER SIX
Day Four

The man stared through the window with bloodshot eyes. Low growls vibrated from his chest while his hands—stained rusty brown—pressed to the glass. I suddenly wished for the scissors that I had previously been unsure I could use, but I had lost them in my struggle to unlock the front door.

I couldn't stay sitting out in the open like this. My car was effective in keeping out one crazed person, but more would come and I wasn't sure it could stand up to a mob. I was shaking so hard that I missed the ignition the first time I tried to get the key in. The second attempt wasn't much better as a scream from the man a foot away from my ear made me jump.

The third time was the charm.

Thankful that my paranoid visions of the car inexplicably not starting did not come true, I shifted into reverse and backed out of the driveway. The car crunched over the man's foot on the way out and I flinched at the sound, but the guy didn't react. Instead, he just kept pace with my window with an even more exaggerated gait than before.

What was wrong with everyone that made them impervious to pain? Evie had not been bothered by her tumble down our stairs, and whoever this guy was, he didn't even notice his broken foot. And I didn't even want to think about the horrifying injuries I'd seen on Austin.

That word I was trying to ignore whispered in the depths of my mind again. Shifting, I got out of there in a squeal of tires.

It soon became obvious that whatever was going on, it was happening all over town. Everywhere I went, I attracted immediate attention from bloody, screaming people. I was reluctant to actually run anyone over, so I ended up having to drive across the high school football field to get away from a group who almost managed to bog down my car.

It was while I was bumping my way over the track that circled the football field that I realized that someone on the radio might have a clue to what was going on. Blaming lack of food and sleep for my sluggish thinking, I reached for the radio knob.

". . . advise all residents to stay indoors and keep their windows and doors locked. Do not open the doors for anyone unknown or exhibiting symptoms of the virus. The infected are considered highly contagious and contact with blood should be avoided. If someone in your home may be ill, it is recommended they be taken to the nearest emergency treatment facility. Residents should expect to be in their homes for up to two weeks. Water, food, and medications for everyone in your home should be gathered. Check back into this broadcast frequently for any updates."

That annoying beep that always accompanies emergency broadcasts blared as I dodged a woman in her housecoat who was missing a conspicuous amount of flesh from her neck. I was starting to see the validity of the warning to stay inside. Every turn I made seemed to only find more people who wanted to attack me.

I was going to need to find someplace to hide, but where? Going back to my own house was not an option. I didn't have a lot of family members and wasn't close to the few I did have. Plus, none of them lived anywhere nearby anyhow. My friends were limited to work friends. We saw each other five days a week and talked amicably over lunch but that was it. I had no idea where any of them even lived. I really had no good place to go.

Unconsciously, I found myself driving a roundabout route toward my office building. Once I realized where I was headed, I pushed a little harder on the gas. It had been the weekend when this whole disaster started. The building should be empty, and I was one of the employees who happened to have a key to the back door.

The numbers of sick people increased as I drove further into town. Running along and shrieking at each other and me, they drew more attention than I liked. By the time I made the last turn to my work street, there were enough people giving chase to fill my rearview mirror.

I turned toward the alley leading to the back door and realized that it was barely wide enough to fit my car. I had forgotten about the dumpster that all the businesses used back there.

Halfway down the alley, I couldn't drive any further, so I snatched the keys and leaped from the car. The hair-raising sounds coming from the way-too-close-for-comfort mob behind me told me that I had seconds before the first of them reached my car.

I raced toward the plain steel door as the sounds of people bouncing off my car hit my ears. The car would slow the masses down, but it wouldn't be enough. Some of them would still get through too fast. Fumbling with my set of keys for the second time, I tried to jam the right one into the lock, but it wouldn't turn.

Desperately, I pulled the key. It was the right one. I tried again, but it still wouldn't turn.

"Please. Please. Please," I chanted as I wrestled with the key when, suddenly, footsteps pounded on the blacktop.

Looking up wildly, I saw the first of them had edged past my car. I was out of time.

Turning, I bolted down the alley, and with a harsh breath, I ran with everything I had. The alley was full of the typical trash—cardboard boxes that had been broken down and bags of shredded papers but nothing that could help me.

I could already feel my limited energy failing. I wasn't going to be able to keep going for long.

Then I saw it.

Hanging down from the five-story building, just ahead, was a fire escape. Without thinking —there wasn't any time—I raced to the ladder and jumped. Somehow, my hand managed to close around the metal bottom rung of the ladder. The whole contraption lowered with a jolt and a loud crash.

Scrambling, I flung myself as high up as I could reach in one jump. Climbing faster than I had ever climbed a ladder before, I was nearly out of reach when the first person got there. The man's fingers snagged the bottom of my shoe and the sneaker being pulled from my foot nearly had the power to pull me from the ladder. Gripping hard, I hung on until the pull on my foot disappeared along with my shoe, then I continued climbing.

As I climbed up a few more rungs, I risked a look below me, terrified that the people would be coming up the ladder behind me. They weren't but what I did see was almost as bad. Below me, at least a dozen of them stood, most of them perfectly still while new arrivals kept coming and screaming as they found me hanging out of their reach. A dozen pairs of bloodshot eyes stared up with that unwavering focus that I was beginning to recognize. Blood smeared across their cheeks, coated their hands, and ran from a variety of wounds.

Shuddering, I turned away from the sight and climbed the rest of the way to the roof.

CHAPTER SEVEN
Day Four

Climbing that ladder zapped what little strength I had remaining. I tumbled onto the roof gracelessly, grateful to have made the climb instead of falling to certain death below. I hadn't been entirely sure I would make it the last few rungs.

As I lay there panting, I took stock of my situation. I was filthy, exhausted, and starving. A horde of rabid people out on the street wanted to kill me, and I now only had one shoe. On the bright side, I had somehow actually made it onto the roof. Those same rabid people didn't seem to know how to climb, and I happened to know that my fellow employees who smoked in this building tended to wedge the door open so they could easily come up here to sneak a smoke. Management sent out emails about it once a week. Emails that everyone chose to ignore week after week.

Groaning, I rolled to my feet. I was going to be sore after using so many new muscles today. Suddenly, I noticed my knee. Now, I could add a skinned knee to my list of complaints.

When did that happen?

At least, I managed to keep my hands on my keys, unlike the scissors from earlier. The keys were the only possession I still had, and I was reluctant to give them up.

Other than a couple of hotels dotting the landscape and the hospital in the distance, my work building was one of the tallest buildings in the area. The roof was empty except for the lone door

29

and a few huge vents. I had a really great view all around. The noise coming from street level continued to increase.

Looking out, I could easily see that more sick ones were making their way in my direction. Like a snowball rolling down hill, the noise attracted attention, which made more noise, and the crowd was quickly getting bigger.

Individual screams were becoming harder to distinguish in the cacophony of sound.

I was hoping that, like Evie and my bathroom, they would eventually lose interest if they couldn't see me.

The rooftop door was a heavy, security-conscious thing that automatically locked on this side when shut. As I got closer, the peak of a mangled pack of cigarettes that someone had used to stop the lock eased some of my anxiety. At least I wasn't trapped on the roof.

I eased open the door. The stairwell on the other side was pitch-black. Bolstering my courage, I reached inside and felt along the wall where I thought a light switch should be.

Nothing.

My key chain had a tiny flashlight on it. Pressing the button turned on a weak beam of light. Flashing that light all around inside the door, all I could make out was the dingy stairwell disappearing down into darkness. I couldn't see nearly far enough for comfort, but the tiny flashlight would have to do.

Debating with myself for a second, I finally pulled the cigarette pack from the door jam. Just in case someone I didn't want getting into the building made it to the roof. Hopefully, no healthy people found themselves trapped up there, though I doubted that could happen any time soon with the numbers of sick people waiting outside. I stepped inside and let the door swing shut with a solid click.

The blackness in the stairwell was absolute without the sun's light. My flashlight was no match for it, and the already meager beam of light seemed to be losing the battle with the dark. A drop of sweat rolled down my neck as I began descending.

My footsteps echoed in the space no matter how I tried to keep silent. The sound only added to the tension for its unevenness, one foot's sneaker causing an echo, the other silent in just a sock. Walking around in only one shoe was quickly becoming annoying.

By the time I reached the door that would take me to the top floor, my filthy clothes were drenched in sweat and my nerves shot. It had been the longest flight of stairs in my life, sure as I was that at any moment someone would rush up from the darkness below. The door out of the stairwell had one of those long, narrow windows in it. A peek through showed me an open floor plan, the space divided by short cubicles.

There didn't seem to be any movement from inside, and the light coming in through the large tinted windows was a welcome sight. I escaped the nightmare-inducing stairwell and stepped into the light.

The well-worn beige carpet muffled my steps as I prowled the aisles between the cubicles. Short enough that I could easily see above them clear across the large room, they were tall enough that anyone sitting at the work desks would be hidden. My mind played tricks on me, showing me glittering red eyes in the dark spaces under desks, and convincing me that I heard the roll of desk chairs moving somewhere just out of view.

By the time that I had finished searching the office, I had been sure a dozen times over that someone was in the room with me, only to not be able to find anyone. My circuit of the office had brought me back to the area near the door. The only space left to look was the bathrooms.

The men's room was nearest, so I hesitantly pushed the door open. To my surprise, when the lights came on, I found myself in the most utilitarian bathroom I had ever seen—on the right wall, a row of sinks; on the left, urinals followed by two stalls.

31

It took me all of a half a second to discern that I was the only one in the room.

Backing out the door, I reached for the women's bathroom. As expected, the women's room was going to take more than a cursory glance to search. The ante room wasn't large. A red day couch and a fake potted tree stood in the corner. A floor-length mirror covered the back wall. Other than squeezing behind that couch, there wasn't any place to hide in the room. Not leaving anything to chance, I looked behind the couch before creeping to the next door.

In the bathroom, a row of sinks lined one wall, a row of stalls on the other. Every stall door was at least partially closed, causing me anxiety as I moved down the line, bumping each open with the toe of my socked foot. I tried not to think too hard about the fact that I was walking in a public restroom minus a shoe.

The final stall proved to be empty, and I heaved a sigh of relief. The building seemed to be deserted, at least on this floor.

Back out in the office area, I wandered from desk to desk, searching for stashes of junk food that I knew would be in most of the desks. The brief twinge of guilt that I felt at taking the first Snickers bar was quickly buried by my hunger. Before long, I had accumulated enough snack food to stuff myself with and retreated back to the women's bathroom.

The doors to the bathrooms had locks on the inside. Turning the lock, I settled into the couch and wolfed down enough candy to make myself slightly sick. Feeling a little better but completely exhausted, I curled up on the couch and was instantly asleep.

What had to be hours later, I woke up, confused as to why I was sleeping on a restroom couch for several long seconds. Sitting up, the past few days came back to take my breath away. I stumbled to my feet and into the first stall. Still groggy, I splashed some cold water onto my face. It was while I was hanging over the sink, water dripping off my chin, that I heard the voices outside the bathroom door.

CHAPTER EIGHT
Day Five

"There's someone in there."

The low voice carried to where I stood dripping into the white sink. The sound had my head snapping up and my gaze glued to the door. As far as I had been able to discern, the rabid people never spoke actual words. They just grunted, growled, and screamed. Intelligent conversation meant hopefully sane and safe company.

Unevenly walking to the bathroom door, I stopped to try to listen to the whispered conversation happening on the other side. All I could catch was a word here and there. It was not nearly enough to follow what was being said. I hesitated with my hand on the lock, the urge to be with other people somewhat tempered by the knowledge that they were strangers.

The whispering on the other side of the door continued. The desire to finally not be alone in whatever was going on won out. I turned the lock and pushed the door open.

"Whoa! Look out!"

"It's coming out!"

Two distinctly male voices shouted over each other. Frozen in the partially opened door by the sight of someone fifty pounds heavier than me brandishing a baseball bat, I cringed and waited for the inevitable sound of my own skull caving in.

When the impact didn't come, I warily cracked an eye open. Standing a few feet away, the two men stared back at me with a mix of alarm and disbelief.

"That was close." The thin one looked rapidly between the still raised bat and me.

"Jesus! Don't pop out at someone like that, especially looking like one of them!" Bat-wielding guy's shoulders slumped, and he glared as he gestured with the bat in my direction.

Reflexively I looked down. The days-old blood covering most of my clothes turned a rusty brown. The long strands of my hair hung in clumps, matted with dried blood and greasy from going half a week without a shower. My missing shoe caused me to limp.

I rubbed my damp palms on my jeans, uncomfortable with the realization that I looked disturbingly similar to Evie the last time I'd seen her.

"Um, hi." I had no idea what to say.

Bat guy snorted. "Hi? I almost killed you!" He began pacing in the circle of light cast by the bright bathroom lights. That was the first I noticed that it was very dark in the office, no sunlight coming in through the wall of windows. I had been asleep for a long time. "Where did you come from, anyway?"

I looked between the two men, confused by the hostile reaction I was getting from the one with the bat.

Seeing my look, the other one told me, "We've been here since the beginning. Just us. The building was empty. We checked. You startled us when you started making noise in that bathroom. We thought a dead one might have gotten in somehow."

"The roof door is usually unlocked. I work here, and when I needed some place to hide, this is where I ended up. I couldn't go home, so . . . wait, what do you mean dead ones?" I ended my ramble with a question.

"Lady, are you okay?" *Great, bat guy was talking again.* "Were you bitten? Do you have the fever?" The two of them eyed me like I could attack at any second.

Keeping a close eye on that wooden weapon of destruction, I sagged tiredly against the door frame. "I'm not okay." Seeing their alarm, I hurried to elaborate. "I'm so confused! My roommate was sick and then she freaked out and started attacking people. I had to hide in my bathroom for days before I could get away from her, then I got outside and looked for help, but all I found were more crazy people who tried to attack me. They chased me onto the roof. Some of them . . . the injuries they have . . . it's not possible. I just need to know what's going on!"

Bat guy moved a little closer. "But you do realize what's happened, right?" When I just stared at him, he went on. "It's a freaking zombie apocalypse. Those people aren't sick. They're dead. And you don't want them to get their teeth into you. You aren't bitten, are you?"

I slid to my butt on the hard carpet, using my sneaker-less foot to hold the door open. Zombies. It was out in the open, that word that I had been avoiding for days. Now that it was out, there was no putting it back.

"No, I didn't get bitten." I looked up to the two men who had moved to stand nearby.

"That's good. People who get bitten don't make it."

An uncomfortable silence fell then, the three of us staring at each other, no one knowing what to say. When I couldn't take it anymore, I pulled myself to my feet and looked the guys over more carefully. Bat guy was maybe ten years older than me, probably six feet tall, and had the athletic build of someone who worked out regularly. He was wearing sweatpants and a black T-shirt bearing the logo of the gym that was located on the second floor of the building.

The other guy, who was shorter and thinner, had a receding hairline and was wearing typical office attire. I guess their clothing explained what they had been doing in the building in the first place. Bat guy was a gym rat. And the other one was likely working overtime at one of the cubicles currently hidden by darkness.

Despite nearly bashing my head in, which admittedly was mostly my fault, neither of them set off any warning bells for me. And bat guy had a bat. If I was going to find myself stuck with strangers, I could have done worse than these two.

Brushing at the seat of my pants, I stepped away from the door.

"I'm Bri, and I'm really glad to have run into you two. What do we do now?"

CHAPTER NINE
Day Five

Using his bat to nudge the door opened, Shawn led our little group into the stairwell. Behind me, Jack clicked on a flashlight and used it to illuminate a section of the pitch-black stairs.

The guys had barricaded an office on the third floor, and that was where we were all headed. My shoe in one hand and the stolen supply of desk snacks in an emptied copy paper box in the other, we descended two levels. They had told me that they had been systematically searching the whole building for food and water, which was why they had been creeping around the top floor.

This descent was somehow still just as creepy as my first trip down the dark stairs, despite having a better flashlight and not being alone. The absolute black both above and below us caused visions of something just out of view, watching. I was more than relieved to follow Shawn out of that stairwell.

"I'm gonna take a quick look around." Shawn glanced behind himself at us before winding his way into the aisles of office furniture.

Behind me, I heard the lock on the door click into place.

"We always double check that no one else got in here when we've been on another floor. Can't be too careful," Jack explained when he saw me look his way. "The office we've been using is back here."

I stayed close as Jack led the way to the back corner office. The blinds covering the glass walls had been closed tightly, giving the space the illusion of privacy once we stepped inside. A small sitting area sported a leather couch and a pair of matching chairs. A huge wooden desk had been shoved to the far wall and was covered with the variety of packaged food the guys had scavenged. An office water cooler sat next to the desk, the in-use five-gallon jug half-full. Another one, a full jug, sat on the floor.

I watched as Jack went to the blinds over the back wall and pulled them apart just far enough to watch outside worriedly. "There's a lot of them out there."

I couldn't tell if his comment was meant for me or himself. Dropping my box by the desk, I joined him at the window. Jack was right. The street outside was alive with zombies. The light from the moon was enough to show me just how many of them were actually out there.

How had I managed to make it to the building without being trapped?

Lost in thought about my apparently incredible luck, I didn't notice at first that Shawn had come in the office.

I jumped at his voice. "It's clear out there. Did you lock the door?"

"Yeah."

I heard the office door click softly shut and the lock on it turn too. "We try to avoid anything that could draw attention."

Realizing that that comment was directed at me, I let the blind close. Nodding, I turned around to face the men. Propping the bat up by the door, Shawn folded his arms over his chest and stared my way. "We stick to one flashlight at night, keep the blinds closed, and try not to make any noise. We didn't really think there was any way for someone to get inside, but you're here, so I guess we were wrong."

"I locked the roof door behind me." I felt compelled to tell him that I didn't leave the door unsecured.

39

"Good."

"We should check the news again." Jack crossed the room in a few strides and pulled the doors on a cabinet open. Inside was a small flat screen. With a push of the power button, the screen came to life.

"There's still news?" I guess I was surprised to hear it. From what I'd seen, it looked like the city belonged to the dead. I moved closer to the screen.

"Well, there hasn't been anything local for two days, but the last we checked, we could still find working stations from Europe."

The volume was turned down to a level that made hearing the woman speaking almost impossible. The three of us crowded close to the TV, listening to the report.

I had been trapped in my blood-soaked bathroom by my roommate for days, spent I wasn't sure how long driving the ravaged streets of the city, and barely escaped a horde with my life, and I still was shocked by what I was hearing on the TV. It really was the end of the world. Every developed country on the planet was losing the battle to control the outbreak. Third-world countries had reports of zombies too, but slow news reports from those areas made it hard to determine just how bad things were in some areas of the world.

When the exhausted-looking woman on screen reported that the US president was unaccounted for, Shawn reached up and turned the TV off.

"Nothing new."

The guys drifted about the room, helping themselves to the sugar overload piled on the desk and sneaking looks between the blinds now and then. I found myself perched on one end of the couch, thinking about the information that I had been bombarded with.

At some point, the sun rose into the sky, lighting up the office even through the closed blinds. Jack had fallen asleep in one of the chairs, head lolling to the side in a pose that was sure to kill his neck when he woke up. Through the long hours of sitting, I had come to several conclusions.

One, it was a miracle that I was alive. I should have been dead, many times over. And I wasn't about to squander my second chance.

Two, I was glad to have run into the two men. The only thing worse than a zombie apocalypse was being alone *in* a zombie apocalypse. Surviving would take a combined effort.

And three, there was no one coming to rescue us.

CHAPTER TEN
Day Seven

The plan was insane. Why had I allowed Jack to convince me to go along with this suicide mission?

I peered through the door's window, into the first floor cafeteria. Inside, round tables surrounded by ugly grey plastic chairs crowded the floor space. The outside walls were glass, letting in more light than I'd seen in days and giving me a great view of about a dozen zombies wandering the sidewalk with that odd gait they all seemed to have.

Our destination, the kitchen, was behind a wall to the left.

"The electricity is still working. There should be a ton of food still good in the kitchen."

Crowded beside me, Jack looked through the window too. Behind us, twirling that bat in his hands, Shawn looked more than a little skeptical. Now that we were down here, I had to admit that going into an area that we were sure to be seen in seemed like an idiotic thing to do.

"I don't know, Jack. They are going to see us."

"Maybe not."

I peeled my gaze from the window to look over at him. Yesterday, we all raided the locker area of the gym. Finally having clothes that weren't stiff with old blood trumped my squeamish thoughts over wearing someone else's things. I even found a pair of sneakers that were only a little too big. The guys also found something to change into, though Jack ended up less than enthusiastic about the bright red sweats he was currently wearing.

With our mismatched outfits that didn't quite fit, unwashed hair, and the guys' scruffy faces, we resembled nothing more than a trio of homeless people.

"Jack. They are going to see us."

"Do you have a better idea?" He flashed brown eyes first to me, then to Shawn, before looking back into the cafeteria. Neither of us had come up with a better plan and he knew it.

Our pilfered pile of junk food was nearly gone. Even with all of us limiting what we ate, there had only been so much food hidden in the desks upstairs. The real gold mine was just through those doors, in the kitchen that had supplied lunch for most of the employees daily.

The first floor was the one level that had been off limits. The walls were mostly glass, the curtains and blinds had been left open. The roving bands of zombies on the street would too easily be able to see anyone moving around the first floor, but now, the food was running low and the reality that we were about to get very hungry was setting in.

We were going to have to either find a way to get out of the building without getting bitten, or we were going to have to make it into the kitchen.

I sighed. The kitchen still seemed like a better bet than going outside.

"Okay, how do we do this?" I asked.

"I think our best chance is to wait until there are as few zombies out there as possible, then just make a run for it. Once we are in the kitchen, we can stay in there as long as it takes for any of them who see us to lose interest."

Shawn chose that moment to step up right behind us. He looked through the window silently for several seconds. "As long as there doesn't get to be too many at the windows, it should work."

Troubled grey eyes met mine. Neither of us was confident in the plan, apparently.

"Yeah, okay. That's the plan then."

The three of us stayed crowded at the door in the dark stairwell for a long time. The zombies on the street seemed like they would never go away. And then they did.

My muscles, already cramped from standing still so long, tensed. There was only one zombie in view, a teenage boy who had dyed his hair green in life. It was now or never.

Glancing over at us to check if we were ready, Jack reached out and opened the door into the cafeteria.

Moving quickly, in a single file line, we made it most of the way to the beckoning door before the green-haired zombie spotted us. I knew the moment he saw us because my own eyes had been desperately glued to his bloated form every second. The zombie snapped his head in our direction.

His blood-curdling scream carried through the thick glass walls.

"Go, go!" Shawn shoved me from behind.

Stumbling forward into Jack, we bolted as fast as possible through the maze of tables. The kitchen door approached fast but not fast enough.

A spine-tingling thud sounded as the green-haired zombie collided with the glass. Two more thuds immediately followed. Wide-eyed, I watched over my shoulder as more shrieking zombies began to come into view, their attention fixed solely on the cafeteria.

Jack reached the door and ripped it open, diving headlong into the room beyond. I followed him through, and Shawn barreled in last, yanking the door closed behind him.

Inside the kitchen, the lights had been left on. Gleaming stainless-steel surfaces covered the long room. One wall was dominated by a row of ovens, the grill, and what I guessed was probably the door to a walk-in refrigerator.

44

Panting a little, I swung around to try to look out the tiny window high in the door, but Shawn's shoulders were in the way.

"Are we okay?" I needed to know if we had just made a bad situation worse by drawing their attention.

"There's at least a dozen that I can see, but the glass is holding. I think we are okay. We'll just have to stay quiet in here until they get bored." Shawn double checked that the kitchen door was securely latched before stepping away from the door.

I breathed a sigh of relief when he turned around. There could be worse places to be trapped. At least here we had plenty of food.

The shelves in the room had been full when things went bad. Bread and rolls, apples, and bags of chips beckoned. I grabbed an apple, happier than I would have ever thought to see the fruit after days without food, followed by days of just junk food. The first bite into it tasted like heaven. I didn't even care that the fruit was slightly past its prime.

Also crunching on an apple, the bat resting on his shoulder, Shawn wandered between the countertops. He stopped to read a label on a giant-sized box of something before moving on.

Jack grabbed a bag of rolls from its shelf. "I bet I can find something to make sandwiches." He grinned up at us, the first happy expression he had in the last couple of days I had known him, and started toward the big silver door set in the wall.

The fridge door opened with a click. With a bounce in his step, Jack started to step into the dark space beyond.

Our only warning for what was about to happen was the rumbling snarl just moments before a blur of tangled blonde hair launched from the darkness and crashed into Jack.

CHAPTER ELEVEN
Day Seven

A short startled scream ripped from my throat. From somewhere behind me, Shawn started yelling at Jack about not letting her bite him while in front of me, Jack struggled to keep the zombie's face away from his own.

The creature snarled and clawed, teeth snapping together audibly as she did her best to take a bite out of her prey. Standing frozen in the aisle, I watched in horror, the spray of blood when Evie killed Austin playing in my mind.

A hard shove to the side broke me out of the trance I had been trapped in. Dropping his half-eaten apple, Shawn raised the bat as he hurried toward Jack. The zombie paused in her assault, looking up with red eyes and bloodstained face. She hissed warningly, and my blood ran cold.

I thought zombies were supposed to be stupidly single-minded and have little self-preservation instinct? Then again, every zombie movie I ever watched portrayed them as clumsy and slow. The zombies in real life may be less coordinated and capable than before they died, but they were far from slow. Hollywood got it all wrong.

The slow-motion horror scene playing out just a few feet in front of me sped back up. Shawn reached where the zombie was still clinging on top of a thrashing Jack. Releasing her death grip on him, the zombie darted to her feet, eyes locked on Shawn, but it was already too late for her. Yelling at the top of his lungs, Shawn swung the bat as hard as he could, connecting with the matted blonde head as she was rising.

The sickening sound of bat meeting skull was every bit as bad as I had imagined it would be.

The zombie dropped to the tiles with a thud, the muscles in her legs twitching. A pool of too-thin-looking blood began to spread around her cracked skull. Jack shoved away from the body and lurched to his feet. Wild-eyed, he began searching his arms and hands for any signs that the zombie had bitten him.

"Did she get you?"

"I think I'm okay."

Both men spoke at the same time, anxiously checking for broken skin. I was unable to look away from the growing circle of red on the white-tiled floor.

Now that she was still, the zombie was more easily distinguished as a woman who had been around my age. Her long hair would have reached her waist. Being locked in the cold fridge must have preserved her, or maybe she hadn't been dead all that long because she had none of the signs of decay that the zombies wandering outside were starting to show. Not all that long ago, she had been a person. Now, she was a twice-dead monster who hadn't really had time to live her life.

*   *   *

The wide streak of blood left behind when the guys dragged the body to the farthest corner of the room was mostly dry, and so was the spot on the floor that I had cleaned up the best I could after Shawn vomited.

Once the adrenaline started to wear off, he started to shake. Shaking turned into nausea when the realization sunk in: he had smashed some girl's head with a bat. Sure, she was a zombie and she had been trying to kill one of us, but mostly, she still looked like the pretty young woman she used to be. Hitting her went against every decent human instinct.

Skirting the wet patches, I walked to where Shawn was watching the zombies outside through the tiny kitchen door window. Jack leaned against the nearby counter, lost in thought. He had been quiet since the attack.

"How's it looking out there?"

Neither of them looked at me as Shawn responded, "There are more of them. I don't know if they heard us in here, or the ones who saw us are attracting the notice of new zombies, but I think the numbers keep getting higher."

That was not what I had been hoping to hear. We needed the zombies to lose interest and go away so we could take our food and retreat back upstairs. Now that there was a dead body in the corner, none of us was too excited about being trapped in the kitchen.

Wandering back to the counter, I absentmindedly put the bag of rolls back in its place on the shelf. We all seemed to have lost our appetites for the time being.

Shawn's quiet expletive did nothing to help the already tense atmosphere.

"What is it?" Jack finally broke from his trance.

"The window is cracked."

"What!" I hurried back to where the guys were crowded around our only view outside of the kitchen. "Are they going to get in?"

"We need to go. Right now!" I hadn't heard Shawn ever sound as panicked as he did at that moment. "If they get through those windows, we won't ever get back to the stairwell."

"Wait!" Jack grabbed Shawn's arm to stop him from opening the door. "If that many of them see us, they'll come through the glass for sure."

I shouldered my way in front of them and peered fearfully out into the cafeteria. The sight made my breath stop in my throat. Zombies lined up shoulder to shoulder, pressing on the glass as their frightening eyes searched for what had drawn so much attention in the first place. More zombies pushed them from behind in an attempt to see inside. One large pane of glass had a spiderweb of cracks spread across its surface. That section wouldn't be able to take much more.

I looked over my shoulder to the wide eyes behind me. "They're already almost through. It's just a matter of time."

In an unspoken agreement, Jack let go of Shawn's arm. Shawn pushed the door open, and the noise rose to a nearly deafening level. Alarmingly observant, the zombies noticed the movement the second the door opened.

Screams competed with the banging of bodies solidly colliding with the glass. The large panes rattled in their frames under the onslaught. I had just set one foot onto the faded cafeteria carpet when the tinkling sound of glass falling to the floor told me that we were too late. That broken window was much closer to the kitchen door than we were to the stairs.

Reacting on instinct, I spun around and dove back through the kitchen door. Feet crunched across the glass and pounded on the floor as zombies flooded into the cafeteria. Shawn bolted through the door behind me. Gasping for air, I looked out and wished that I hadn't.

Dozens of zombies already made it inside. In the lead, a tall man, who was decayed enough that his skin had sickly black patches, was too close to reaching the still open kitchen door. Yelping, I yanked the door shut.

Seconds later, the first zombie's face appeared in the round window. Nearly eye to eye with the creature, I flinched as it opened its decaying mouth and hissed menacingly. Hands grabbing my shoulders from behind made me yelp again, but I recognized the voice in time to keep myself from reacting more.

49

"Get away from the door!"

Shawn roughly dragged me back until we had one of the large stainless counters in between us and the only entrance into the room. It was while the two of us huddled there, watching the zombies at the door fearfully, that I realized that Jack was not in the kitchen.

CHAPTER TWELVE
Day Seven

I gasped. "What about Jack?" I started toward the door, to do what, I didn't know, but Shawn stopped me with the grip he still had on my arm.

"He's still out there. He ran for the stairs."

I stopped pulling toward the door. The bloodstained hands clawing at the window reminded me that anyone who tried to go into the cafeteria had a grim future.

Where at first the kitchen had been almost peaceful, so long as you ignored the dead body, the noise now hurt my ears. The clanging of tables overturning, bangs of the zombies at the door, and the shuffling of a whole lot of feet only added to the sound. As I listened, one sound distinguished itself from the rest.

I covered my ears in a failed attempt to block the sound of still human screaming.

I dimly realized that tears were streaking down my cheeks but didn't want to take a hand from my ears to wipe them away. Backing further away from the door, I sank to the floor. The panicked cries for help lasted for another minute before fading.

Shawn stayed behind the counter, gripping the bat tightly and watching the door. It didn't have a lock we were able to engage. The zombies didn't seem capable of turning a doorknob, but that didn't mean one of them wouldn't get lucky. If they got the door open, we were both dead.

"We have to find a way out of here."

I looked up from my study of the floor. "How? There's only one door and no windows."

He began looking around the room for any way to escape. We both already explored the entire kitchen. I was positive that the door blocked by zombies was the only way out. I watched Shawn looking around with a sense of helplessness. The situation was worse than it had been when I was trapped in the bathroom.

"I think this is a drop ceiling."

"What?" I looked up to find Shawn staring up.

"A drop ceiling." He gestured up. "It's a false ceiling. Above it is a space that has the ducts and pipes and stuff. It might be big enough for us to crawl up there."

Climbing to my feet, I walked to stand next to him as he assessed the ceiling. Not looking at me, he suddenly climbed on top of the counter and reached up. The ceiling panel lifted up easily when he pushed on it. Shoving the panel aside, he stood up all the way, and his head disappeared into the hole.

Shawn looked at me. "This could work. We'll have to be careful. The ceiling panels won't support any weight, but the ducts and pipes should."

A particularly forceful bang on the door made me look fearfully over my shoulder. The door stayed closed, but the bloodshot eyes of a zombie peered in directly at us. I scrambled on top of the counter.

"Okay. Let's go."

"Try to be quiet. We should be out of their reach up here, but still. Take your time. When we get inside, we will have to find a way out or up."

I was significantly shorter than Shawn, and even standing on the counter, climbing into the ceiling was going to be a challenge. Seeing my predicament, he gestured that he would help me up.

The air inside the ceiling was dusty and stale. The boost helped me climb high enough to be able to perch on a bunch of old-looking pipes. The surfaces that I had held onto to get up there felt filthy. The space was an allergy attack in the making.

The metal infrastructure groaned ominously as Shawn pulled himself into the crawl space, but it held. Holding onto the bat with one hand, I was impressed at how easily he made the climb.

"Now what?"

"I think we'll know when we've found what we're looking for." Carefully, he began to inch his way across the labyrinth of metal.

Right next to the hole that we made, there had been enough light. But I quickly discovered that it was really dark up in the ceiling. The lack of light made our already slow progress even slower. The groaning of the ducts and the commotion from the zombies that was coming from directly below us now had my nerves wound tight. When Shawn accidentally hit something with the bat, the clang made me jump so hard I almost slipped off of the pipes.

"Sorry," he whispered.

I didn't reply. I just concentrated even harder on staying safely hidden in the ceiling.

The smell of decay had been steadily increasing. Before long, I was fighting back the urge to gag.

I didn't know how long we had been navigating through the darkness, but it was long enough that my muscles started to burn with exertion. Crawling along the inside of the ceiling was more physically demanding than I would have guessed. I nearly cried in relief when I heard, "This is it! I think this leads to an air vent in the stairwell."

In the blackness ahead, I thought I could see a relatively large metal duct that ended at a wall. How Shawn knew it led into the stairs, I didn't know. He must have kept a better sense of direction up there than I had. There was just one problem—the metal air duct blocked our way out.

"Okay, but how do we get out?"

"We're going to have to get the duct to come off the wall." He spent several minutes feeling around in the darkness, looking for a clue how to remove the metal. A frustrated sound let me know that it wasn't going well. "It's bolted fast. I can't get the bolts loose."

After a few more seconds, he stopped his search. His vague outline in the dark appeared to turn in my direction. "I could probably get it off there, but it's going to make a lot of noise."

"Do we have any other options?" I was way out of my comfort zone here and had no suggestions.

"We could keep looking, but any place that could be an exit is going to have the same challenges. I'm pretty sure this one leads to the stairs. We could go up, get our stuff, and find a better way out of the building."

I nodded, but then realized that he probably couldn't see me. "Do it."

Turning around so his feet were toward the duct, Shawn got a good grip on some pipes and began kicking at the metal. The noise was awful as he repeatedly hit the duct, and the metal began to slowly warp and bend.

The noise from below, already loud, increased as the zombies were worked up into a frenzy by the noise. They could hear but not see us, and the sounds they made had me readjusting my grip. Falling through the ceiling would be bad.

Starting to huff from exertion, Shawn began to use the bat to pry the metal further from the wall. With a tortured sound, it finally gave way.

The end of the duct fell down, revealing a vent. Dim light and much-needed fresh air streamed in through the holes. With one hard blow, the vent popped free from the wall and clattered to the floor below.

Sticking his head out the hole, Shawn looked around and then back at me. "It's clear. I'll help you down."

The hole in the wall was maybe a foot by two and a half feet. Not that big at all. As I turned around and stuck my feet through, I was suddenly glad for the weight that I lost over the last week. With help, wriggling through the wall and dropping to the floor wasn't hard. My sneakers slapped the hard floor of the stairwell. He was right, and I immediately raced to the door and locked it. Catching sight of me, zombies swarmed the door, and it rattled in its frame.

Inside the cafeteria, not all that far from the other side of the door I was standing at, a red stain spread across the previously clean carpet. A familiar shoe was jostled across the floor, kicked by zombies as they surged in my direction. Pulling my gaze away, I turned back to check on Shawn, still trying to get out of the ceiling. I didn't want to see any more.

CHAPTER THIRTEEN
Day Seven

Shawn's significantly wider frame was giving him problems squeezing through the hole in the wall. Feet dangling toward the floor, he had to work to get his shoulders through. Just when I was starting to worry that he would be stuck, he broke free and dropped to the ground.

He immediately looked to the door where zombies beat on the safety glass. When he took the first step toward it, I stopped him.

"Don't go over there." My voice shook a little. "I already locked it." There was no need for both of us to have nightmares about that shoe rolling around in the puddle of blood.

"Alright. Let's get our stuff and try to figure out how we're getting out of here."

The stairwell was creepy without Jack's flashlight to chase back the darkness. The only light came from the small windows in the door at each new level. We didn't waste time and bounded up the stairs to our floor.

Back in the office, our safe room, I couldn't resist pulling apart the blinds to look outside. Overlooking the same side of the building as the cafeteria, the street below was full of zombies. Attracted by the noise and confusion, more zombies rounded corners and darted up the street on their way to the broken window. "We need to get out of here."

56

"Come on." While I had been looking outside, Shawn threw the last of the supplies we had left piled on the desk into a gym bag. He roughly pulled the zipper and jogged to the door.

As I turned to follow him, Jack's original clothes—washed in the bathroom sink and hung over a chair to dry—caught my eye. I faltered. First Evie, then Austin, and now Jack. Everyone I knew was dying.

"Bri!" The yell from the next room got my feet moving again. I wasn't dead yet, neither was Shawn. But if we didn't find a way to escape the building and it was overrun, we would be next. I caught up with him by the exit to the stairs. "We need to get a good look around. Can we get back onto the roof?"

"Yeah. The door locks from the inside."

"Stay close."

He didn't have to tell me twice as we wound our way back to the heavy door that led to the roof. At the last second, I remembered to jam the cigarette pack back into the lock. Getting trapped on the roof during a zombie apocalypse wasn't high on my to-do list.

A peek over the edge of the roof reminded me that I wasn't all that fond of heights. More than fifty feet below, the zombies crowded the street.

"Don't let them see you!"

The amount of noise coming up from the street made me have to yell to be heard.

Nodding in understanding, Shawn ducked down as he worked his way around the edge of the roof. By the time we made it to the opposite side, I could tell from the noise level that there were significantly fewer zombies down this way.

A look over the wall confirmed my guess. A few of them darted through the narrow alley, but it was nothing compared to the swarm on the other side of the building.

Even so, it didn't really matter. A dozen zombies or a hundred, either way, it was too many. If we climbed down the ladder, the few zombies in the alley would be waiting for us at the bottom. I eyed my abandoned car just up the alley wishfully. I had been hoping that we could somehow make it to the car and drive out of there, but I couldn't see that happening anymore.

Shawn continued his circuit of the roof while I stared forlornly at my abandoned car. Making his way back to where I stood, he looked at me with worried eyes. "I have an idea, but I don't think either of us is going to like it."

That sounded ominous. When I didn't say anything, he continued, "I think this alley is narrow enough that we could lay something across to use as a bridge."

"What? No way!" I started shaking my head, but he cut me off.

"Do you have a better idea?"

I didn't. "What do you have in mind?"

"While Jack," he said, grimacing slightly at that name, "while *we* were searching for food, we found a janitor's closet. There was a long ladder in there. I think it will reach."

I looked across the open space to the roof of the next building over, a full story down.

"Is that even possible?" The idea of falling five stories was almost as terrifying as the zombies.

"I think it's the only way we are getting off this roof."

In the end, he was right. Our best bet for escaping the building was to make it to the next building over. The horde of zombies below was steadily growing. It was only a matter of time before they started finding their way upstairs. When that happened, we really would be confined to the roof. It was better to get out of there before it came to that.

The janitorial closet that Shawn mentioned turned out to be on the fourth floor—the floor I worked on. It was funny. I sat at a desk for nearly two years, just yards from the closet that held the ladder that may save my butt from becoming zombie chow. I had no idea that closet was even there.

Handing me a bundled-up extension cord, Shawn hefted the ladder and started back up to the roof. I decided against asking what the orange cord was for. I probably didn't want to know.

We made a lot of noise going back up. The ladder banged off the stairs and railing in the dark. Each bang made me cringe as I imagined the zombies on the first floor breaking through the door and following the noise straight to us.

The quality of the light outside started to change subtly by the time we clanged our way back to the roof. I silently cursed the failing light. We didn't have a lot of time before we were going to be fumbling around in the dark.

The ladder made a loud sound as Shawn extended it nearly as far as it would go. I wasn't sure how happy I was to see that it did look long enough to reach between the two buildings. A small part of me was still rebelling at the idea that I was about to trust that ladder with my life.

"They've noticed us."

I moved closer to the edge and looked down to where a couple of zombies looked up. Bloody, ragged clothing, and beginning to decompose, they were more frightening than before every time I got a clear look at them. The zombies were doing that creepy, completely motionless stare that they tended to do when they were thinking. I shuddered and turned my attention to Shawn.

He had the ladder across the gap and was tying the world's biggest knot at the end of the extension cord he had wrapped around a rung of the ladder. Moving to a nearby pipe sticking up out of the roof, he tied the cord around that as tightly as it could go.

"That's as good as it's going to get."

We both stared at the ladder for a second. The lightweight metal seemed far too flimsy to hold either one of us.

"Maybe you should go first." Before I had a chance to get offended, he clarified, "I weigh more than you. If I go first and the ladder breaks, you will be trapped up here."

In a kind of twisted sense, his logic was sweet. Dying a slow death trapped on the roof wouldn't be a fun time. At least, if the ladder gave out, the fall would probably kill me.

"Okay," I squeaked. Heart pounding in my chest, I reached for the ladder.

"I'll hold on to this end."

Refusing to look down, I fumbled with trying to figure out how best to cross. The downward angle made it awkward. Finally settling for semi-crawling, feet first, I started across.

CHAPTER FOURTEEN
Day Seven–Eight

A ray from the setting sun stabbed me in the eyes, effectively blinding me, but I wasn't complaining. If I couldn't see, I couldn't see the ground far below or the growing crowd of zombies who tracked my progress with dead eyes.

The ladder shuddered and creaked as I inched past the halfway point. It buckled sickeningly under the strain, but somehow it held. Sweat covered the palms of my hands, and I felt a trickle of it roll down my neck. I barely dared to breathe until my too-loose, stolen sneakers planted on the roof of the next building over.

"Made it," I called across the alley unnecessarily. Shawn had been holding onto the end of the ladder, watching me cross. I took a second to shake out the muscles in my shoulders and gripped my end of the ladder. "Your turn."

I squinted against the sun and watched as Shawn swung the bag of supplies over his shoulder. With a quick look down, he climbed onto the metal frame.

The end of the ladder jerked in my hands, harder than expected. I gripped harder as if I could somehow prevent it from dropping my companion to his death. I suddenly understood why he attempted to tie the other end of the ladder down. Each time he inched farther down, the rung in my hands jumped. I was sure that without the other end being tied, I wouldn't have been able to control my end.

I squinted into the light, my hands clammy and cramping from their death grip as I watched Shawn near the halfway point. The ladder developed a pronounced sway. My stomach dropped as I watched the metal bend further. How far could it go without giving out?

A hiss from below elicited several answering shrieks. We were drawing too much attention. The whole point of risking this rooftop crossing was to stay below the zombies' radar. More and more of them were being drawn to the alley and consequently could see that we were moving to the next building. If the crowd got too big, we would be in the same situation as before, just in a completely unfamiliar building.

"Watch out!"

I whipped my gaze back to find that Shawn had somehow finished crossing while I was watching the zombies watch us. He needed me to move my hands so he could step down.

Breathing slightly easier, I flexed my fingers to restore blood flow. I looked back at the gap between buildings that we had both miraculously survived crossing. The ladder was bent frighteningly.

"Let's not ever do that again, okay?"

"You're telling me." He was already walking toward this building's rooftop door. I jogged a few steps to catch up. "It's locked."

Why couldn't this group of employees have been as careless as mine? The locked door was going to be a problem. I banged my fist on the door in frustration and then jumped back as something banged into the other side. Growling and frantic scrabbling told me all I needed to know about who was making the noise. "Crap."

"Yeah. We'll have to find another way down."

On the far side of the roof, we found what we were looking for. There was a problem though. Zombies roamed the streets. Far too many of them. We were effectively trapped on the roof.

*　　*　　*

It had gotten much colder than I expected overnight. In the pitch black, with clouds covering the moon and the sounds from the undead all around, neither of us managed any real sleep. By the time the horizon began to lighten in the east, there was a marked decrease in the noise from below.

Shivering from the dampness that the early morning dew coated us with, I rubbed my hands together and watched the sun break into view. I had never been happier to see the light. It had been a cold, scary night.

As the sun rose, we edged carefully to the side with the fire escape ladder and looked down. Only a few zombies were in view. They moved along with those birdlike movements, seemingly not focused on anything in particular.

"If we can find a break in them, we might be able to get down and sneak out of here." Shawn was lying next to me, looking out over the edge.

"Then what?" We hadn't talked through the plan further than escaping the building. I was starting to worry. I spent some time driving around the city before. I knew firsthand that nowhere was zombie-free, but I was beginning to worry if my companion really grasped the scope of the problem. He had been locked up in the building since the start. "It's like this all over. We won't last long down there on foot."

"I've been thinking about that. I think we need to get out of the city. Go someplace where there is less population."

"Okay, but how will we get there?"

Looking to his right, he pointed. "Do you see the green Jeep parked at the curb over there?"

If I concentrated, I could make out the back corner of what was probably a dark-green Jeep sticking out around the corner of the building. I nodded.

"That's mine." He pulled a set of keys from his pocket to show me.

I looked back to the Jeep again. It had to be fifty yards from the bottom of the ladder to the vehicle. In a zombie apocalypse, fifty yards felt like a mile. The both of us would have to climb down the fire escape, run the distance, and get inside the Jeep, all before getting caught by any zombies. It seemed impossible.

There really wasn't a better option.

The sun rose, slowly burning away the moisture from my clothes as we lay on the roof, watching for our moment. It seemed like as soon as the few zombies within view wandered far enough away, another one or two would round a corner, and we would be right back to square one. I was starting to think that we would never get a chance to run for it when the final pair of zombies disappeared out of sight.

"Now."

CHAPTER FIFTEEN
Day Eight

The morning dew left the fire escape slippery. Concentrating on moving downward one foot after the other, as fast as I humanly could without falling, left me no time to worry about the zombies that were surely just around the corner.

Eerily still, the usually busy section of the city was a ghost town. The sound of our sneakers squeaking on the metal rungs and the not-so-distant noises from the zombies were the only things breaking the silence.

The light thud from Shawn's landing on the pavement sounded too loud for my hypersensitive hearing. Sure that it would have been heard, I finished my descent frantically. Muscles locked up from nerves, I neglected to bend at the knees and nearly toppled over upon landing. Strong hands pulled me upright by the shoulder and propelled me in the direction of the Jeep.

Down at street level, the smell was intense. A faint odor of garbage and decay plagued us all night up on the roof, but down between the buildings where airflow was restricted, the smell became overwhelming. I tried not to gag as I ran. There was no time to be sick.

The street was stained with dried pools of blood here and there. Trash had been strewn everywhere. A swarm of flies buzzed heavily around an overflowing dumpster.

I missed stepping on a severed hand by inches, the skin mottled and grotesque.

We made it most of the way to the Jeep when the hair-raising scream that I had been dreading sounded behind us.

"Don't look back!" Still gripping my shirt, he pushed me forward when I started to look over my shoulder.

The sound of a third set of feet pounding their way up the street struck me with terror. Never the most athletic person, my near-miss escapes from before taught me that the zombies were really fast. Running from them was not easy.

Beside me, Shawn held his hand out in front of him and pressed the button on his keys. The taillight flashed. Just a few more steps and I pulled the passenger side door open desperately, flinging myself inside. A long second later, the driver's door flung open and the heavy bag he had been carrying sailed across the center console and crashed into my lap, the end of the bat poking me in the side.

Zombies that had been drawn by the commotion banged into the side of the Jeep moments after Shawn pulled his door closed. Decay had truly set in for most of them, and their bloated faces left greasy smears on the glass as they tried to get inside. The zombie that chased us up the street snarled at me without her lips as the engine started and the Jeep bumped through the growing press of bodies.

Transfixed, I watched the one missing part of her face until she became just one of the crowd that was chasing us as we retreated from the city.

I stayed quiet, gripping the bag of our supplies with white knuckles as I recognized that we were working our way toward the highway. At some point, I became aware that I was sitting on a mangled pile of some sort of paperwork, and the floor around my feet was littered with half-empty water bottles. I didn't even care. I was just glad to be in a vehicle and leaving the city.

The streets were empty of other traffic, but they were not deserted. Quiet cursing from my left sounded every time we made a turn onto a street with too many zombies. It was fortunate that we were in a car as we climbed over curbs and plowed through junk to escape being trapped. Winding a circuitous route through the madness, it took twice as long as usual before I spotted the sign for the highway.

We dodged a short zombie and picked up speed on the on-ramp. The highway was just as deserted as the city streets, except with less of the undead wandering around. Occasional cars had been abandoned, but we encountered nothing to significantly slow us down as the miles flew by.

Twenty minutes after getting onto the highway, I finally spoke up, "Where are we going?"

Concentrating on the road, he spared me a glance. "There was this summer camp that my parents used to make me go to each year. It's in the mountains. The nearest town is really small. There shouldn't have been many people in that area when this all started." He glanced at me again. "Do you have a better idea?"

"No. The summer camp is fine." I spent most of my life in one city or another. I had no idea which way to go to find a less populated area.

I fiddled with the radio for a while but found only silence. Even the recorded emergency broadcast from a few days ago was gone. I shifted the bag on my lap to give my side relief from the end of the bat and absentmindedly rolled an empty water bottle from side to side with my shoe. Sliding in my seat, I tried to get more comfortable atop the pile of papers.

The drive was starting to wear on my already-frayed nerves when I felt the Jeep begin to slow down. Lifting my eyes from where I had been watching that water bottle roll under my sneaker, I looked up, hopeful that we were near our destination.

The mountains that had been in the distance were closer now, but that was not the reason we were slowing down. Up ahead,

67

a solid wall of stopped vehicles blocked both lanes of the highway as far as the eye could see.

"What is that?" I asked.

"I think it must be a roadblock. I heard on the TV that they were setting them up at all the state lines to try to contain the sickness."

We rolled to a stop yards from the last vehicle and sat in the Jeep, staring at what was undoubtedly hundreds of abandoned cars. Nothing moved ahead of us except for a single zombie who wobbled on a badly broken leg.

After several minutes, it became apparent that the people who were there before were long gone now. Looking around, I noticed that the other side of the highway, a short distance away across an overgrown grassy center, was completely empty.

"Is there any reason we can't drive on that side?" I asked, gesturing to it.

Shawn looked where I pointed. "I doubt whoever was guarding the roadblock is still there. That should work."

Easing his foot off the brake, he turned the wheel to the left. I noticed as we bumped off the pavement that the grass had been crushed by a few other vehicles that pulled the same maneuver before us.

CHAPTER SIXTEEN
Day Eight

Driving on the wrong side of the highway threw me off balance. A lifetime of sticking to the right side of the road ingrained in my mind that doing otherwise was dangerous. As we rolled along the deserted stretch of pavement, I kept expecting to suddenly find myself in a head-on collision, despite common sense telling me that wasn't likely to happen anymore.

Over on the other side of the road, the line of stopped cars stretched on. A few zombies emerged from the traffic jam as we drove by. Some car doors stood open as if the occupants fled in a hurry, but I didn't see anyone who appeared to still be alive.

We drove for more than a mile before finally coming to the reason for the stopped traffic. Military trucks had been parked sideways, blocking the road just past the next exit. Orange cones attempted to direct traffic down the off-ramp, but stubborn drivers apparently refused to exit, instead of backing up traffic in the long lines of cars we had just passed.

Our side of the highway was open, and we breezed right on by the roadblock. Further up the road, we were forced back to the correct side of the highway when we found the matching roadblock for traffic that had been traveling in the opposite direction. The jam of cars on that side seemed significantly smaller, leaving me guessing that more people had been attempting to run away from the city than toward it.

The landscape around us had been changing. More and more of the view through the windows was filling with trees. The tires hummed along the deserted road, the silence eventually wearing on my nerves. I couldn't remember the last time I had been in a car without music. That was one of the things I noticed about the end of the world; it was quieter now.

A car sat abandoned in the middle of the right lane ahead. The driver door stood open. We hadn't passed any parked cars since the roadblock, and this one stood out for that fact. Shawn slowed down as we drove by, and I pressed my face to the glass, attempting to pick up any clues about whoever had been inside.

The hot pink steering wheel cover and a small stuffed butterfly hanging from the rearview mirror caught my eye as we drove by. There wasn't a person in sight, and I felt a flash of pity for whoever owned the car. Seemingly, she had been female . . . and young. I hoped that she wasn't out there alone.

I looked back to the guy on my left. I was grateful to not be on my own. I doubted I would make it very long without someone to watch my back. We all had to sleep sometime. Now that we were out of the relative safety of the office building, we would have to be on guard every second. And it didn't hurt that fate dropped me in front of someone who had proven capable, with enough decency to team up with a strange woman.

The guys could have chosen to ignore the pitiful-looking wreck that tumbled out of the bathroom. Or worse.

Shaking my head to clear those thoughts, I asked, "Are we close?"

"Yeah. If I remember it right, we take the next exit. There will be a really small town and then nothing but mountains."

True to his word, a few minutes later, Shawn drove down the off-ramp. We slowed down as we entered what appeared to be the main street of the smallest town I had encountered in my life. I wasn't sure it even qualified as a town. Maybe a village?

70

On the right, a long, single-story brick building squatted in a lot of overgrown weeds. A crumbling area of blacktop led to rusted playground equipment. The sign out front declared it to be an elementary school, but by the looks of the place, it had been out of use for much longer than a week.

To the left, a tiny square building was labeled as the post office. Rusty red smears marred the white paint on the door. Next to the post office was a gas station with only two pumps and an attached diner that looked like the type of place truckers would have frequented. The large pane of glass on the front had been broken.

A few small roads, practically one lane and with no lines, shot off left and right from the main road. We passed a fire station, its one bay door open and the truck not inside. A few older houses stood next to a trailer court. That was where we spotted the first group of zombies. There were half a dozen of them, and my stomach clenched as I got my first good look at a small child who had become one of the undead.

She cocked her head and watched our vehicle with the others, then sprinted along behind them as they chased, her too-short legs not able to keep up.

Turning away from the window, I stared resolutely ahead as Shawn stepped on the gas, leaving the group behind. We were abruptly through the town, and the trees closed in around the road. It couldn't have taken more than twenty seconds to drive from end to end, even at a slower speed. He hadn't been kidding when he said it was a really small town.

The road gradually began to incline. Steep, rocky ground rose sharply to our left. The trees were thick and only occasionally broken by cabin-like homes perched on the side of the mountain. The ground on the other side of the road fell away into more trees.

We had been driving for a while, and I was sure that it had to be nearly noon, but the trees blocked a lot of the light. It made it

71

seem much later in the day than it actually was. We traveled miles from that little town when the car finally began to slow again.

"I'm not sure where the turn is," Shawn answered my unasked question when I looked his way.

The first indication that we finally arrived was the large wooden sign partially covered by growing trees to the right of the road. Right below the sign, a gravel road wound through the brush and disappeared into the trees. The gravel crunched under the tires when we made the turn.

A bridge that looked less than trustworthy crossed a shallow stream. I held my breath until we crunched onto the gravel on the other side and looked ahead as we rounded the final turn to our destination.

A low log building was directly ahead, several small cabins flanking it and fading into the gloomy trees. We made it to the summer camp.

CHAPTER SEVENTEEN
Day Eight

The largest of the buildings lay directly ahead. A circular drive passed by right in front of the main entrance, a sign posted on the bulletin board hanging by the door proclaiming that the camping season was only two weeks away. With any luck, there hadn't been anyone living at the campground yet, and there wouldn't be any nasty surprises waiting for us within any of the buildings.

Shawn stopped the car a small distance away from the entrance and the two of us sat there, neither willing to get out of the Jeep until we were fairly certain that we were alone. A tense silence descended as we both looked around. I was looking over my shoulder, back the way that we came, when a short blast from the horn caused me to jump in my seat.

Heart beating wildly in my chest, I glared at him. "What was that?"

He grinned sheepishly at me. "Sorry. Didn't mean to startle you. I just thought that it might be a good idea to make some noise and see what happens before we get out of the car."

"Don't do that again," I said grumpily. Silently, I admitted to myself that it was a good idea. If there were any zombies in the area, they would come running at the sound from the horn and we could drive away, but I wasn't about to admit that to him.

"Sorry."

He didn't really look all that sorry.

After another few minutes, we decided that it was probably safe to get out of the Jeep. There really was only one way to test that theory. Shawn turned the ignition off and grabbed the bat from my lap. "Ready?"

"No." But I reached for the door handle anyhow. We couldn't just sit in the vehicle forever.

The trees surrounding the camp were old. They branched out in a thick canopy, blocking a significant amount of the light. It was only midday, but it looked closer to nightfall. I closed my car door as quietly as I could and stretched muscles tight from the uncomfortable ride. My heart rate, which had calmed down from my scare from the horn, ratcheted back up. I walked around the front of the Jeep and waited for my companion to meet me.

He had been looking carefully around the small clearing. When he joined me at the front of his Jeep, we headed toward the main entrance of the largest building in an unspoken agreement. It seemed like as good a place as any to start.

The main door was unlocked, both a blessing and a possible curse. If the door was unlocked, did that mean that there was already someone here? Or that there had been someone working here at the time of the outbreak, and they now waited for us in some dark corner of the summer camp?

The door pushed open with a creak, revealing a large open room. Round tables crowded the space, each with a half a dozen folding chairs leaning against them. A closed door immediately to our left had a brightly painted wooden sign labeling it as the office. Far to our right, another closed door looked exactly like the one that we used to get into the kitchen at my office cafeteria. It was silent and dark in the room, the light filtering in through the high windows enough to just see by. We were the only things moving.

Moving toward the office door, Shawn listened at it intently before rapping the surface with his knuckles. The sound wasn't loud, but in the silence of the building, I was sure that anything that

74

had been inside the office would easily have heard it. There was no response, and he carefully turned the knob and pushed the door open. Inside was exactly what I would have expected from the office for a kid's summer camp.

A couple of chairs that had seen better days sat in front of a heavy old desk, the top littered with papers. A shelf along the back wall was lined with plenty of well-used books that featured pictures of wildlife and plants on the covers. To the right, an open door was labeled 'nurse'. It was apparent immediately that there wasn't anyone in the office. I edged toward the darkened nurse's room, nightmare flashbacks of the zombie who sprung out of the walk-in cooler at Jack plaguing my mind. I breathed a sigh of relief when I found nothing but a small desk, chairs, and a couch in the room.

We continued our search of the building slowly, afraid at every corner that we would run into someone who wanted to eat us. After a thorough search, the entire building turned out to be empty. I sagged into one of those folding chairs back near the entrance. The day had been an emotional roller coaster, and I was exhausted. I was pretty sure that there were still hours left before the day officially ended.

"This seems like a good place to stay for the night." We kept mostly silent since getting out of the car, but Shawn must have felt that it was safe to speak now that we cleared the building. "We can keep looking around tomorrow, but I think we've both had enough for today."

I didn't argue with him. It had only been a day since we stood in that kitchen and listened to a friend die. We spent every second since just trying to keep ourselves alive, but the loss was beginning to catch up with me. I hadn't known Jack for all that long, but he seemed like a good guy. He hadn't hesitated to welcome me into their small group and did his best to make me feel like one of them. No one deserved to die a death like he had, and I wiped the tear away that managed to sneak past my control, hopefully before Shawn noticed. I had never been someone who cried. I didn't plan to start now.

While searching the kitchen earlier, we noted unopened boxes of muffins and breakfast pastries stacked on the counter. Confiscating one of the boxes of muffins, we retreated into the office. There wasn't a lock on the door, but I figured out how to wedge one of the chairs under the knob. The improvised lock wouldn't keep out a determined attacker for long, but it would slow them down. We each stuffed ourselves with as many of the muffins as we could keep down. They were the healthiest thing either of us had eaten in a week and drank the last of the water that we brought along in the bag. We would have to make finding drinking water a priority in the morning, but for now, all either of us wanted to do was get some rest.

"I'll take the first watch. Get some sleep. I'll wake you up when it's your turn."

Shawn settled into the remaining chair, turning it toward the only way in or out of our refuge and keeping one hand on the bat lying across his knees. He looked exhausted, his clothes dirty, his hair a mess, and the strain of the last week written all over his face. I hesitated, wondering if I should be the one to take the first watch but ultimately gave in to my own need to shut down for a few hours.

The faux leather couch in the nurse's office wasn't the most comfortable place I had ever slept. The material was hard and cold, and it wasn't long enough for me to stretch out completely, but none of that mattered when I curled up on it. Using a blanket that I found folded up in the closet in the corner for a pillow, I was asleep as soon as my head hit the material.

CHAPTER EIGHTEEN
Day Nine

I slept like the dead for long enough that when Shawn shook me to wake me up, the day had long since turned into night. Outside the high office window was the deep black of the middle of the night. The office was pitch-black, causing my other senses to make up for my lack of sight. Quiet noises that I couldn't place came from outside the building from time to time, keeping me on high alert as the endless hours crawled by. If it wasn't for the fact that another person was sleeping on that couch just a foot away in the next room, I might have lost more than a little of my sanity waiting for the sun to come up.

With great relief, I finally noted that the pitch-black outside of that window was turning a deep blue. I concentrated on the gradual change in color, watching as it slowly morphed into dawn.

The light was not as bright as I expected, but the trees stretching their branches over everything in the area blocked a lot of the afternoon sun the day before. So I shouldn't have been surprised. Either way, I was just glad to see the sun.

In the next room, Shawn slept like the dead since he dropped into my vacated spot on the couch. He barely moved. I wondered briefly if I should wake him as the sun rose but decided against the idea. We had both been completely exhausted the day before. Even after sleeping for what must have been more than six hours, I still felt like I could have slept for another entire day. I knew that he must be feeling the same.

I passed the time by poking around the small office. There wasn't much in there that I thought could be of much use for us. I did find a small flashlight in one of the desk drawers that I scooped up and added to our bag of supplies. After the night before, spent sitting in the dark, I was indescribably happy with my find. I was perched on the corner of the desk, slowly picking apart a muffin and eating it while listening to a bird singing loudly nearby, when I heard Shawn getting up in the next room.

He emerged from the darkened room a minute later, still staggering slightly from sleep and rubbing his face vigorously.

"Morning." He didn't spare me a glance as he greeted me with a voice still rough from sleep.

"Morning." I watched as he wandered the office. He checked the chair that was still jammed under the doorknob, stood on his toes to peer outside, and finally stopped his pacing long enough to take a few bites out of a muffin. "Nothing happened while you were sleeping." It was probably unnecessary to tell him this. He would have known if anything went wrong in the night, but I felt compelled to say it out loud. For both of our benefit.

I received a grunted reply as my answer.

Taking the hint, I already figured out on previous mornings that Shawn was not much of a talker when he first got up, so I kept quiet. By the time that he finished his breakfast, he was looking decidedly livelier.

Dusting the crumbs off his hands, he finally looked my way. "We should get busy. We need to find water, and we should take a better look around the camp. Just to be sure that there aren't any nasty surprises waiting out there for us."

I slid off my perch on the edge of the desk, ready to get out of the small room. Being shut in, in the oppressive dark, left me jittery. I was used to more light and freedom, and after nearly an entire day spent in the car just the day before, I was looking forward to being able to move around today. Of course, moving around came with the drawback of having to be on the constant alert for zombies, but way out here in the middle of nowhere, I was hoping that we wouldn't find anything of that variety.

Our first stop was the kitchen, where we made a more thorough search for supplies. It was obvious that the food meant for the campers started to be brought in, starting with the less time-sensitive items. Prepackaged snacks made up most of our find. I opened one cabinet to find giant-sized containers of the powdered stuff that was meant to taste like tea with lemon. I hated lemon tea. And there wasn't any water anyhow.

I tried the faucet, but no water came out. Seeing that, Shawn went to the nearest light switch on the wall. We had long ago agreed not to use lights at night for fear of drawing too much attention, but now, he flipped the switch.

We both looked overhead at the row of industrial lighting that lined the ceiling.

Nothing happened. Looking around, in search of anything that may have been turned on by the switch, I felt fingers of unease furl through me. Nothing seemed to have been activated by his flick of that switch. Striding to a refrigerator near me, I pulled the door open. The inside light didn't activate. While not exactly warm in there, it wasn't as cold as a refrigerator should be either.

"I think there's no power."

With a grim look on his face, Shawn answered me, "It was bound to happen, but I was hoping it would take longer."

I didn't know why it hadn't occurred to me that things like electricity would eventually go away. If there were no one to keep working to provide modern conveniences, those conveniences wouldn't last. I spent my entire life within city limits, comfortably surrounded by things like electricity and running water. I couldn't fathom living without a flushing toilet.

Disappointed by our overall lack of success in searching the main building, by mid-morning, we moved our search to the

79

smaller outbuildings scattered across the grounds. They had, so far, proven to be all exactly the same. It was small with one window and one door and three sets of bunk beds holding dusty mattresses crammed inside. That was it. Somewhere around the tenth cabin, I felt myself losing enthusiasm for our task.

Birds flitted through the thick tree canopy overhead. We worked our way along the string of cabins, heading deeper and deeper into the forest surrounding the camp. To someone who spent some time in the woods before, it would probably have been peaceful. To me, it was anything but. The inability to see more than a dozen yards kept me on edge. I couldn't shake the feeling that there was someone or something out there watching us.

My palms were sweating. Shifting the kitchen knife that I grabbed from the kitchen from one hand to the other, I watched around us nervously. I was so focused on the danger that I feared may be lurking in the trees that I missed the danger that was right under our noses.

Taking the two steps up to the newest cabin door, bat slung over his shoulder by one hand, Shawn reached for the cabin door with the other. He had no more than turned the knob when the door burst open, and a zombie came leaping through.

Knocked off the steps by the force of being hit by the door, Shawn landed on his back in the dirt, a stunned expression on his face. Hissing, tangled hair flying behind her, the zombie landed crouching over him. Shawn's reflexes brought the bat from his shoulder to stop her from advancing any further, but it was at an awkward angle. I could immediately see the strain as he pressed the bat into her chest, just managing to fend off her assault.

I watched the two of them fly off the top step and land in the dirt in shock, unable to believe for a moment what my eyes were telling me. When the zombie let out a terrible scream, inches from his face, the spit visibly flying from her mouth and into his cringing face, it shocked me out of the immobility that held me in its grip.

"No!" I lunged forward, unsure what I was going to do but knowing that I had to do something. I couldn't just stand back and watch as the only friend I had left in the world was killed.

CHAPTER NINETEEN
Day Nine

The zombie clawed at Shawn in her mindless frenzy to kill. Trapped on the ground in a very compromised position, it was taking all his concentration to keep her filthy teeth away from his flesh. Bony fingers topped with ragged nails scratched at his chest and neck.

"Stop!" Rushing forward, I raised the kitchen knife in my hand menacingly. In hindsight, yelling at the zombie wasn't my brightest move. Up until then, she had been focused solely on the body struggling underneath hers, but my yell drew her attention to my approach. Swinging bloodshot eyes my way, she screamed again, making me hesitate.

I never even considered any sort of violence against another person before in my life. Even if the woman in front of me was already dead, I still hesitated to attack her. Taking a weapon and using it against another person went against everything that my life ever stood for.

Apparently torn between killing the body she already had pinned and going for the one standing feet away, the zombie shook her head like a confused dog. She watched me for a long second with unblinking eyes before making her decision.

The allure of prey that she already had trapped proved too much. Dismissing me, the zombie returned to her attack on Shawn. Her momentary distraction allowed him to get a better grip on the bat that he was using to hold her back. Despite her clutching at his shirt with determination, I saw that he was making some progress, driving her face a few precious inches further from his own.

The demonic-sounding hiss that she unleashed raised the hair all over my body. Sweat ran in rivulets, sticking my shirt to my skin and making my already clammy hands slick. Now that I was no longer faced with the dead stare of the woman, I found it somehow easier to readjust my grip on the knife and inch closer. If she wasn't staring at me with those too-human features, I thought that I might be able to do the unthinkable.

"Kill it," Shawn hissed at me when I finally made it into his view.

Looming over the top of the struggling pair, I could clearly see that he was going to lose the battle. It was only a matter of time. The zombie was just too strong. She was unfazed by the length of wood pressing into her chest in a way that should have been painful. She didn't appear tired in the least. Instead, she continued to pull herself toward her goal with determination.

I raised the knife. *Go for the head*, I reminded myself. It was a lesson taught by every zombie movie I ever watched, and only enforced by the things that I had seen in the last week. What should have been mortal wounds to other areas of the body failed to even really slow the zombies down. The only one that had been stopped was the zombie from the office kitchen and only after a hard crack to the head.

Aiming, I brought the knife down.

I learned something at that moment. Putting a knife through a skull was not as easy as it looked on TV. The knife met her head and skidded along the bone with a grinding sensation that made my stomach churn. An ugly gash opened up in its wake, too-thin blood immediately pouring out to run down the back of her shirt.

Swinging around, the zombie glared malevolently at me. Hissing, she let go of where she had been clutching at Shawn's shoulders and twisted her body. I watched with wide eyes as she gathered herself to lunge my way.

I reeled back, trying to get out of her reach but already knowing that I was not going to be fast enough. A hysterical sound escaped my lips as I watched the zombie flying toward me, mouth gaping open and bloodstained teeth on display.

When she suddenly jerked to a stop and flopped unceremoniously to the dirt, I stared uncomprehendingly. I had been sure that those gruesome teeth would be the last thing that I would see.

Shrieking, I watched as the zombie flung herself back around, toward the leg that Shawn managed to grab, stopping her lunge from killing me.

He had had to drop the bat and use both hands to grip her foot. Now, sprawled across the dirt on his stomach, he was in an even worse position than before, completely unable to defend himself in any way.

Still hanging onto her limb, he managed to make it awkward for her to swing around and attack him. That split second, when they grappled for control on the ground, was all I needed. Adrenaline surging, I stopped my backward momentum and flung myself forward. This was it. If we didn't manage to kill this zombie right now, I knew deep in my bones that at least one of us would not be escaping this confrontation still alive.

Raising the knife again, I plunged it with all my strength down toward her filthy head. This time, the blade bit into the bone. The knife sunk into her skull, and the zombie fell instantly limp.

Kicking away from the body frantically, Shawn scrambled backward before managing to pull himself to his feet shakily.

"Holy shit," he gasped as he leaned over, bracing his hands on his knees.

"Are you okay?" I circled the body warily, afraid that it would somehow come back to life and come for me as soon as my back was turned.

Standing up straight again, Shawn began searching his arms for any evidence of a bite. His shirt was torn at the neck, and dots of the blood that I had spilled with my first knife strike flecked the material. Grass stains covered his jeans and his hair stuck up wildly in all directions. He was paler than I had seen him yet, but thankfully, neither of us found any evidence that her teeth made contact with his skin.

"I think I'm okay." He sounded understandably relieved as he patted his hands across his own face.

I felt my shoulders sag at the words. I had no idea how we managed to escape this time without any bites, but I was thankful.

Turning, I looked at the zombie. She was middle-aged. A T-shirt bearing the camp logo twisted around her shoulders. She couldn't have been dead more than a couple of days judging by the lack of decomposition that I noticed yesterday while we drove through the masses of zombies in the city. "I guess now we know that there was someone here." We were wondering since we arrived the day before if there had been anyone else hiding here. Now we knew. I wondered if there had been more than this one woman.

"Thank you."

The quiet words made me look to my side, where Shawn was still standing, staring at the zombie with an unfathomable look on his face.

Finally breaking his stare, he turned in my direction, his eyes meeting mine.

But those eyes weren't what drew my attention. Instead, I felt my gaze pulled toward where the rip in his shirt had shifted, giving me a glimpse of a trio of deep scratches that had been gouged into his shoulder.

CHAPTER TWENTY
Day Nine

The stricken look on my face must have been enough to let Shawn know that something was very wrong.

"What?" He glanced over his shoulder, looked back to me, before finally realizing that I was looking at him, not past him. He looked down.

Reaching to pull his shirt further out of the way, the little bit of color that started to return to his face faded out again. I moved closer but stopped just short of being able to reach out and touch him.

"Are they new?" My voice shook a little.

He didn't answer me. He just continued to look at the lines scratched into his skin, but I didn't need an answer anyhow. Tiny beads of blood welled to the surface of the scratches. They were fresh.

"Um, it's not a bite, so everything's going to be okay. Right?"

"I don't know." His reply was so quiet that I had to strain my ears to hear him, even in the near silence of the trees. "The news said that bites are contagious, but I can't remember hearing anything about scratches."

Suddenly frantic to do something, anything to help, I reached out and grabbed him by the hand. Turning around, I hauled him back the way we had come, pausing long enough to yank my knife from where it was still lodged in the zombie's skull.

"Come on. We need to get that cleaned up."

I kept a firm grip on his hand as we wound our way through the trees, back toward the big building. We left the door closed but unlocked. Shoving it open violently, I kicked it close just as violently and continued to pull my companion behind me. We stormed through the office and into the dark nurse's room.

"Sit," I ordered, releasing the hand that I had doggedly been hanging on to. The squeaky material of the couch alerted me to the fact that he listened to me. Not looking back, I was on a mission. I went to the closet where I found the blanket the night before.

Inside, clear plastic bins held all the basic first aid supplies that a nurse for a kid's camp was bound to need. Looking into the bins, I selected peroxide, antibacterial ointment, and the largest-sized Band-Aid. Snatching a clean-looking white towel from a pile, I took my armload to the couch and dropped it next to Shawn.

"Take this off." I gestured to his shirt. The movement brought my own hands into view, reminding me that they were covered in dirt and zombie blood.

Turning back to the closet, I pulled out a pair of latex gloves. We had no water for me to use to wash the filth off. Covering my hands with the gloves was going to have to do.

When I turned back around, Shawn's shirt was off. Under any other circumstances, I would have instantly become a nervous, babbling mess. I had not been wrong in my earlier assessment that the guy spent some serious amount of time in the gym, but right now, I had tunnel vision, my eyes skipping over all the good parts to land on the scratches that marred his skin.

I used most of the bottle of peroxide, insisting on applying it over and over, hoping that any possible infection would be carried away by the bubbles. A generous layer of the antibiotic ointment and one really large Band-Aid later, I was out of things that I could do to try to fix the situation. Sitting still for the first time since starting on my mission of cleaning those scratches gave me time for it to finally sink in. Both of us hadn't escaped our encounter with camp counselor zombie 100 percent okay.

I felt the familiar burning behind my eyes that told me that I was too close to crying for comfort. Pushing off where I had been sitting next to Shawn, I walked quietly out of the room. I stopped when I reached the door leading outside, well aware that going out there alone wasn't the best choice, even if I was desperately in need of a few minutes of privacy. Leaning dejectedly against the wall, I looked up to get myself back under control.

At some point, I slid down the wall to sit on the hard floor, my back resting against the wall still. Inside those latex gloves, my hands sweated profusely. When I pulled the first one off with a snap, I found that the mud and blood coating it mixed together inside the wet glove. I wiped the muck off the best I could onto my jeans, repeating with the other hand. The idea of having the zombie's blood all over me was making me sick to my stomach.

Footsteps approached as I was concentrating on wiping away as much of the gore from my second hand as possible. I heard a sigh and then the slide of material along the wall next to me. Looking up, I found Shawn, his torn shirt back on, sitting in nearly an identical position to my own. He slid down the wall just on the other side of the door.

I watched him as he contemplated the floor for a while. As the minutes ticked by, I found that I couldn't keep quiet anymore. "We don't know that anything bad is going to happen."

My voice sounded naively hopeful even to my own ears.

He finally turned his head my way. "No. We don't know anything for sure yet."

We lapsed into silence again for a while, both of us lost in our own desperate thoughts.

When Shawn spoke, enough time had passed that it startled me. "Have you seen it happen?"

I knew instantly what he meant. He wanted to know if I watched anyone die from the infection before. I cleared the sudden lump in my throat as I thought about my dead friend. "Yeah."

He was quiet for a moment and then said, "I haven't."

I looked over in surprise, wondering how anyone still alive at this point managed to not see anyone be killed by that horrible virus or whatever it was.

"I don't really have any family or anything like that." He shrugged. "I heard the news reports the first day, but I didn't see any of it personally. I thought they must have been blowing the whole thing way out of proportion. I mean, who would believe this if they didn't see it? I decided to go to the gym late that night. There wasn't anyone around. When I went to leave, a zombie was waiting at the front door for me. He scared the crap out of me, and I decided to go back upstairs and wait for him to go away. Obviously, I never made it out of the building until you and I went to the roof." He lapsed into another silence while I digested what he just told me. Looking back at the floor, he mumbled, "What's it like?"

That lump in my throat was back in full force. Sliding sideways, I didn't stop until my shoulder rested lightly against his. "It shouldn't be long. If you're going to get sick, we'll know."

CHAPTER TWENTY-ONE
Day Nine–Ten

Thirst was what finally drove me from my position on the floor. The light coming in from outside that was already weakened by the thick trees started to grow dimmer. Shawn and I spent hours sitting there . . . waiting.

"How does it feel?" I gestured toward Shawn's shoulder.

He hadn't said anything since asking me about death by the virus.

Raising a hand, he gingerly touched over the bandage. "I don't know. I mean, it feels okay. A little sore."

A tiny bit of hope bloomed in my chest. It had been hours since he was scratched. Maybe you couldn't contract the virus that way. "That's gotta be good."

I had plenty of time to think during those days I spent trapped in my own bathroom and then later in the office. Evie had not been bitten. I was sure of it. She would have mentioned it to me if something as noteworthy as being bitten by another person happened to her. That meant that she had become ill some other way. And the only thing I had been able to come up with after sleepless nights spent wracking my brain was that flu shot.

I knew that Evie had gotten the shot over her lunch break. Early that evening, she seemed perfectly fine, but not long after, she became obviously sick. I figured that it couldn't have been more than eight hours from the time she got that shot until Austin had half-carried her stumbling form back into our apartment.

It made sense. How else had so many people all fallen ill at the exact same time? They had to have all been exposed at about the same time but without a bite. The long lines of people waiting for their flu shot that day at the grocery store haunted me. Had all those people been somehow infected by the thing that was supposed to protect them?

Stiff from the hard floor, I stretched, feeling the crack of my spine as it shifted. Feeling a tiny bit better but still thirstier than I remembered ever being in my life, I looked down to where Shawn still sat on the floor.

"I'm going to see if I can find anything to drink," I said.

Nodding, he climbed to his feet. We had already searched the entire building and had not found any water, but that didn't stop me from looking again. I just couldn't fathom how there could possibly be nothing drinkable anywhere. Especially in a building that was obviously designed to feed large amounts of people. By the time I finished my latest search of the kitchen, disbelief had morphed into worry. We had already gone almost an entire day without water. We were going to have to find some really soon or face dire consequences.

Back in the office that we had claimed as our new home, I picked up an empty plastic bottle and twirled it in my hands as I tried to come up with an idea. We crossed a small stream on our way in, but even I knew that you couldn't just drink water from outside. The risk of catching something was too high. The last thing we needed was to get sick. Going to a hospital wasn't really an option anymore.

"Um . . ." Shawn had been following me around as I searched. I found him staring at the bottle in my hands now. "Out in the Jeep, I know I left at least a few bottles there that I didn't drink all of."

91

My initial reaction was to recoil from the suggestion. I mean, sharing a drink with someone was kind of gross, but feeling like someone stuffed a bone-dry, dirty sock into my mouth had me reconsidering in a hurry. Water from a half-used bottle had to be better than water from a stream, and at this point, those were our only two options. I clearly remembered that there were several half-full bottles of water in the Jeep. They had sloshed and rolled around my feet during yesterday's drive.

Thank goodness he kept his car a mess.

"Okay."

The attack—from out of nowhere—earlier that day left the camp tainted with the feeling of impending doom. And the lack of light didn't help. Stepping back outside had my nerves jangling. I was afraid that another zombie would come bursting around a corner at any second. Luckily, nothing of the sort happened, and I stood watching as Shawn rooted around in his car. When he finally stood back up, arms loaded with his find, we beat a hasty retreat back inside the building. Apparently, I wasn't the only one feeling the strain of being exposed.

Back inside our office, we spread the found water out on the desk. In all, he had come up with seven bottles in varying stages of being consumed. I eyed the water, eager to get my hands on a bottle. I knew I couldn't be the only one that needed it badly, but both of us showed some restraint. We had already begun to learn the value of rationing in this new world.

"How should we do this?"

I thought about my answer for a second. "Let's combine them so we know exactly how much is there." We worked together and, in the end, came up with just under three full bottles of water. "Why don't we each take one bottle for today, and in the morning, we will divide the last bottle? It will give us something for then until we can figure out our next move."

I didn't have to read his mind to know what he was thinking. Shawn didn't think that he would still be alive in the morning, but neither of us said anything about it.

"Okay," he echoed my earlier answer and handed me a bottle.

Logically, I knew that I needed to take it easy. That one bottle was going to be it for me until the morning, but, at that point, I was so thirsty. It only took a few swallows before my bottle was more than half-empty. Screwing the cap back on with a resigned sigh, I set the water back on the desk. At least now, my mouth didn't feel like the Sahara.

The rest of the day was spent waiting. As time crawled by, I alternated between pacing and sitting stiffly in the uncomfortable office chair. My gaze inevitably always ended up back on my companion, watching for any sign of the virus. As the sun descended, leaving us surrounded by the darkness, my eyes started to get heavy, but I couldn't risk going to sleep. What if Shawn got sick while I was unconscious?

Despite my worst fears, he didn't seem like he was ill, although the strain of the day showed in the shadows under his eyes.

Shawn was never a big talker, and now, he was even quieter than usual. He was mostly spending his time watching out that window that was too high for me to see from. Occasionally, he would rotate his injured shoulder, as if trying to work out muscle stiffness.

But there was no fever. I was positive that by now, anyone who had gotten the vaccine would have been terribly sick. Every so often, I made him let me take his temperature with a thermometer I found in the nurse's closet. It remained steadily under 100 degrees. Maybe slightly elevated, but by no means anywhere near as high as the temperatures that ravaged Evie's body that first night.

It was then the longest night of my life, sitting in the dark with nothing to do but wait. Even worse than my first night spent

93

huddled in my bathtub, covered in blood, and listening to the world go crazy all around me. I hadn't truly grasped just what was going on then. Now I did.

Right now, there was only one person left alive in the world that I knew and waiting for that person to either live or die and being completely helpless to do anything to save him was a nightmare.

When the first chirping from birds drew my notice to the lightening color of the sky, I almost couldn't believe it. It was morning.

CHAPTER TWENTY-TWO
Day Ten

I almost couldn't believe it. The sun was coming up and Shawn still didn't seem to be sick.

"How do you feel?" I waited with bated breath for his answer.

"I feel okay." He rotated his shoulder again and then grinned at me. "It's a little stiff, but I feel fine otherwise."

A grin immediately spread across my features. All night long, I had been telling myself that if he made it to the morning without any symptoms, he was probably going to be okay, not daring to really hope that that would actually happen. But now it did. Light was beginning to filter into the room, and I felt nearly giddy with optimism.

Impulsively, I bounded the few steps between us and wrapped my arms around him in a hug, my exuberance overriding my usual shyness for a second. I had a tendency to keep to myself, and my unusual display must have caught him off guard because it took a long second before I felt his arms return the hug.

By then, my mind already had plenty of time to regret my impulsiveness. Looking anywhere except at his face, I pulled back a couple of big steps and tried to cover up my blunder.

"Um, I'm really glad that you don't feel sick. I think that you would by now if you were going to."

95

"I gathered that much." He was still smiling at me with humor. I couldn't blame him. He had just avoided what we had both been sure was a death sentence. He was allowed to be in a good mood.

Breaking eye contact, thankfully, because it was making me a little uncomfortable, he strode to the desk and picked up the bottle of water that we allocated as his last night. It hadn't escaped my notice that he had only sipped from it all night, even though I knew that he had to be thirsty. Now, he unscrewed the cap and chugged the rest of the bottle without coming up for air. When he was finished, he wiped the trickle of water that escaped down his chin with one hand while handing me the remaining one with the other. "Here, you take this."

Shaking my head was one of the hardest things I could remember having to do. One bottle of water in an entire day was not enough. I tried to make it last, but I ran out in the middle of the night. Eyeing his outstretched hand and the liquid relief he held in it, I forced my mouth to form the right words.

"No, we agreed that one is for both of us."

He grabbed my hand and placed the bottle in it. "I'm good . . . for now. Besides, I've been thinking about this situation all night. We are going to have to come up with a better source of water . . . today. I think I know where we should look for answers." When I just stared at him for a second, he continued, "There has got to be some sort of wilderness survival guide on these shelves." His hand swept out to indicate the loaded bookshelf on the far wall.

Swinging my gaze to the books, I felt like giving myself a good kick in the rear. Why hadn't it occurred to me that the books found in a wilderness summer camp for kids would likely be a treasure trove of information useful to our situation? I began scanning the titles on the spines. In only a matter of seconds, I pulled a likely candidate from its place. Thumbing through the pages, another grin spread across my face. This was exactly what we had been looking for.

*　　*　　*

I grimaced down at the corpse of the camp counselor zombie. Despite neither of us being too excited to come back out here, we made the walk down the wooded path, back to the last cabin that we checked yesterday.

In my haste to get Shawn back to the office and clean up his scratches, I had totally forgotten about the bat that he dropped in the grass. We were going to have to drive back into that hole in the wall that the locals called a town, and he was going to need it.

Flies buzzed around the crusty wounds that my knife had left on her skull. When I glanced up at the cabin door, still standing open, all I could picture was the moment when she came barreling out of the door and knocked Shawn off the steps.

I couldn't wait to get away from here.

"Okay, got it. Let's go." Straightening up with the bat in hand, Shawn checked to be sure that I heard him and started back the way we came. I didn't hesitate to follow.

Scanning through the survival guide, I quickly found exactly what we needed. The chapter on purifying water was simple. We either needed to boil the water for ten minutes or put four drops of bleach into a quart and wait for half an hour. Either solution would be well within our grasp, provided we could come up with a few basic necessities.

Despite our thorough search in the entire building, we were surprised when we were not able to find a single box of matches or a bottle of bleach. There was a closet full of all sorts of cleaning chemicals but no bleach.

I guess we used up all our luck earlier when Shawn somehow didn't turn into a zombie overnight. But luckily—even though it looked like we were a hundred miles from anywhere—we were actually only a short drive from civilization. There had to be someplace there to find what we needed.

The drive back out of the mountains left me feeling edgy. I couldn't forget the gang of zombies that we had seen before. I knew that they were still out there, along with many more people that had turned in this town. And just because there were less of them than what we faced in the city, that didn't mean they were less dangerous.

"There was a little store on the back of that diner, next to the gas pump. I'll bet we will find everything that we need in there. Won't take more than a few minutes and we'll be back in the Jeep and out of there." Shawn tried to cheer me up when he noticed my plummeting mood.

I gave him a weak smile. A few minutes out here was a long time, long enough for the zombies to find us, but I wasn't going to say that, so I kept my thoughts to myself.

The trees ended and we were back in the open air of the main street. After only a little over a day, my eyes had already adjusted to the dimmer light in the trees. The midday sun felt blinding, making me blink rapidly. By the time my sight cleared up, we were already pulling into the spacious parking area surrounding our destination.

There was a big truck that had been abandoned in the parking lot, but other than that, the lot stood empty. Shawn pulled right next to the glass door leading into the store. He seemed to debate with himself for a second before leaving the engine running. I had been eyeing the store with distrust but scurried to climb out when I realized that I was the only one still in the Jeep.

I didn't like what we were doing at all, but I wasn't going to let him go out there on his own. Not when I had so recently gotten a vivid idea of how I would feel if I were to lose him.

The sign on the door read open. I could clearly see from outside that calling the room a store from where I was standing was generous. Certainly, the living room that I shared with Evie was larger.

When Shawn pulled on the door, it swung open with a cheery-sounding jingle. Eyeing the bells hanging from the top with my best death glare, I followed him inside.

My first impression had been spot on. A single shelf ran down the center of the store and was loaded with every kind of snack food and candy known to man. The outer walls of the store were also lined with shelves loaded with everything from cat food to windshield washer fluid. The upside to it was that it only took a matter of seconds to find the shelf holding the cleaning stuff. Triumphantly, I pulled several of the pint-sized bottles of bleach from the shelf.

Turning around, I found Shawn stuffing packages of beef jerky into the bag that he brought along. When I stepped up to his side, he looked my way.

"Got them." I held the bleach in my arms, trying to hold on to all the bottles and my knife.

"Good. I found matches and a few other things that we might be able to use." He glanced behind us, back to the Jeep. "I think that we should get out of here."

I couldn't have agreed more. The edgy feeling that I had since we decided that we would have to come back into town had gotten worse. Now that we had the means to make water from the stream safe to drink, all I really wanted was to go back and hide again. It felt way too exposed out here.

Those infernal bells loudly jangled again on our way out. I jumped at the sound. Muttering under my breath, I dropped the bottles of bleach into the back seat of the Jeep before climbing back in the front. Shawn dropped his bag in the back, too, and was behind the wheel in seconds, ready to make our escape when a woman came running around the corner of the diner.

Three zombies sprinted after her.

CHAPTER TWENTY-THREE
Day Ten

The woman was probably younger than me, and the look of absolute terror on her face eliminated any thoughts I was having that she was anything but human very quickly.

"Hang on." Shawn was watching out the window with a look of serious concentration on his face.

Guessing at what he was planning, I grabbed for the dash in an attempt to steady myself. I hadn't had time to put on my seatbelt yet. The tires squealed as the Jeep lurched forward, toward the girl. It only took a second before he spun the car sideways, expertly stopping it broadside to the running girl and giving her a clear shot at the back door.

The maneuver left me wondering where he learned to drive like that, but the thought only had a brief chance to flash through my mind before the girl wrenched the door open and dove inside.

The trio of zombies had been right behind her. She didn't have time to get the door closed before one of them was reaching inside. The girl grappled with the door, trying to pull it shut, but the creature managed to get its head and shoulders too far in. The smell that rolled off the zombie instantly filled the interior, making me fight back a gag. Each time I encountered one of them, they seemed to be even more revolting than the last. The ear-splitting shriek that it blasted us with made my blood run cold as I envisioned just how bad being trapped inside of a vehicle with a zombie could get.

Cursing, Shawn stomped on the accelerator and the Jeep lurched forward. The other two zombies bounced off the side as they tried in vain to find a way in.

The rotting zombie lost its footing as the car shot forward. Letting go of her death grip on the door, the girl swung around in a move that I wasn't sure I could have pulled off and planted both booted feet squarely in the zombie's face. Kicking hard, she sent it flying the rest of the way out the door.

I turned around in my seat to watch the struggle, holding up the knife and trying desperately to figure out a way to defend us if the zombie actually made it all the way into the backseat. Behind us, the zombie rolled and tumbled along the pavement, tripping one of the others who had been chasing us at top speed. Reaching out, the girl grabbed the open door and slammed it shut before slumping back into the seat.

Her cheeks were flushed, and she was breathing in gasps. Closing her eyes, she visibly tried to get her breathing under control. I took the second her eyes were closed to look her over. I was right; she probably wasn't any older than seventeen or eighteen. Shoulder-length—nearly black—hair was in a wild tangle all over her head, prompting me to wonder briefly what my longer locks must look like by now. I was guessing that her skin was that beautiful and perpetually tanned olive tone that always left me a little jealous, though right now, it was hard to tell because of all of the dirt.

I glanced over at Shawn who had been switching between driving us away from this death trap of a town and trying to watch the newest member in the mirror. He glanced at me, and I noticed the worried crinkle on his forehead.

It didn't occur to me until that moment that we just let a complete stranger into the backseat. She didn't look all that dangerous but looks could be deceiving. Every zombie show ever created made it clear that people were your most dangerous enemy during an apocalypse. What if she was crazy? What if she was some sort of a decoy? What if she had been bitten?

A little alarmed now, I looked back at the girl just in time to see her wide brown eyes.

She focused on the two of us in the front for the first time. "Thank you."

Shawn looked in the mirror at her again, a slight frown mostly hidden behind the beard that was starting to grow out of control. "You're welcome."

I looked down at my own stained clothes and only slightly less dirty fingers. I hadn't been anywhere near a mirror in a couple of days, but I was guessing that we weren't any cleaner than the girl in the backseat.

"I'm Fallon. You two just saved my life." She pulled herself up a little straighter in her seat. "I don't think I could have kept running for much longer." She sounded like she really meant what she said.

"I'm Bri. This is Shawn," I chimed in. My instincts had always been pretty good about people, and they were saying that Fallon wasn't anything to be scared of. She was just like us, struggling to stay alive in a world gone mad.

I noticed that Shawn studied me for a second before nodding almost imperceptibly. By then, we had already made several miles back into the mountains.

Suddenly, Shawn stepped on the brake so abruptly that I almost toppled from my backwards perch on the seat. Stopping in the middle of the desolate road, he threw the vehicle into park and turned around to face Fallon.

"Are you bitten?" he asked.

If the abrupt question caught her off guard, she didn't let it show.

Shaking her head, she said, "No. None of them got close enough."

102

I couldn't find any trace of deceit on her face. Apparently, neither could Shawn. Looking at me again, we shared a moment of silent communication where I knew we were both thinking the same thing. Taking a stranger back to our hideout was a gamble, but could either of us live with ourselves if we left this girl behind? I couldn't help but think about how Jack and Shawn found me in that restroom, bloody and exhausted and still a little clueless about exactly how bad things actually were. Neither of them had known a thing about me but they gave me a chance that probably saved my life in the process.

Really, the decision had already been made for us, and we both knew it.

Turning back around, Shawn put the car back into gear and kept going. I noticed some of the tension leave the stiff set of Fallon's shoulders as she seemed to realize that we weren't planning to kick her out of the vehicle. I sat down in my seat, keeping my torso twisted so I could still see the girl in the backseat.

"There's a place we've been staying at. It's not far."

She nodded at me and pulled the bag that she had been sitting on top of out from underneath her, dumping it next to her on the seat. I hoped that there hadn't been anything breakable in there, not that she had time to move the thing before diving into the Jeep.

"Thank you," she said again. "I've been hiding in different places in town for a few days, but none of them lasted for very long. I don't, um . . ." She hesitated, a flash of some unhappy memory crossing her face, before finishing the thought. "I don't have anyone left, and after my car ran out of gas up on the highway, I started walking. I ended up here. It seemed like it would be a safe place to stay at first, but I guess no place is safe anymore."

I nodded at her in understanding. For a brief time, I dared to hope that the camp would be safe, but that lone zombie had set me straight on that in a hurry. There was no such thing as safe anymore—only marginally less dangerous.

103

CHAPTER TWENTY-FOUR
Day Eleven

Fallon splashed in the water behind me. My shirt stuck to me, wet from the water still dripping off my hair. I peeled the material away from my skin. I always hated that feeling, but I was willing to put up with it for now because there was no way I was standing on the side of this stream without my clothes. More splashing came from Shawn nearby. He was also taking advantage of the opportunity to try to get some of the dirt off.

For the first time in several days, we had the time for luxury like a bath, even if you could hardly call it a bath by normal standards.

Yesterday, all three of us downed bottle after bottle of the stream water that we had treated with bleach, making up for days of dehydration. Although it smelled like the chemical stuff, so far, it hadn't made anyone sick.

While acting as the lookout while Shawn and Fallon got cleaned up, a branch snapped nearby, catching my attention. If a zombie was anywhere nearby, it was up to me to protect them.

Looking in the direction of the sound, I peered through the trees. After nearly a minute, with no more sounds and no signs of danger, I relaxed again. There were more random noises in the woods than I would have guessed—something that I still wasn't used to. Every time a branch creaked or a squirrel chattered, I found myself bracing for an attack.

I heard Shawn splash his way back to the bank, and a minute later, he appeared at my side, using a small towel to rub the water from his hair. He smiled at me before taking up a spot just a few feet away, scanning our surroundings. We stood like that in amicable silence while I listened to Fallon finishing her own bath up behind us.

We had only known Fallon for less than a day. A bit reluctantly, Shawn agreed to her request to let her take a turn on watch overnight. I knew he hadn't actually slept while she was on guard, though I didn't say anything. Truth be told, I had been reluctant to go to sleep without Shawn watching my back too, but through the open door between the nurse's room and our office, I saw how seriously Fallon seemed to be taking the duty. She remained alert, pacing between the door wedged closed by the chair and the high window, constantly checking for any sign of danger. After a couple of hours, I started to feel silly for doubting her.

It amazed me how quickly Shawn and I had become "us" while everyone fell into the "them" category. It hadn't escaped my notice that I completely trusted someone who I had known for less than a week while finding it difficult to extend the same trust to another newcomer. I always felt that actions speak louder than words, and while Shawn may have been a stranger just a week ago, in the short time we had known each other, he had proven himself over and over. I had no doubt that he would have my back in any situation we came across.

I didn't feel the same about Fallon, even though she did nothing to warrant my mistrust. Maybe that would change with time, but for now, there was only one person I wanted watching my back.

Before long, the three of us were making our way back to the main camp building. Walking along, I kept having to pull my jeans up as they sagged. I noticed that I wasn't the only one losing significant weight. While we were eating, it wasn't enough. Either we eat more now and take the risk of running out of food sooner,

106

or we could ration ourselves and have something to eat longer. There really wasn't much of a choice there. I had no idea what we would do for food once our supplies did run out. It's not like I had ever grown a garden or killed an animal before. My lunch had come nicely prepackaged from the grocery store for all my life.

After our run in with the three zombies in town the day before, none of us was in a hurry to go back out there. I tried not to think about the fact that we were going to have to go back eventually. If for no other reason, to search that tiny town for things like canned goods and various supplies that would be necessary to stay alive in this new world.

Thinking about it now, I never knew just how easy electricity and running water made my life until it was taken away.

Having all these thoughts in my head, my attention then was pulled to the girl walking just ahead of me. Fallon walked through the brush with ease—her wet hair wrapped up in a towel— as if this was not her first time doing such a thing. She dodged thorns and stepped over obstacles partially hidden under long dead leaves with the ease of practice. I couldn't help but compare her progress to my own as I tripped over a buried rock and snagged my jeans on a thorn bush again.

Carefully pulling the wickedly jagged branch free from my leg, I hurried to catch up with the others. There was no way I wanted to find myself alone in the trees, even if we were only a short walk back to the camp office. The forest was still way too creepy.

We had only questioned Fallon a little about herself the day before, so I didn't know much about the girl, but it was easy to tell just by comparing her actions to my own—she had a different skill set than I did. While I cringed at the first bottle of creek water with my extreme thirst as the only reason I finally gave in and drank it, she didn't hesitate to tilt a bottle back and finish it in few long gulps. Even now, up in the front, Shawn could occasionally be heard muttering under his breath about something that he had stepped on or gotten snagged in, and it was obvious that I was no good in the woods. But Fallon moved through the trees and thorns like it was second nature to her. Plus, she had survived on her own for how many days—something that I wasn't so sure I could have accomplished.

It all added up to make me more curious about our new companion's background.

CHAPTER TWENTY-FIVE
Day Twelve

A hair-raising shriek from outside had me sitting bolt upright in the chair. The book that I had been attempting to read in the dark, both to pass the long night hours alone and to hopefully gain more useful knowledge, dropped from my hands and landed on the floor with a thump. Cringing, I froze, hoping that the sound would go unnoticed by the zombie who was too close for comfort.

Luck was not on my side because another scream instantly blasted through the night and the zombie thudded at once into the side of the building. Soft footsteps from behind me sent my already racing heart into orbit. I looked up and saw Shawn and Fallon emerging from where they had been sleeping in the nurse's room. The moon must have been especially bright out tonight because more light than usual was making its way through the window, making it possible to make out the worried expressions on both of their faces.

Other than the one zombie that surprised us in the little cabin our first morning here, we didn't run across any zombies way out here. The rugged terrain and low population seemed to be working like we hoped, keeping the numbers of the undead low. Of course, we knew that we were bound to run into at least a few zombies, but that didn't mean that we were any more prepared for another run in with them than before.

"What do we do?" Fallon hissed, her eyes locked on the door that was wedged close with the other chair.

"Maybe it will go away?" I thought back to Evie and how she lost interest in the bathroom door when I had been quiet for a while. The zombies didn't seem to have much of an attention span. If we all stayed silent, maybe it would go away on its own.

Lapsing into a tense silence, we all waited to see what would happen next. Thumping and bumping its way along the outside of the building, the zombie let out rumbling growls and the occasional scream that we could easily hear in the silence of the night. It seemed to have worked its way away from the end of the building that we were in, the noises becoming more muffled, and I sagged a little in relief. It was only a matter of time before the zombie wandered off into the woods, but it would still be out there somewhere and, therefore, still be a danger.

A particularly hard thump followed by a splintering sound made the hair stand up along my arms. That did not sound like anything that would bode well for the three of us. More thrashing and shrieking were accompanied by more splintering, and suddenly, the screams were louder than they had been before.

Cursing—something that I learned Shawn did when things were not going in our favor—he crept closer to the barricaded office door. He leaned close, pressing his ear to the surface, and listened. After a second, he pulled back and motioned for us to stay quiet. Completely unnecessary, but then again, I was the one who dropped the book.

"It's in the cafeteria."

It sounded like a table and a bunch of chairs were knocked over as more low growls came from just on the other side of our flimsy office door. As much noise as the zombie was making, if there happened to be any more nearby, it wouldn't be long before they joined the party. I wasn't the only one that that thought occurred to as Fallon whispered, "That thing needs to shut up."

It felt like an eternity as we stood there, huddled together in the dark, listening to the zombie trash the cafeteria. The creature worked its way around the room, blasting shrieks and clanging chairs, marking its path. When the noise from the outer room suddenly stopped, it was somehow even creepier than the sounds the zombie created.

Looking at the two standing beside me, Shawn's and Fallon's faces showed the strain of the last couple of minutes. We were all well aware of the implications of having a zombie roaming the building around us. And now, the thing had fallen silent, and that was even worse. Before, we at least knew where it was. The unknown, as it turns out, was worse than knowing.

Several more minutes passed, but the zombie continued to keep quiet. Some small part of me began to hope that the best may have happened, and I finally couldn't help but verbalize my thoughts. "Do you think it's gone?"

I saw hope light up Fallon's eyes at my question, but it was short lived as Shawn answered.

"It was at the wrong end of the room when it went quiet. Near the kitchen, not the door out. I don't think we can afford to assume that it's not inside anymore."

He was right, of course. I knew I certainly wasn't going to be getting any sleep until I was sure that more than a hollow wooden door held close by an office chair was between the zombies and me.

"We need to go out and check." Fallon didn't sound any happier with that thought than I was.

Nodding, Shawn eased closer to the door and pressed his ear to it to try to listen once more. He had emerged from the nurse's room already armed with his bat. Backing toward the desk, I picked up my knife from where I had sat it earlier. Seeing my action, Fallon gripped her own knife—one that she lifted from the kitchen the day before with an unsteady hand.

111

Standing back up, Shawn looked over his shoulder to us. "Are you ready?"

The whispered words sent the knot of dread that had formed in my throat straight to my gut, but I nodded anyhow. Getting a similar response from Fallon, Shawn slowly eased the chair out from under the doorknob, trying to be as silent as possible. Setting the chair out of the way, he eased the door open a crack, just far enough that he could see into the cafeteria.

A couple of frantic heartbeats later, Shawn pulled the door the rest of the way open.

The moonlight coming in through the high windows illuminated the outer room well enough that I could see the destruction caused by the zombie. The formerly neat rows of tables surrounded by their chairs had been bumped into. Tables had been shoved out of line, chairs toppled. The door leading outside, the one that was closed, now stood open. Splinters of wood scattered over the floor nearby, letting me know that something about the door had failed when battered by the zombie, and that was how it had gotten in. There really wasn't any surprise there. Security had obviously not been a high priority when the camp was built. Whoever made those sorts of decisions probably thought that, way out here in the middle of nowhere, the risks of any sort of intruder were minimal.

How could that person have known that, one day, a trio of people would rely on those doors to keep out the undead?

The zombie wasn't anywhere in sight. Staying close together, we worked our way across the cafeteria. Stepping carefully, I made sure not to bump into anything that would make any noise. The swinging door that led into the kitchen beckoned. If the zombie were still somewhere inside the building, the kitchen seemed the likeliest place it would be.

We reached the door and paused just outside. Unlike the kitchen door at the office building that Shawn and I had narrowly escaped from not so long ago, this door did not have any sort of window that we could use to see inside. The only way to know was to go in.

Looking at each other in some sort of unspoken agreement, we moved toward the swinging door together.

CHAPTER TWENTY-SIX
Day Twelve

What in the hell was it doing up there?

My first thought was one of confusion as I looked around Shawn and caught a glimpse of the zombie. It managed to climb up onto the long center island that ran the length of the kitchen and was reaching toward a set of pots that hung gleaming in the faint moonlight from ceiling hooks. This one had obviously been dead for a while. Its bloated and greasy-looking flesh seemed like it wanted to slide right off the bones. Most of its hair fell out, leaving just a few sparse clumps to cling limply to its scalp. Gore crusted its ragged clothing, and I couldn't tell blood from any hapless victims it managed to sink its teeth into from what was its own leaking bodily fluids.

I thought that we were silent, but maybe we weren't quiet enough. The creature slowly swung its head in our direction and focused its one remaining eye on where the three of us stood frozen in the doorway.

Maybe we confused it as much as it standing on top of that counter confused me, or perhaps it was just having trouble seeing. Either way, the zombie cocked its head slightly to the side and went utterly still, staring right at us, then its rotten lips peeled back from its teeth and snarled exactly the type of sound that one would not want to hear coming from the dark.

Lurching forward, the zombie crashed to the tiled floor in an ungraceful heap. It took it a few seconds to disentangle its limbs, but far too soon, it was clambering disjointedly back to its feet. I didn't even realize that I backpedaled back through the swinging door until I was already back in the cafeteria. Behind me, Fallon was backing away too, and the door didn't have a chance to swing all the way shut again before Shawn followed.

I guess none of us was too eager to get anywhere near the zombie.

The door swung shut all the way this time as the three of us regrouped near the center of the cafeteria room. At that point, we came to our senses enough to know that we were going to have to stop our retreat at some point. The zombie was going to have to be dealt with, whether we like it or not.

A scream came from behind the kitchen door just before the door burst open. Lurching through the doorway, the zombie focused its one good eye on us. It moved with none of the speed than I had come to expect from the zombies. Instead, it jerked along in those characteristic fits and starts but much slower and almost uncoordinated in its movements. The creature shambled toward us, paying no mind to anything that was in its path. It tripped over downed chairs and bounced off the heavy tables to reach us.

The sight was horrifying.

As the zombie came within a dozen feet of our group, Shawn stepped forward and raised his bat. Its eyes held the dead gaze of a predator, as it focused on his movement. Swinging the bat hard, he hit it right in the creature's skull. A wet, splattering sound followed quickly when the zombie hit the ground. It was for-real kind of dead instantly.

All of us were breathing fast and just stood there for a few seconds, staring at the rotting corpse that now lay just a foot from us. A pool of blood began to spread across the floor. The hard hit had split the zombie's skull.

Hyped up on adrenaline, I hadn't noticed the stench coming from it . . . until now. The zombie smelled like an animal that had been killed on the highway and then laid in the summer sun for a week.

Fighting back a gag, I pulled the neck of my shirt up in a futile attempt to cover my mouth and nose.

Poking at it with the end of the bat, Shawn looked back at us. "It's dead."

Next to me, Fallon gave an audible sigh of relief. "Do you think it was just the one?"

"I think so, but we should probably look around. Just to be sure." Shawn looked over to where the door was still hanging open. "Need to do something about the door too."

I chimed in through my shirt. "We need to do something about the zombie. It can't stay in here."

Nodding, Shawn handed me his bat. He reached down, grabbed the corpse by its filthy shoes, and began dragging it toward the door. The smear of blood that was left in its wake looked nearly black in the limited moonlight. Trailing behind him with some vague thought of watching his back, I watched as Shawn paused at the open door. Looking out, he looked around carefully before dragging the zombie outside. He dropped its feet when he pulled it a dozen yards away from the building. "When the sun's up, I'll come back out and finish dragging it further away, but this will have to do for now."

Back inside the building, we found Fallon looking nervously into every shadowy corner. The bathrooms were still and empty; the kitchen was now thankfully the same.

Upon closer inspection, we found that the door had been forced open when some of the screws in the jam were pulled free. Shards of wood from the door frame still littered the ground. Fixing the door properly with what we had on hand wasn't really an option. Surprisingly, Fallon was the one who came up with the idea that at least allowed us to keep the door closed. It was by no means secure, but anything was better than letting it hang open for any passing zombies to stroll right on in, and the fix was as good as it was going to get anyhow.

By the time we were finished, there wasn't a lot of the night left. No one wanted to go back to sleep, so we all sat in the office, sharing a bag of beef jerky and talking about what just happened.

"Why was it different from all the other zombies I've seen?"

Fallon asked the question that had been mulling around in my mind.

I shrugged before answering, "I don't know. Maybe it was so decomposed that it was starting to have trouble getting around. I've not seen one like that before either."

She nodded. It made sense anyhow. Who really knew anything about why the zombies were the way they were. I was convinced that the flu vaccine was what started this whole disaster, but the why still escaped me.

Was it some random fluke, or had someone engineered the apocalypse? I wasn't sure that we would ever find out the answer to that question.

CHAPTER TWENTY-SEVEN
Day Fourteen

The rain had been pounding the metal roof over our heads for over a day. At first, the sound lulled me into the best sleep that I had in weeks, but now, the constant drumming started to wear on my nerves. Our already gloomy hideout was even darker, the rain clouds keeping the sunlight from even making it to the trees above. With no way to really get dry quickly and no spare clothes, we all stayed indoors even more than usual. I was starting to feel trapped.

Wandering to the door that led outside, I fiddled with our makeshift fix. It did the job but wasn't going to keep out anyone determined to get inside. Looking behind me, I found Shawn and Fallon playing cards at one of the round tables. The discovery of the well-worn deck was giving them something to do to pass the time, but I never really liked card games. I was on my own.

Suddenly unable to stay cooped up in the dark building for another second, I opened the door.

Outside, the rain still came down in the wind-driven sheets. The small overhang above the door kept the worst of it off me as I stepped out. Leaving the interior was just what I needed, and I instantly felt lighter. I didn't even mind that I was already wet from the knees down because of the wind carrying the rain to me despite the roof.

The entire world looked gray. The rain kept me from being able to see it clearly. The dense underbrush that marked the start of the forest appeared blurry, even though I knew that it wasn't all that far. Leaning back against the open doorframe, I crossed my arms and settled in to watch the rain.

I had been standing there for several minutes, lulled into a semi-trance by the repetitive sights and sounds of the storm, when movement in the distance caught my attention. Standing up straight, I focused on where I was sure something other than the rain had moved. I didn't have to wait long before I saw it again. Down the road, far enough away that I couldn't make out anything clearly, a distinctly human shape emerged from the gloom.

"Guys."

I kept my voice down, and my eyes trained on the figure. They moved along slowly. I couldn't tell if it was a zombie or someone still alive.

My low level of worry ratcheted up to blatant alarm when three more figures took shape in the rain.

"Guys!" I hissed louder and dared a look behind me to see if they heard me this time. When Shawn looked up with alarm, I knew they heard and swung back around to watch the figures in the distance.

I backed back through the doorway, keeping my gaze locked on the four distant shapes as Shawn appeared by my side. Raising an arm, I pointed, drawing his attention to what had alarmed me. We watched the distant figures slowly draw closer for a few seconds, before we closed the door and secured it the best that we could.

"What is it?" Fallon asked.

"I don't know. Maybe people. Maybe zombies."

"Zombies, as in plural?" She looked at me in alarm.

"Yeah."

"How many?"

"I saw four," Shawn answered her as he began to drag one of the heavy tables toward the door. "We need to be ready. If they're zombies, our best bet is to stay quiet and hope they don't figure out that we are in here."

I cringed at the screech the table made against the floor. Moving to it, I grabbed one side and lifted. Shawn followed suit, and we carried the table the rest of the way to the door. We set it down up against the door. I didn't know if it would be any help, but it seemed better than doing nothing.

I couldn't see out of the high windows that this building had. Pulling a chair over, I used it to gain the needed height. Shawn and Fallon were already looking out another window. It took me a second to locate the figures because I was looking in the wrong area. They were much closer to the building than I would have figured. Silently, the three of us watched as they drew closer.

As the four figures turned off the little back road and into the camp driveway, they finally were clear enough to start to make out details.

I didn't think that they were zombies. They moved like people. The one in the lead was taller and broad-shouldered. Close behind him, two smaller figures huddled close together, and a tall thin figure was in the rear. All of them seemed to be doing their best to avoid the wind and rain while moving steadily toward our building.

I practically held my breath, worried absurdly that they would somehow be able to hear my breathing. At the next window over, Shawn and Fallon both held completely still, warily watching the people approach. When the closest figure drew within a few feet of Shawn's Jeep, he paused to look in through the windows. He appeared to say something to the people behind him, but I couldn't hear what it was over the roar of the rain on the roof. As one, the group looked back to the door of our building. They seemed to huddle closer together as they watched. I could only guess that they were probably looking for any signs of life, unsure if whoever drove the Jeep would still be among the living.

After a long minute of staring, from both sides, the leader slowly began to walk toward the front door. Alarmed, I looked over to my companions. There were four of them and only three of us, and our weapons consisted of a ball bat and two kitchen knives. If the newcomers wanted to cause us any trouble, we would have difficulty defending ourselves. Sharing a silent glance between us, I knew that the three of us were all thinking the same thing.

Another look outside told me that we were out of time. The man was near the overhang. No one seemed to know what to do.

Panicking a little, I yelled, "Stop!"

Fallon made a noise that I interpreted as distress, but my yell had the desired effect. The man came to a startled stop. Squinting through the rain, he looked around himself before focusing on the door again. One of the smaller figures came up to stand next to him, and she was finally close enough for me to see that it was a woman.

There was another long moment of silence while we all stared again. The people outside shifted uncomfortably from one foot to another, no doubt soaked and freezing and probably nervous about being standing out there while we watched them from inside.

I started to feel a little bit bad for them. They were people, just like us. I couldn't see any weapons, but that didn't mean much with the rain and gloom concealing the details from me. But the fact that there was a woman with the big man made me feel slightly better, even if that thought was a little ridiculous.

The woman next to the man was the first one to break our stalemate. "We don't want any trouble. We're just looking for a place to get out of the rain."

None of us knew what to do. I could see it plainly written on their faces. Shawn looked over to me, seemingly asking me what I thought we should do, then I looked at Fallon.

121

A couple of days ago, we didn't know her either, but she hadn't proven dangerous. In fact, she was the one who fixed the broken door. And if we hadn't helped her, she would probably be dead by now.

If we stopped helping each other, humanity was as good as dead. We needed each other more than ever, if any of us were going to survive this zombie apocalypse.

"I think we should let them in," I whispered.

CHAPTER TWENTY-EIGHT
Day Fourteen

Fallon shook her head rapidly at my whisper, obviously not agreeing with me. Shawn looked out again before turning back to face me.

"Are you sure, Bri?"

We were a team and had learned to trust each other in the short time that we'd known each other. Both of us would probably be dead by now if it weren't for the other.

"No." I looked worriedly back outside. The people were still standing there, waiting for our response. "But I don't think we can turn them away."

"Okay." He raised his voice to be heard over the downpour. "Are you armed?"

The people looked at each other for a second before the big man answered, "We have two knives, a machete, a hatchet, and a gun."

The gun, in particular, was what I was most worried about.

I watched as the two remaining people moved closer. There was another woman, and the rail-thin, tall figure seemed to be a teenage boy. They all looked miserable, soaked, and exhausted. When I looked back to Shawn, I found him looking at me. He looked concerned, but I knew him. He wasn't likely to leave those people outside.

"We will open the door if you leave the gun outside." Until I had a chance to get to know them a little, I wasn't crazy about them having a weapon like that.

Out in the gloom, the burly man looked to the closest woman. They exchanged a few words before he pulled a small handgun from under his jacket. Holding it up for us to easily see, he took the last steps under the overhang and set the weapon on the floor.

I jumped off my chair and went to the table. Shawn and a frowning Fallon followed me. The three of us pulled the table away from the door. Arranging ourselves just inside the door, nerves jangled just under my skin as Shawn began to open the door. It was a risk we were taking, letting the bigger group in.

The door swung open, revealing the group of people crowded under the overhang just on the other side.

The man was first. He glanced warily behind himself before slowly stepping across the threshold. My first impression of him hadn't been wrong. The guy was huge in every way possible. The rain had matted his black hair to his head, and he hadn't bothered to zip his jacket back up. He was already soaked clear through anyhow. Brown eyes darted around the cafeteria, taking in the three of us and looking for any hint of danger.

Behind him, the three others hurried inside, eager to get out of the rain and probably to get to relative safety indoors. The one woman, in particular, stayed close to the man. She wasn't all that small, but compared to him, she looked tiny. When she stepped through the door, I noticed the hatchet in her hand that had been hidden by the weather. She clutched the weapon in a shaking hand, her own eyes searching the room.

The teenager looked like he was ready to drop where he stood. These people all were drained and unhealthy looking, but the teen was by far the worst. His eyes were sunk back in his skull and a complexion that probably used to be tanned was too white. His clothes were baggy on his frame as if he had lost a significant

124

amount of weight. The last woman came up behind him and wrapped a supporting arm around his torso. She was the oldest member of the group. Even soaked from the rain, filthy, and tired, I could clearly see the gray that streaked her hair and the lines that started to spread on her face.

"Stop! Are you bitten?" Shawn's alarmed question had me searching for whatever he had seen that I missed.

There. The leg of the teenager's pants was torn. It was hard to see, but the rain hadn't completely washed away all traces of the blood that had soaked through the material.

The man raised a placating hand. "It's not a bite. He got cut running from the zombies in that little town yesterday."

I looked warily at the teen. Seeming to sigh, he slowly leaned down and pulled the leg of his pants up. The wound underneath made me cringe. The gash was deep and ran through the middle of his calf. They hadn't made any effort to treat it. Maybe they didn't have any medical supplies to do so, and the skin around the wound was already turning an angry red. Open to contaminants like it was, it was only a matter of time before his leg became seriously infected.

"I'm Bill," the man told us when he saw that we were placated seeing the teen's leg. "This is my wife, Maya, and this is Carrie and Devon." He gestured to the other three. "We've been walking for a while now. Thanks for letting us in."

"I'm Shawn. This is Bri and Fallon." He didn't seem to know what else to say, and he stopped there.

I jumped in when the silence threatened to become uncomfortable. "We have some basic medical supplies. I can take a look at your leg if you want me to." I directed my statement to Devon.

He smiled weakly at me. "That would be great."

"Okay. I'll be right back." I hurried into the office with a backward glance at my people. In the supply closet, I pulled out everything that seemed helpful to treat a serious wound. I was no

125

doctor, but it looked to me like the teen could have really used a trip to the hospital. I hoped he had his tetanus shot.

When I stepped back into the cafeteria, I found everyone sitting around the tables in a wary truce. No one looked comfortable, but at least Shawn and the newcomers were talking. Fallon sat slightly to the side of everyone else, and she still didn't look all that happy with how things were working out. I didn't have time to worry about her at the moment. I wanted to get Devon's leg cleaned up the best I could and was eager to get back to Shawn. I didn't like leaving him essentially all alone to deal with the new people.

"Okay, let's see what we can do with these." I dumped my armload of supplies on the table and scooted a chair closer to the teen. He had used another chair to prop his leg up and pulled his jeans above the wound again. Up close, the cut didn't look any better. Whatever he had sliced it on must have been really sharp. There was one deep gash that went right into the muscle of his calf.

While I went to work on his leg, I listened to the conversation that I had interrupted with my entrance.

"We ran out of gas a few miles before the exit to that town. We thought that we would probably be able to find some somewhere and carry it back to the car, but as soon as we hit the main street, the zombies started coming from everywhere." Maya shuddered a little in remembrance. "We didn't know which way to go. I thought that it was going to be the end for us, but then we heard someone shouting at us. It was Devon, and he led us away from the zombies, but he got hurt. We ran into the woods and just kept on going."

"You just met them?" I questioned Devon as I tried to figure out how best to bandage his leg.

He nodded. "Yeah, yesterday. I was starting to think that I was the only one left alive in the whole town and then there they were. I'd been hiding in my attic and then I heard voices. I didn't want to be alone anymore."

126

I gave Devon a tight smile of understanding. My few days alone in my bathroom had been one of the worst times in my life. I could only imagine that a couple of weeks—all alone and hiding in an attic—had been brutal for the teen.

CHAPTER TWENTY-NINE
Day Fourteen

The rain finally stopped sometime in the late afternoon. Bill and Maya had been keeping a watch out from the windows, and I had to admit that having the extra sets of eyes was a big help. With only three of us, it made the shifts tediously long. But the four new additions had jumped right in with helping out, and I was already noticing the difference.

With more than twice the people now hiding out in the cafeteria, there was near constant chatter. Someone was always talking to someone else. Even Fallon seemed to be starting to thaw toward them, and she was currently sitting at a table with Devon, the two of them making use of the deck of cards.

Shawn had been talking with Carrie for a while. I could hear bits and pieces of their conversation from where I was adding drops of bleach to our water supply. More people meant that we would need more of everything, and I wanted to be prepared. We didn't have much, but the water was one thing that we did have in abundance. Maya had produced a few cans of fruit from the backpack that she carried, and they had readily shared with us. They seemed like genuinely good people, and after only a few hours with them, I was already glad that we had decided to let them in.

From what I had been able to gather, they had a rough road getting this far. Their group was larger when they left their homes in search of a safer place to stay. Their group had consisted of Bill, Maya, Carrie, Carrie's husband, and another man who also lived on the same street as the rest of them. I didn't have to ask to know that the two men being absent from their group was a bad thing.

The group worked their way west in search of a place with fewer zombies. They stopped a few times, but it never lasted long before they were overrun and had to leave. When they ran out of gas on the highway, they planned to siphon a few gallons from a car in town and continue on their way, but the crowd of undead had foiled their plans, chasing them in the opposite direction of their vehicle, and they met Devon in the process. They had escaped the zombies in the trees and had been walking since, hoping to find a place to get out of the rain and decide what to do next, then they had emerged from the woods onto the little back road that led them directly to the camp.

Shawn relayed the basics of our own story to Carrie, and she made a noise of sympathy when he told her that we lost someone too. She was disheartened when she found out that we had been running in the opposite direction from her group and that there was no safer place than this one, as far as we had found.

Finished with my task with the water, I walked over and pulled out a chair next to Shawn. "The water will be ready in half an hour."

Carrie nodded to me. "Thank you. I don't know where we would be if you all hadn't decided to let us in."

Getting dry wasn't easy, and the woman sitting across from me still looked damp. Her long graying hair was drying in greasy-looking strands that lay limply plastered to her skull. The strain and loss of the past couple of weeks had left her with a haunted cast to her features.

Basically, she looked awful. All four of them did, not that I thought that we looked much better. At least Shawn, Fallon, and I were reasonably rested. I looked to Shawn. "Why don't you and I take the first watch tonight, and let everyone else sleep?"

I didn't add that they needed it more than we did.

"That sounds like a plan. Carrie, we've been sleeping in a nurse's office connected to the main office. There's a couch and the floor is carpeted, so it's definitely more comfortable than sleeping anywhere else."

"This is a camp, right? Aren't there beds somewhere?" Bill had wandered over to our table.

"Yeah, but they're all in cabins spread out around the area. We've stayed in this building because it's bigger and seems more secure."

Bill seemed to think before nodding in agreement. "It makes sense for us all to stay together. And this place is better than some of the others we've stayed in lately."

"Shawn and I are okay with taking the first watch if you want to try to get some sleep."

He nodded again, and I could see his frame droop a little with exhaustion. "That would be good, thanks. Would you all be okay with me bringing in my gun? I understand why you wanted it left outside, but I'd feel better if it was back within reach."

Shawn answered him, "Yeah, go ahead."

"Alright. I'm gonna go get that and then if you don't mind, I think Maya and I will try to get some sleep."

*   *   *

After hearing the rain drum on the roof for so long and hours of talking, the silence of the night seemed somehow ominous. The chirps, croaks, and peeps from the wildlife blended into quiet background noise that I no longer noticed unless I thought about it. Perched on top of my chair once again, I watched through the window for anything that could cause us trouble. So far, the fog that had been slowly building into a white wall was the only thing that moved out there.

I yawned and stretched before coming down from the chair. It was deep into the night and almost time for us to wake up Fallon and Bill for their turn. Maya, Carrie, and Devon were all going to get an uninterrupted night's sleep—something that we hadn't been able to do very often with fewer people.

I wandered over to where Shawn had been watching out a window toward the other end of the cafeteria. "Hey. It's all quiet out there, but the fog's starting to get really thick."

He turned around and leaned against the wall next to me. "Yeah. I hope it doesn't last too much longer. I don't like not being able to see out there."

"First that crazy rain, now this." I shrugged slightly. There wasn't anything any of us could do about it anyhow. "The new people seem okay."

He nodded thoughtfully. "They do. I wonder if they will stay. Having a few more people would make a lot of things easier."

I was a little surprised by his statement. It never occurred to me that the new group might choose not to stay. Where else did they have to go?

I didn't respond as I thought over the possibilities.

We stayed like that, backs against the wall, in companionable silence for a few minutes. When I figured that it had been long enough, I pushed off of the wall and walked back to my window.

Back up on my chair, nothing seemed to have changed. The slow creep of the fog still concealed too much of my view. The moonlight still glinted dully off the puddles here and there.

I sighed and settled in for more less-than-stimulating looking out the window. Being on watch at night was my least favorite job in this new world.

Suddenly, a deer burst from the hazy underbrush. Running full speed, the animal crossed the open driveway in a few bounds, swerved to miss the Jeep and disappeared into the fog.

As the deer bounded out of sight, I rested my hand over my now pounding heart and silently laughed at myself for being startled by a deer, but then I realized that the usual night sounds from bugs and small animals had gone completely silent.

CHAPTER THIRTY
Day Fifteen

"Bri." Shawn was already hurrying toward me in the darkened cafeteria.

"I saw it," I whispered back, clambering off the chair.

"Go wake everyone up. Make sure they stay quiet." He took up a position watching out my window.

Careful not to bump into anything, I hurried into the office. The door to the next room was open, and I could see the shapes of sleeping people on the floor. The room was not that large, and floor space was basically nonexistent with so many bodies stretched out in there.

I hissed through the doorway, "Get up!"

It didn't take much to rouse everyone after living on the edge like we had been. My second whispered hiss had everyone coming to attention.

"What's wrong?" Fallon shoved her hair from her face as she sat up on the couch.

"I don't know, but something's not right."

They all struggled to their feet, weapons coming out from where they had stashed them. The new group seemed particularly on edge, reminding me that they had been on the road for a lot longer than I had been.

Maya began stuffing her backpack with everything she could get her hands on. It took me a second to realize that she was preparing to have to run. It had happened to them before, and I suddenly felt ill-prepared if we did have to leave the camp. Grabbing Shawn's backpack from where he left it on the desk, I started stuffing bottles of water and the last of the food in it.

Everyone else had crept from the office by the time Maya and I had filled the two bags. Zipping mine closed, I followed Maya through the door.

The thought of having to leave the camp was terrifying. At first, this place had been creepy, but we started to settle in here. I knew that being out on the road had to be worse.

Everyone crowded around a few windows near the door. Tension crackled in the air as they watched outside.

I climbed back on my chair. The night outside was still too silent.

It couldn't have been much more than a minute, maybe two, since that deer charged from the gloom. Now, as we all watched, something else moved in the darkness.

A lot of something elses.

Zombies emerged from the fog by the dozen. They stumbled over fallen branches, got tangled in thick briar bushes, and limped along on damaged and rotting limbs. A few still moved with the fluid, fast movements that most of the zombies I had seen before used, but most of them now more closely resembled the zombie that managed to break into the cafeteria. I shuddered at the sheer number of them.

I didn't know who gasped to my right, but I could only imagine that whoever it was, was as terrified as I was. We all froze in place, afraid that the smallest movement would give us away to the horde.

They wandered into the clearing, meandering along, clearly with no destination in mind. The silence was more unnerving than anything else. I had gotten used to the screams and snarls that always seemed to announce their presence. For whatever reason,

134

the zombies outside made none of those noises. A few low growls made it through the walls, but that was all.

I didn't even want to think of the implications if the zombies became silent predators.

One uncoordinated zombie tripped over her own feet and crashed onto the hood of the Jeep. The noise seemed to stir the others up a bit, and their movements collectively became more hurried. One zombie, who zipped around the clearing with speed, screeched.

In a domino effect, more growling and screams began to sound. The zombies' movements became frenzied as they milled around, disappearing and reappearing in the thick fog.

"This is bad," Devon breathed so lowly I wasn't sure for a second that I'd heard him.

"If they hit that door, they're going to get in," Shawn whispered to the group. "It didn't stop a single zombie when it wasn't broken."

"Is there a back door?"

"Yes, but it's locked," I answered Maya. The narrow hallway that led past the kitchen and past a pair of bathrooms ended with a door out. A chain and lock kept that door closed, something that originally I had been pleased with because it made me feel safer. I was re-evaluating my position on the lock now though.

"There has to be a key."

I pulled my gaze away from the window to look at her. "We haven't found it."

At that moment, a zombie stumbled its way up onto the tiny front porch. It clattered around out there, gently bumping into the door and causing it to rattle in its broken frame. The resigned expression on Maya's face was highlighted by the moonlight coming in through the window.

"It's time to go." She looked away from the chaos outside, toward the big man who had been silently watching next to her.

Bill nodded slowly. "Yeah, it's time."

Their group backed away from the windows and melted into the darkness further into the building.

Fallon, Shawn, and I were left staring at each other with wide eyes. I was not happy to think about going outside with so many of the undead there. Clearly, I wasn't the only one.

"Should we go?" I had no idea what the right decision was. Going outside seemed suicidal, but if we became trapped inside by this many zombies, we were as good as dead too.

"I don't want to go out there."

"I think we need to go."

They answered me at the same time. I looked back and forth between them, my head spinning with possibilities. I opened my mouth, but no sound came out.

A harder thump rattled the door, and the zombie on the porch snarled.

My mind was made up instantly. The zombies seemed intent on hanging around the camp. It was only a matter of time before they got in. Even if they never got inside, with so many of them prowling the area, going out for food and water would be dangerous.

Maya had been right. It was time to go.

I reaffirmed their decision and turned to follow their retreat. Shawn immediately fell into step beside me. A second later, Fallon's booted steps sounded behind us. Unhappy as she was about going outside, I had no doubt that she was more afraid of being alone again.

It became pitch-black as we got further from the windows, slowing us down. I held a hand out in front of me, afraid of running into something in the darkness. By the time we made it down the narrow hallway, I was feeling along the wall to keep oriented.

A whisper of noise ahead of me stood the hair up on the back of my neck, images of just what could be lurking ahead in mind. Suddenly, a bright light turned on directly in my face.

"Thank God, it's you. I wasn't sure." Carrie turned the blinding light away from me and toward where the rest of her group was crowded around the chained door.

"Can you pick it?" Maya whispered to Bill.

He looked at the lock intently for several long seconds before answering, "I don't know. Maybe."

Maya produced something from her pack that I couldn't see in the crush of bodies, and he took it and went to work on the lock.

I had no idea what exactly it took to pick a lock, but their group seemed like this was something that they had done before. I kept quiet, worried about what would happen if he couldn't get the lock open. And I worried about what would happen if he could.

The door was solid, giving no way to look outside before we could open it. What if the zombies found their way around to the back of the building? We would run outside and straight into them. I gripped my knife a little harder and looked nervously behind me. The glow from the flashlight didn't reach that far, and I couldn't see my friends.

A familiar hand reached out to settle lightly on my shoulder, making a little of the anxiety ease up. Shawn must have noticed my building panic.

An excited murmur ahead was followed by the rattle of chains being removed from their place on the door.

They did it. The back door was unlocked.

"Is everyone ready?" Bill looked around to each of us.

When no one objected, Carrie switched off the flashlight. "Okay."

The door opened silently, something I would be eternally grateful for, and moonlight spilled into the hallway. At the front, Bill hesitated, peering out into the night cautiously. He had just taken his first step outside when a crash from out in the cafeteria told us that the zombies had made it inside.

"Go!" Fallon hissed from behind me, and we all surged out into the night.

The air was heavy with moisture and the stench of so many rotting corpses was like a slap in the face. I felt like I was too close to hyperventilating as I crept along behind Carrie. The fog made it impossible to see more than a few feet away. I didn't want to lose sight of anyone, afraid I would never see them again.

Out of the shifting white curtain, to my right, a shuffling zombie materialized. It was already upon us by the time we saw it, and I gasped as it set its sights on Devon. The zombie growled as it reached for him. I watched, horrified, sure that he was going to be bitten, then the zombie slumped to the ground in a heap.

Blinking rapidly, I had to stare for a second to be sure that my eyes weren't playing a cruel trick on me.

Carrie leaned over the zombie, tugging to release a machete from where she had sunk it into the zombie's skull.

CHAPTER THIRTY-ONE
Day Seventeen

We were all tired of being soaked to the skin. The trees all around us seemed like they would never end, and they constantly dripped with the light rain that was determined to continually fall from the sky. Huddled together under a particularly thick old tree, we did our best to shield ourselves from the chilling rain, but it wasn't really working.

"That was the longest night ever," Fallon groaned.

Shifting slightly, she attempted to stretch her muscles that must have been stiff from spending the night crunched up in the cold. I certainly felt like I had gone a couple of rounds with a professional fighter and lost big time.

"Does anyone know how far it is between towns out here? Devon?" Carrie asked as she stretched too.

"Um, I'm not sure exactly how far up the road the next town is. It takes about twenty minutes to get there by car."

A shred of hope lit in me upon hearing his words. If it took about twenty minutes to drive from Devon's home to the next town over, it couldn't have been more than fifteen miles between towns. We walked along the road for hours the day before and before that, and had been trying to work our way in that direction through the forest. Granted, that first night and day in the trees, we had been hopelessly lost and could have been traveling in a variety of directions. Still, the town couldn't be that much further up the road.

"We have to be getting close," Shawn echoed my thoughts.

"I think we are, but I'm not sure. The trees all kinda look the same."

Devon wasn't kidding. I had been very relieved when we finally stumbled on the little road the day before. The close trees and the foreboding sky made me feel trapped. The open road gave us a bit of breathing room and a sure direction to travel.

Someone started passing around one of our few remaining bottles of water, and I took a few small sips when it was my turn.

In an unspoken agreement, our two groups had merged into one, sharing our limited resources and watching out for each other. I was grateful for the four new people, even if their coming to our camp was probably what led the horde of zombies to us in the first place. They certainly didn't mean to get our hideout overrun, and their skills had been what kept us alive that first night as we desperately tried to avoid the undead in the thick fog. The time that they had spent on the road taught them more about killing zombies than the rest of us learned while hiding in the camp.

Not that that meant that we were completely helpless. We had encountered a few zombies wandering in the trees, and all of us had taken out at least one of them by now. The rotting man-zombie in overalls that had been my second ever kill had been just as terrifying as the camp zombie, but I managed to get the job done.

"We should probably get moving," Bill said, interrupting my thoughts.

Everyone climbed to their feet with audibly protesting joints. A long series of cracks from my own spine accompanied my standing up. My sneakers squished uncomfortably, and water trickled down my neck from my hair. While a town came with a higher number of zombies, it also had shelter from the rain and food. After a couple of days spent never managing to get dry,

140

having a roof overhead and some dry clothes sounded worth the risk.

The backpack that I had slung over one shoulder was getting lighter. Seven people went through a lot of food, and there wasn't much left. Following the rest of the group down the steep bank that led back onto the pavement, I unzipped the bag and pulled out one of the remaining granola bars. While I held the bag out, everyone else took their share. When I put the bag back on my back, it felt completely empty. Maya's bag was still full, but I was sure that she had mostly packed things like medical supplies with maybe some food and water filling up the remaining space.

Walking along the road was infinitely easier than traversing the forest, and we were covering a lot more ground. We walked for maybe an hour before a curve in the road appeared ahead.

"This is it. The town is just around that corner," Devon excitedly told us as he sped up.

"Devon, wait!" I knew—out of all of us—that he had the hardest time these last couple of days. His leg hadn't really had time to heal, and he was walking with a more pronounced limp now than he had been when we first met him. Thoughts of finding a dry place where he could rest were probably all that crossed his mind, but we needed to approach the town with caution.

The bend in the road wasn't far, and before long, we were rounding the corner, and a town that was even smaller than the other one came into view. If that was even possible.

The streets were silent.

Cautiously moving forward, our group worked our way into the town.

Someone had been killing zombies here. It was the only explanation for what I saw in the road where zombies with bullet holes to the head slumped where they had fallen. In the driveway to my right, someone had dumped what must have been at least a dozen corpses together in a reeking pile. Ahead, a crow pecked at

141

the remains of someone who had died wearing a single pink fluffy slipper.

Skirting around a rain-diluted pool of blood that had come from the zombie nearest to me, I looked around warily and stayed close to the rest of the group. This place had an eerie feeling to it.

The main street was basically rows of closely spaced homes on either side of the road. No one stood out from the others, the houses stretching out ahead of us before ending abruptly. The trees on the other end of the town looked just as formidable as the ones that we had left behind us. I kept looking for any sort of store, even a small gas station, but there didn't seem to be anything like that here. Just the houses. It was really bizarre to someone who had grown up surrounded by city concrete, townhouses, and carefully planned suburbs.

I almost bumped into Bill's back when he came to a sudden stop just in front of me.

"Well, does anyone have a preference for which one we try?" He gestured around himself.

We all looked around, but the houses seemed identical that it made them all practically indistinguishable from my view. Blank stares and shrugged shoulders seemed to indicate that everyone else felt the same way.

"Alright." Critically eyeing the two nearest homes, Bill settled on the one on our left, and we moved up the short driveway together.

Keeping her voice low, Maya gave a quick explanation of the routine that they had adopted when breaking into a new place to me, Shawn, and Fallon. "We need to try to see if there are any zombies inside. If there are, we'll move on to another house. It's not worth the risk of letting them out with us. If it seems clear, we'll go in and search the entire house. Just to be sure. If it's clear, we can set up camp and look for any supplies that might be useful."

I nodded absentmindedly while listening. Her words all made sense. At that point, Bill was standing at the front door of the house, and Carrie had gone to one of the windows. When Bill knocked lightly on the door, she peered inside. After several seconds, Bill knocked again.

"It looks empty." Carrie looked back toward the rest of us.

"I don't hear anything."

"Guys, this place gives me the creeps. Let's get inside and off the street." Maya had been facing away from the house, watching our backs. She glanced over her shoulder to us to punctuate her words. When she turned back around, I saw her gaze go to the pile of zombies that was still visible back the way we had come.

People were nothing if not predictable, and a quick search near the front door revealed a key that had been hidden under a flowerpot on the steps. Shawn handed the key up to Bill, and he used it to unlock the front door. He pushed the door open and stood at the threshold for a second. The inside of the home was deathly silent. My eagerness to finally get out of the rain warred with the fear of the unknown as we crept inside.

The people who lived in this house had obviously taken great pride in it. We fanned out, splitting into smaller groups as we searched for any danger. Shawn and I worked our way through the small living room together, and I couldn't help but notice that everything had been left neat and very clean. Other than a faint, unpleasant odor that I couldn't place, you would never know that the world had gone to hell outside if the only thing you had to go by was this living room.

I could hear the others as they worked their way around the house. No sounds of alarm or struggle could be heard, increasing my confidence that the house had indeed been empty. I was sure that, if a zombie were lurking around inside, we would have found it before now. At the other end of the room from me, Shawn peered behind the couch. His actions might have seemed silly, but it was better to be safe than sorry, even if there was not much chance that a zombie was lurking back there. A short dark hallway led off the back corner of the living room, and I walked toward it with more confidence. The lighting was low, but there was enough for me to see that a washer and dryer stood against the wall along the hall. A closed door at the far end was the only other way into the space.

Shifting my knife into my other hand, I tiptoed down the narrow space past the appliances and reached for the doorknob. It was likely just a closet, but every corner needed to be checked, and I wasn't going to be the one who got lazy and failed to open every door.

Turning the knob, I pushed the door open.

A low growl sounded from the pitch-black space beyond.

CHAPTER THIRTY-TWO
Day Seventeen

A horrible smell came from the darkness in front of me as I blinked rapidly, trying to adjust my eyes enough to see what was coming.

Backpedaling, I banged into the side of the washer, sending a metallic bang echoing down the hall. The growling continued, but the expected attack never came.

"Bri!" Hands yanking me further backward, I found myself shoved behind Shawn as he waited for the zombie to emerge from the room with the bat raised. The others began rushing into the living room, drawn by the commotion. I peered around Shawn's shoulder, not wanting to take my eye away from the dark doorway.

Something about the sound of the growl was nagging at the corners of my mind, but the rush of fear wasn't letting me think clearly. When the low sound cut off, I was still trying to figure out just why the growls bothered me.

"What the . . ." The bat lowered a fraction as we caught sight of the shadowy form that was slinking into the hall.

"It's a dog."

The dog came into the hallway with cautious steps, head low as he eyed us with wary curiosity. His ears and legs seemed too big for his body, making him look almost comical. A second later, I realized why that was. The dog was very thin.

His ribs and hip bones jutted out against the black and tan coat. The limited light glinted off a chain collar that hung loosely around his shrunken neck. Sympathy swelled inside me for the creature that had been apparently left shut in the dark room for weeks. I had been trying not to think about the fate of so many animals that had been left with no one to care for them. The thought of their suffering made me want to cry every time but standing in front of me now was the cruel reality of the situation. The most helpless of those around us were suffering horribly.

"Bri."

I ignored the warning tone in his voice as I ducked around Shawn and crouched down. Keeping my posture loose, I held a hand out and froze, offering to let the dog come to me at his own pace.

"Hi, boy. It's okay. You can come out now." I kept my voice even as I coaxed the dog to me. He cocked his head slightly to the side at my voice but remained where he had stopped. After a few seconds, I looked back to the group that was hovering just behind me. "It's okay. You guys can finish checking the house. I'm going to make friends with the dog."

"Are you sure?" Maya sounded skeptical.

"Yes. This many people all staring at him will just make it worse."

"Alright." They didn't look all that sure that they should be leaving, but the group slowly started to disappear from my view.

All except for Shawn.

"I'm not leaving you alone with that dog. What if it decides to attack you?"

"He's not going to attack me." I was confident in my words. I had grown up with dogs. I also volunteered at a vet clinic as a teen. The only reason I hadn't owned a dog when all this started was because we weren't allowed pets in the rental. This dog was scared and weak, and he was defensive, but he gave no indication that he was going to get aggressive. He just needed time to adjust to having strangers in his house.

"Well, I'm still not leaving."

"That's okay, but you need to stop being so tense."

He laughed shortly. "How exactly am I supposed to do that?"

"Sit down. Lean back against the wall and try to relax. And stop staring at him. It's best if you don't look at him at all for now. This might take a while."

Looking skeptical, Shawn followed my instructions and slid down the wall a few feet away from where I crouched. Satisfied, I turned my attention back to the dog.

I talked softly to the dog. Not much of it really made a lot of sense, but the content wasn't what really mattered anyway. Before long, the dog had taken the few steps needed to be able to stretch out his neck and sniff my offered hand. His tail banged against the dryer weakly a few times before he moved closer and sank down into an exhausted heap next to me. We stayed like that for a while—me rambling on to the dog before he finally relaxed and let his head rest on my knee.

"Good boy," I crooned to the dog as I let my fingers lightly stroke the fur just behind one ear. "That's a good boy."

"Okay, he's okay now. Just don't make any sudden moves." Clambering to my feet, I waited for the dog to get up, too, and started back toward the dark doorway.

"What are you doing?" Shawn cautiously got up from the floor too.

"I still need to check inside there." There was basically no chance that a zombie was lurking in the darkness, but I was still going to check.

The dog followed behind me as I went back to the doorway. This time, my eyes were fully adjusted to the lack of light, and I could see inside.

It was a bathroom. A sink was to the left and a tub to the right. I wrinkled my nose as I stepped inside.

The dog had been doing his business in the tub—that accounted for the smell. I noticed that the toilet past the sink was bone-dry. That little bit of water had obviously been the dog's saving grace. Without it, he would have never survived so long shut in this room. A rumpled bath mat and a stuffed monkey dog toy were on the floor by the tub. A large metal bowl was overturned in one corner. The air inside was horrible and my eyes were already burning. Picking up the bowl, I left the bathroom.

"Let's get you something to drink."

We didn't have much water left, but I was hoping that the others would have found something to remedy that situation by now. With the dog sticking close to my side and Shawn following behind, I went back through the living room and turned in the direction that I guessed would lead me to the kitchen.

The sound of low voices let me know that I was on the right track. Everyone else was probably in the kitchen searching for something to eat.

The conversation died out as I walked into the room with the dog at my heels. "Ignore him, everyone. Act like he isn't here at all."

As wary as the dog was, it would be best if everyone left him alone for a while.

They started talking again, and I listened as I looked around the room for something to take care of the dog with. One cabinet door that was hanging open had rows of canned dog food lined up inside, and I pulled one can out and set it on the counter. What he needed most, at this point, was water. After I sorted out the water situation, I would look for a can opener.

I didn't find what I was looking for in the kitchen, but a glance out the backdoor solved my problem. I could see another dog bowl overflowing with rainwater. Nothing seemed to be moving in the tiny backyard, so I opened the door. Shooting outside, the dog greedily lapped at the bowl until it was more than half-empty. With a final slurp, he raised his head and looked around himself. For a second, I was afraid that he would take off, but he sniffed the air once before turning around and coming back to where I had been waiting in the doorway.

"Good boy." I patted his head and reached for the tags that dangled from his chain. "Rex. Good boy, Rex." He wagged his tail when he heard his name, and he looked up at me with a bit of life returning to his eyes. "Let's go find a can opener."

*   *   *

Running my fingers through his hair, I snuggled closer to Rex and tried to turn my mind off.

When nighttime came, we had decided to stay in the house. I was currently tucked under the covers in one of the bedrooms when the dog happily curled up by my side.

Another day came that passed more pleasantly than usual in our new reality. We had eaten until we were all stuffed and pilfered clothes from the closets to replace our own filthy ones, except for Bill. There hadn't been anything in any of the closets that even came close to fitting his frame. We also entertained ourselves with books that we found around the house.

Rex's behavior had also improved quickly. Whenever he was done with his can of food, he would take a long nap and wake up ready to be the life of the party. He warmed up to the entire group quickly, and them to him. Everyone had been more than happy to comply with his pestering attempts to get them to pet him.

That night, it was my turn to get a full night of sleep. I was more than tired, but I still couldn't seem to relax enough to fall asleep. Too many questions were racing around in my brain. Who had killed all the zombies outside? And where were they now? We made sure to keep someone on watch all day but had yet to see a single live zombie here. What happened to Rex's owners? I couldn't help but think about them. We were eating their food, wearing their clothes, and sleeping in their beds. I wondered if they were out there, somewhere, trying to get back to their home. And I wondered what was going to happen to us.

The last couple of days had been harsh. A day inside, with dry clothes and plenty to eat, had done a lot to revive everyone. But we all knew that it was only temporary. Eventually, we would be forced to move on.

It was a harsh lesson that we were learning the hard way.

CHAPTER THIRTY-THREE
Day Eighteen

"You should probably stay off this leg for another day." I gave Devon's leg a serious look. "It hasn't healed at all from the first time I saw it. If you aren't careful, it's going to get infected."

"Okay. Thanks, Bri." He pulled the leg of his jeans back down but, to my satisfaction, didn't move to get off the couch.

When Fallon had finished taping the clean piece of gauze over the wound on Devon's leg, she dropped onto the other end of the couch to keep him company. Tossing the rest of our makeshift first aid kit back into Maya's bag, I stood up to return it to the spot by the front door where we had piled all the things we would want to take with us if we needed to make a run for it again.

Days spent wading through the damp and filth in the woods hadn't been good for the teen's leg. I hadn't been completely honest when I told him that his leg wasn't healing. It was worse than that. The skin around the wound had taken on a slightly puffy, red color. I was more than a little worried.

"His leg is worse." I dropped into a kitchen chair between Shawn and Carrie.

"I was afraid of that." Carrie looked through the doorway with concern. "Poor kid's really starting to limp."

"What can we do for him?" Shawn turned to me. I don't know how, but I had somehow become the group's unofficial

151

doctor. They all seemed to rely on my advice way more than I was comfortable with.

I sighed. "He needs to rest. If we can keep the wound clean, maybe his body will fight off the infection. Some antibiotics wouldn't hurt."

"I didn't see anything like that when I was raiding the nurse's closet back at the camp." Maya walked into the room and joined our quiet conversation.

"There wasn't any. I doubt a summer camp nurse would have been allowed to give anything stronger than aspirin and Tums." I hesitated. "There has to be something we could use in some of these houses." I turned toward Carrie. As far as I knew, she was the one who searched the upstairs bathroom.

She shook her head. "Nothing like that here. Just Band-Aids and Neosporin."

"Should we try another house?"

I looked back to Shawn. "Maybe."

"I don't know. There's something about this place that makes me uneasy." Maya glanced over to where we could see Bill watching out a window. "I'd really rather just get out of here. There's a car in the garage that we could all fit in. I say we take it and go."

"We need to stay. Devon needs the rest." I looked around. "We all do."

Even in clean clothes, our group looked like we weren't doing so well. Everyone was losing weight at an alarming rate; cheeks were beginning to sink into an unhealthy degree. None of us had bathed or combed our hair. Dark circles had taken up permanent residence under all our eyes. What we really needed was to stay, eat as much as we could, and sleep a lot. Maybe then we would start to look human again.

"I'll go look for some meds for him."

Somehow, it didn't surprise me at all that Shawn was the one to offer help. He was good like that.

152

"I'm going with you." I wouldn't let him out there alone.

"I'll come too."

I glanced over at Carrie with surprise. She looked back at me with some expression that was hard to decipher in her eyes.

"I'm not going to just sit back and let the kid suffer if there's something that I could do." She pushed her chair back from the table and left the room.

An uneasy silence fell over the table as everyone looked at each other. It seemed like Maya had something that she wanted to say.

When I focused on her, she sighed. "Carrie's grandson was about the same age as Devon. They lived in New York City. She lost contact with them at the beginning, but the last thing she heard was they were taking her grandson to the ER with a high fever." She looked over to her husband again. "I'll go tell Bill what's going on. We'll stay here and keep an eye on Devon and Fallon."

A few minutes later, Shawn, Carrie, and I shut the back door behind us with a quiet click. Rex jumped up and pressed his nose to the glass on the other side of the door, watching us leave. I had no idea what we were going to run into out here, so I thought it was safer to leave the dog behind.

The rain had finally stopped, and a pretty blue sky stretched out overhead. As the sun shined once again, the humidity was already climbing, and the smell from the decaying zombies that were scattered around the small town hung heavy in the stagnant air.

Our game plan was simple. We would start searching houses and hopefully find what we were looking for without running into too much trouble. There just had to be someone who lived in this place who had a bottle of antibiotics stashed in their home.

The yard between our hideaway and the next house over had already started to grow out of control. The tall grass was still wet, and my sneakers and lower pants legs were soaked again by the time we crossed the short distance. In either direction, the street was silent and empty.

I grimaced down at Shawn and Carrie as I stepped onto the front porch. The three of us paused to look around before knocking on the door. Each of them was going to look in nearby windows. I tapped my knuckles lightly against the peeling paint of the door when they nodded at me, indicating that they were ready.

Almost immediately, a crash sounded from within.

"No good." Carrie backed away from her window. "There's one in there."

A face streaked with crusty blood pressed up against the window where she had just been standing. The zombie inside hissed and banged its forehead against the glass.

"Let's try the next one."

We followed Shawn to the next house over and repeated the process. This time, there was no activity stirred inside by my knock. The owners of this home hadn't left a convenient spare key hidden by their door, so Carrie used a rock from their landscaping to break the window in the door. I flinched at the sound of glass hitting the floor inside, but there were still no alarming noises telling us to run. After carefully reaching inside to unlock the door, we were finally able to step inside.

The house was much smaller than the one that we were using for our hideout. It took almost no time for us to decide that the house was empty.

The single small bathroom didn't yield the results we were hoping for, though I did scoop up half of a bottle of prescription pain killers I found hidden behind a jar of Vaseline. I had no doubt that they would come in handy at some point, hopefully not anytime in the near future.

Wandering back to the kitchen, I found Shawn had just finished dumping the contents of a cupboard into the duffel bag he brought along. We agreed that, while searching for the medicine, we would also take any food we came across. It didn't make sense not to.

Carrie walked into the kitchen from where she had been looking through the bedrooms. "I found a pack of batteries that are the right size for our flashlights. There's nothing else back there."

"I took all the nonperishables. There wasn't much." Shawn zipped up the duffel. They both looked my way.

I held up the bottle I'd taken. "They aren't antibiotics, but these could come in handy."

"Good. Let's keep moving."

The next house had its front door standing wide open, and we approached it with extra caution. After looking into windows and banging on the doorframe, Carrie decided it was safe to go in. In the upstairs bathroom, we finally found what we had been looking for. I held the bottle up triumphantly, and two answering grins bloomed on the dirty faces looking back at me.

Slinging the backpack onto my back, I felt lighter than I had been in a very long time as we descended the stairs and headed back toward the front door. Behind me, the other two were talking animatedly about the things that we had picked up while searching the houses. At the front door, I glanced through the window to check for zombies. It was all clear, so I swung the door open and stepped outside.

But then suddenly, the tall hedges that ran between this house and the next rustled. I had just enough time to turn to the left before a zombie launched itself from their green depths and crashed into me with all its weight.

I shrieked as I went down hard with the zombie snarling on top of me. Its strength was alarming as it gripped onto my shoulders and brought its gaping mouth closer to me.

Time slowed down. I recognized Shawn and Carrie yelling from somewhere out of my field of view. Using both hands to try to hold the creature back, I knew already that that was a battle I was going to lose. The zombie's rancid breath blew across my face as its teeth gnashed and drool splattered across my chin.

With a final pull, the zombie managed to yank my upper body close enough to bite when, without warning, pain exploded in my shoulder.

CHAPTER THIRTY-FOUR
Day Eighteen

Wide-eyed with horror, I looked down to where the zombie had sunk its teeth into my shoulder. Shaking its head like a dog trying to kill something within its jaws, the zombie reared back. The strap of my backpack pulled forward, pinched tightly in its teeth.

Chomping down hard on the padded nylon, the creature focused its red eyes on my face and growled. Hyperventilating, I shoved it back with all of the strength I could muster.

A hand clutching the knife that I dropped appeared from behind me and stabbed the zombie in the eye. It instantly went limp. I lurched to my feet, frantically kicking out from under its dead weight. A set of hands spun me around, and I was met with worried grey eyes. Muttering his most colorful expletives yet, Shawn pulled at the neck of my shirt to reveal the bite.

Dazed, I looked down.

An angry-looking bruise was already growing where the zombie's teeth had given me a nasty pinch, but there was no blood. Incredulous, Shawn grabbed the backpack strap and looked at the rips bitten into the tough fabric.

"I can't believe it."

"Is she bitten?" Carrie appeared next to Shawn and looked at what we were both staring. She started to laugh. "You have got to be the only person alive to be saved from a zombie by a backpack."

I must have been going into shock because I failed to see the humor in the situation. At least I still had enough sense to realize that my mouth was hanging open and so I shut it.

I wasn't the only one to fail to think it was funny. "We should get back to the others." Shawn glared at Carrie over his shoulder as he turned me to go back.

The walk back took less than a minute, and I felt like I was trying to move underwater. Everything seemed sluggish and a bit fuzzy around the edges. Maya had been watching for us, and she knew that something wasn't right as soon as she opened the door. Her voice sounded like it was far away.

"What happened?"

"Bri had a really close call." Shawn pulled out a kitchen chair and sat me down in it.

"Is she okay?"

That was genuine worry I heard in Maya's voice, and it brought a bit of reality back to me.

I had nearly been bitten by a zombie. The strap of my backpack was the only reason I was not going to become one of them. That was way too close.

"She's fine, just bruised," Carrie huffed as she shouldered her way through the door carrying two overloaded bags: hers and the duffel that I just now realized Shawn must have abandoned three houses over.

My arms felt chilly. I began rubbing my hands over them to try to warm up, but the heavy backpack that I still wore hindered my movements. Shrugging out of it, I fingered the bite mark.

The rest of our group filtered into the room, and before long, everyone seemed to be talking at once. They wanted to know what had happened, and I couldn't really blame them, but the conversation went around me as if I was insulated from anything beyond the torn nylon that was still in my fingers.

A ragged stuffed monkey dropped into my lap.

Rex stood with his nose nearly touching my knee, his brown eyes intently watching my face. Reaching out slowly, I rested my free hand on top of his neck.

When a blanket draped around my shoulders, I looked up. Releasing my grip on the strap, I grabbed Shawn's hand and squeezed it.

"Thank you."

*   *   *

I decided to make a conscious effort to not be mad at Carrie. We had all been through unspeakable horrors. We weren't all going to react the same way to every situation that arose. I knew that she hadn't been laughing about me nearly getting bitten. Not really. The stress of the situation was enough to make any of us have odd reactions.

After she had risked her own safety to look for the medicine that Devon needed, I knew that she was a good person, but I was still having a hard time being in the same room with her. This was my issue, and I was going to have to work it out, but it was going to take longer than one afternoon.

"I think that we should stay here for the night. We can re-evaluate in the morning." Bill looked around to see if we all agreed.

No one objected, so I jumped up off the couch. It was my turn to keep watch, giving me a plausible excuse for a hasty exit.

Roaming the house slowly, stopping to watch out of every window for a minute or two, took my mind off the ache in my shoulder. When the fog of shock had finally cleared from my mind, I discovered that I must have banged my head when I hit the ground. There was a sore spot on my skull and a dull throbbing headache as proof.

Following behind me was Rex, carrying his toy. He hadn't let me out of his sight since we got back. Every time I stopped, he

159

would drop his toy at my feet and sit. I started to pet his head lightly while looking out the window, and I quickly found the gesture quite therapeutic.

It was when I was looking out of the window in the upstairs hallway when Shawn found me a little later into my watch. He didn't say anything, just leaned up against the wall to wait with me. I wasn't sure what I wanted to say exactly, so I kept quiet.

Shawn, Rex, and I made our way around the house like that for several hours. By the end of my shift, I had realized something that, up until then, hadn't occurred to me. The world may have effectively come to an end. Civilization had been thrust back hundreds of years and appeared to be tottering on the brink of complete extinction, but, for the first time in a very long time, I was not alone.

Later on, when I was sufficiently exhausted that I thought I may be able to actually get some sleep, I dragged my feet back to the bedroom that I had used the night before. But when I cracked open the door, I found Fallon already asleep there. Closing the door, I tried the next room. Maya and Bill were there, and I shut the door quickly, feeling like I had intruded. The couple seemed to never get any time to themselves, with so many of us all forced together like we were.

I knew the last bedroom was probably already occupied. Carrie was on watch, and I passed Devon asleep on the couch in the living room. That only left one person who I hadn't already run across in my search for a place to sleep.

Hesitating in the hall, I thought about finding someplace else to curl up for the night, but that wasn't really what I wanted to do. I took a deep breath and lightly tapped my knuckles on the door frame.

"Yeah?" Shawn's voice was groggy.

"Um, I don't really want to sleep alone, so . . ." I trailed off. I was already feeling like some sort of idiot for even suggesting that we share a room. I was glad for the darkness to cover the burn I felt spreading across my cheeks.

I then heard covers rustled in the room. "Come here."

Crossing to the bed before I could talk myself out of doing it, I climbed under the covers that he was holding up for me. His arms wound around me, pulling me back to rest against his front, and I felt his nose rest lightly against the back of my head.

After a tense few seconds, I felt myself relax, and before long, I was drifting into a blessedly dreamless sleep.

CHAPTER THIRTY-FIVE
Day Twenty

When morning came, we were all preparing to leave our temporary shelter. When I carried the last of our bags into the garage, Bill and Shawn were already there, trying to figure out the logistics of fitting seven people, a dog, and the small mountain of supplies we had gathered into one van.

We had rested long enough that everyone felt like they had at least some of their strength back. Devon's leg wasn't really any better, but at least it wasn't worse, and we knew that we were out of options for trying to treat him here. It was time to move on.

We were hoping to find a settlement of some sort. There had to be one out there somewhere. It seemed impossible that the only people left alive would be us—a small group that was barely hanging on by the tips of their fingers. There had to be people out there who were doing better. Maybe they would even have a real doctor, not a girl with limited first aid training and a few years spent observing the veterinarians in an animal clinic.

"Good riddance to this place." Maya walked into the garage with Devon limping along behind her. She had never gotten rid of her dislike for the creepy little town, not that any of us blamed her. Something about it was just off.

In the end, the two largest members of our group took the seats up front. Fallon and I sat in the middle, with Rex taking up most of our floor space; even too thin, the dog was big. Carrie,

Maya, and Devon squished into the back seat. The hatch had barely closed on all the stuff that we shoved back there. I was really glad that we found the keys to the van in the kitchen, instead of having to try to carry all the heavy bags ourselves.

We may have gone a little overboard with packing, but as far as we knew, we would be living out of the van for the foreseeable future. To that end, we had gathered jugs of water, all the canned or boxed food for a several house radius, and a few comfort items such as blankets and hairbrushes. We even made room for a giant-sized bag of dog kibble. Leaving Rex behind wasn't really an option for any of us.

The sound of the garage door opening must have drawn the zombies. There weren't many of them her. Whoever had gone on a spree with a gun had seen to that, but there were a few. Three of them, shuffling along and rotting to the point that strips of their flesh were peeling, met the van as Bill drove it out of the driveway. They offered no real threat to us. The doors were all locked and the windows rolled up, but I still flinched when one of them banged on the window by my face. For a second, I thought I felt the stinking, hot breath of the zombie, even though I knew that that was impossible. I rubbed my shoulder in reflex.

Low growling from my feet pulled me back from my thoughts. Rex had climbed to his feet and was watching the zombie alertly, the hint of sound rumbling from his chest.

"It's okay, boy." I patted his back in an effort to keep him quiet. That was going to be the only drawback to having a dog. We already talked about it. Sometimes, dogs made noise, but a noise made at the wrong time could get us all killed. Rex was going to have to learn to be quiet when there was a threat nearby.

The plan was simple. South seemed like the most likely option for finding a settled group. With no electricity, the north would be a harsh place to try to survive in the winter. If anyone was going to manage to eke out a living in this new world, it would be in the south. A road map found in the glove box had provided our

163

route. We would go back the way we had come, get on the highway, and just keep driving.

It may have taken us days to walk the distance between the camp and the town, but in what felt like the blink of an eye, I saw the turnoff for the camp up ahead. As we drove by, I craned my neck to try to get a view of the place that, for a short time, I had thought would be home.

That wooden bridge that I hated flashed by. The brief view I had of it told me that we made the right choice when we ran. Several zombies ambled across its surface. Their heads snapped in our direction, and I was sure they gave chase, but the trees stole my view.

We were nearly back to the town just off the highway when I noticed the thick black smoke trailing high into the sky. I saw the others looking at it too, but no one said anything. I had a feeling we would find out soon enough what was causing it.

The last time I had been in the other town, Shawn and I had been searching for supplies to make drinking water. It seemed like much longer than it had actually been since we saved Fallon and got the heck out of there. The town looked startlingly different than I remembered it.

Windows in nearly every building had been broken, doors stood hanging open. There was a car abandoned by the fuel pumps that hadn't been there earlier. And we found the source of the smoke. The row of trailers that were closest to the main road was all on fire.

A crowd of zombies milled around the burning homes, some getting too close, their tattered clothing catching on fire.

I looked behind me to check on Devon. This was his hometown that had been reduced to chaos. He stared out the window with a frown on his face but didn't comment.

We glided back up the on-ramp, and the miles passed quickly beneath the tires of our confiscated van. Devon and Fallon talked quietly back and forth, but the rest of us didn't really have much to say. The journey ahead would be dangerous, and with no set destination in mind or even a guarantee that we would find what we were looking for, everyone was troubled.

The highways were still as silent and empty as they had been when Shawn and I first drove them together. The grass along the side of the road was a little taller, the abandoned vehicles dirtier, but the view was more or less the same.

The decision had been made before we pulled out of the garage: we would try to siphon gas from abandoned cars along the way instead of trying to get gas at a gas station. It seemed safer to avoid towns that we had no intention of stopping at anyhow, and Maya's group had worked out a system when they were on the road before.

We had been driving for a couple of hours when Bill announced that we needed to start looking for a likely place to stop. The first car that appeared ahead of us was stopped unceremoniously in the middle of the road. Three of the four doors and the trunk all stood open. Bill didn't slow down, just swerved around the car and kept going.

I wasn't sure why he hadn't stopped. He was the one who just said we needed gas. Shawn must have been confused, too, because he looked curiously over at Bill.

Bill saw the look. "That one was probably empty. We've found out that cars that are left the way that one was were left like that for a reason. We need a car that looks like it was purposefully parked. Like the driver intended to come back for it."

Barely a mile up the road, we found what he had been talking about. A beat-up-looking pickup truck and an SUV were pulled into the grass along the side of the road. Next to the vehicles, a makeshift camp had been set up. But it was obvious that whoever had been there wasn't coming back.

The open tent door flapped in the breeze. Belongings were scattered around and tipped over. One door to the truck stood open. I could see blood splattered on the interior, and a large pool had congealed on the ground.

The fine hairs on my arms started to prickle. Whoever these people had been, they thought that it was safe to stop here and paid with their lives. I hoped we weren't going to make the same mistake somewhere along the road.

CHAPTER THIRTY-SIX
Day Twenty

We stayed in the van for several minutes. Bill had stopped it in the middle of the highway, giving us enough room to be able to look all around the abandoned camp. We needed to be sure that the zombies were gone before we all climbed out of the safety of the van.

My eyes kept going back to the dry blood that had sprayed the interior of the truck. It looked like someone had been so close to survival, only to have their life snatched away from them at the last second. It was a disconcerting thought.

Bill was the first to open his door, the rest of us following him. Maya pulled out the length of hose that she had cut back in the garage and a gas can. She went to work siphoning gas from the pickup while the rest of us fanned out.

Rex darted into the tall grass and began vigorously sniffing the area. I still wasn't sure that he wouldn't run off, so I kept an eye on him as I wandered over to the open tent. It only made sense to check for anything we may want to take with us.

A couple of sleeping bags lay in a heap on the floor of the tent, looking like whoever had been using them got up in a hurry. The empty wrappers from a few candy bars were tossed into a corner. Other than that, the tent was empty. Pulling my head back out of the opening, I looked around to see what the rest of the group was doing.

While Maya stole the gas, Bill stood watch, making sure that nothing was able to sneak up on her. Devon leaned against the side of the van, keeping his weight off his injured leg. The others all poked through the scattered belongings left in the grass, but it didn't look like they were finding much of use.

Rex had wandered close to the tree line that started a dozen yards off the pavement, his nose to the wind as he sniffed intently at the breeze.

"Rex, come here, boy," I called him back to me. If he took off after something, I wouldn't be able to go look for him, and I was already attached to the dog. I didn't want to lose him.

When he trotted back to my side, I walked nearer to where everyone else had congregated at the back of the abandoned SUV. Maya was just finishing pouring the gas into our own tank.

"We should fill the can back up with whatever is left in this one. Who knows when we'll be able to stop again." Carrie patted the side of the SUV as she looked to Maya.

Maya and Bill walked over, and Maya set up to finish taking whatever gas was left in the SUV.

Looking over the top of the vehicle, Bill wondered out loud. "Do you think we should take the tent?"

Looking in the direction of the tent, I contemplated on the question. Did we need a tent? Or, more accurately, was it safe to use a tent? The previous people who had tried it hadn't fared so well.

"I think I'd feel safer sleeping in the van."

Echoes of agreement sounded around me. Those flimsy panels of fabric wouldn't do much to keep a zombie out.

"Yeah, you're right."

Muttering about making space for the now half-full gas can, Bill went to open the back of the van. Devon hopped to the open door and climbed back into the back seat. I watched him worriedly, and I wasn't the only one. We were all staring after the teen when a hair-raising snarl from the dog made us look in the direction he was staring.

A zombie had broken from the tree line and was hobbling toward us as fast as its mangled body could manage. Even from a bit of a distance, the damage that had been inflicted on it was apparent. Bites to its face and neck had removed chunks of flesh. One arm had been gnawed until bone showed through. Likewise, the missing muscle that had been removed from its thigh was deep and was what was causing the relatively fresh zombie's slower pace.

Decomposition hadn't had much of a chance to set in yet, and without the damage, this zombie would have still been frightening for its speed.

"I got it." Carrie pulled her knife from her belt and walked steadily forward to meet the zombie.

It was just one zombie, but that didn't mean that more wouldn't come. Grabbing onto Rex's collar to keep the still growling dog from attacking, I watched as Carrie calmly approached the zombie.

The creature lurched toward her with mouth open, and she allowed its own momentum to drive her knife through its eye. When she bent down to retrieve her knife, I hustled the dog over to the van and put him inside.

"Watch him, please. I don't want him to run off," I told Devon before sliding the door shut. We were just about ready to leave, and having the dog shut in the van would make me feel better.

I was turning back around when I heard the scream.

Whirling, I watched in horror as two more zombies charged from the trees—fast ones.

Carrie was still midway between the trees and the vehicles. What was worse, she wasn't alone.

Somehow, in the scant seconds it had taken me to shut the dog in the van, Maya and Shawn made it to Carrie's side. I bolted in their direction.

I wasn't going to make it to my friends before the zombies. And they stood no chance of outrunning them and making it inside the van. In my peripheral vision, I saw that Bill was also running toward them. We would have to hope that, between the five of us, we could kill two fresh zombies and that the three of them could manage to not get bitten until we got there to help.

The tall grass impeded me as I tried to make my legs run faster. I had never cursed being shorter than average as much as I was at that moment. Pulling ahead of me, Bill held his own knife out.

Without conscious thought, I found the machete that I had discovered in the garage and claimed in my hand. I was near to where my friends had turned to face their attackers when the zombies reached them first.

Swinging hard with his bat, Shawn attempted to take out the first zombie, but it jerked to the side, and his blow bounced off its shoulder instead. The creature kept coming, and with no time to recover, he was unable to stop it from running straight into him. Shawn and the zombie went down in a tangle of limbs, and the tall grass hid them from my frantic sight.

Just feet away from where Shawn had gone down, Maya was struggling to keep the other zombie at bay while Carrie attempted to stab it. But the zombie wasn't exactly an easy target as it fought with Maya, and she had to be careful not to hit Maya instead of the zombie. None of Carrie's stabs had the desired effect.

I could see the desperation on their faces as the zombie inched closer to taking a bite out of Maya. Just when I thought that it was too late, Bill reached them and charged straight into the zombie, ripping it away from the women tumbling into the grass.

I bounded the last few steps to where Shawn had disappeared, heart beating like it wanted to escape from my chest. I couldn't have found family, for the first time in my life, only to have that family taken away so soon. I refused to believe that fate could be so cruel.

Just as I spotted the familiar color of his shirt, Shawn staggered to his feet, breathing harshly. A smear of blood coated his cheek, and more of it was on his hands. And the knife he held.

The zombie lay unmoving in the grass.

"Are you okay?"

He saw me running toward him, and a panicked look crossed his face.

"What are you doing?! Get to the van!" He swung around, checking for any more zombies.

The zombies lay still while Maya was helping her husband get to his feet and Carrie looking wildly around. The five of us bolted for the van where Fallon and Devon were standing, looking unsure if they should try to help or not.

"Get in the van!" Bill's loud order made up their minds, and the two scrambled to climb into the back seat.

When I ran away from the van to help the other, it felt like an eternity for me, and going back toward its safety wasn't any better. I kept waiting for more screams and sounds of pursuit to come from behind us, but, thankfully, they never came. Reaching the vehicle as one group, we piled inside and slammed the doors closed.

I was still clutching the machete when Rex almost cut himself on the blade in his exuberance at greeting me. I tucked it away and buried my hands in his hair in an attempt to stop the trembling that had started.

"Has anyone been bitten?" Maya's low question came from the back seat.

"No."

"I'm okay."

Carrie hesitated before answering, "I'm good. It's not a bite." She held up her hand that she had wrapped in her outer shirt. Red was starting to bleed through the material. "Think I'm gonna need stitches though. That knife is sharp."

"Okay." Bill cleared his throat. "Let's get out of here. Carrie, we'll look for a better place to stop and get your hand taken care of. Hang in there."

It was a relief when he started the van and left the abandoned campsite behind.

Finding a place to stop proved to be harder than expected. We had been traveling a long stretch of highway that was bordered on both sides by endless trees. It was nearly an hour later before we took an off-ramp that led to a tiny gas station in the middle of nowhere.

The front door to the gas station had already been forced open by someone else. The food, drinks, and anything else remotely useful that had been stocked on the shelves were gone. Fortunately, we had enough of those things for now. What we needed were four walls and a roof. The little gas station would work well enough.

Carrie had started to look a little green by the time I sat her down and began rooting through our medical supplies. I hoped she wasn't squeamish about needles. Having to stitch her hand up was going to test the fortitude of my own stomach. The last thing I needed was her getting sick all over me.

"Okay, Carrie. Let's take a look." I grabbed for her hand but pulled away like it was too hot.

Because it was.

CHAPTER THIRTY-SEVEN
Day Twenty

This could not be happening. I shouldn't have been able to feel the heat of Carrie's hand through the shirt wrapped around it. That just wasn't normal, and it could only mean one thing: Carrie was running one very, very high fever.

I hesitated for a brief moment before I reached out to touch the back of my fingers on the exposed skin of her arm. I needed to be sure.

My heart fell. She was too hot.

"Um, Carrie? You feeling okay?"

She shook her head. "Honestly, no. I think I might be coming down with the flu or something."

"Okay." I tried to keep my tone light. "Let's take care of your hand and then I'll see if we have anything else that might help in the bag."

I dug until I found a couple of our remaining latex gloves and put them on. Steadying myself with a big breath, I unwound the shirt, afraid of what I was going to find. Carrie had said that she didn't get bitten, but maybe she had been mistaken. I had only ever felt a fever like that once before, and it had been coming from Evie just a few hours before she died.

I hoped that I was wrong, but to be honest, I was completely expecting a bite or maybe some deep scratches when I finally uncovered her wound.

The wound was clearly a deep cut made by something very sharp. Like a knife. I moved her hand to look for the feared marks, but they weren't there. Just one long gash to the palm of her hand. Maybe luck was with us, and Carrie really was just coming down with a bad case of the flu. She certainly hadn't had one of the tainted vaccines, and she appeared to not be bitten, so that seemed to rule out zombie infection.

"I've, uh . . . I've never given anyone stitches before, so . . ." I trailed off.

"It's okay. Do what you can." She gave me a tight smile.

I got busy cleaning the cut. Around us, the rest of our group had done their best to secure the gas station and search it.

When Shawn wandered over to where Carrie and I sat, I shot him a meaningful look while Carrie was distracted by something that Bill was saying to Maya. Catching my look, Shawn came closer and hovered over my shoulder to watch. I didn't want to cause panic, not until we knew for sure at least, but I needed to tell someone else about my concerns. If Carrie really was infected, she was going to die and then she was going to become a very real danger.

The feeling of the needle and thread pulling through flesh was nauseating. The experience had to be even worse for Carrie. She did her best to hold her hand steady, but she couldn't help the involuntary twitches. By the time I had finished closing the wound, sweat was trickling from her forehead. I couldn't help but wonder if it was a result of my stitching her hand or the zombie virus. Digging for some pain killers, I handed her a hefty dose.

"Thanks. We should start calling you Doc." She smiled weakly at me and swallowed the pills.

"You should rest a while." I did my best to smile at her attempt at humor. Even I could feel that the expression fell flat on my face.

"I think I will."

Carrie got up stiffly and wandered over to where the others had piled a few blankets. The gas station didn't exactly offer any sort of comfort, but they had done their best to make a soft spot to rest. I watched her go while Shawn dropped down to sit next to me.

"What's wrong?"

I leaned closer to whisper, "I think Carrie might be infected."

"What!"

His voice was too loud, and I scowled at him.

"She is running a really high fever, and she says she feels like she is coming down with something. I didn't see any bites, but I've only felt a fever like that one time before."

He stayed quiet, watching Carrie for several seconds. The woman's long hair had fallen to cover her face from view, but even way across the room, we could clearly see the trembling that had started to shake her. "We have to tell everyone else."

He was right, and I didn't stop him when he waved for the others to join us.

"What is it?" Fallon asked.

When I repeated what I had already told Shawn, everyone focused their worried eyes on the woman huddled into the blankets.

"You're sure it wasn't a bite?" Bill asked me. He looked troubled.

"I didn't see anything that looked like a bite." I looked at directly at him. "Yeah, I'm sure. Like she said, she cut herself on her knife." As soon as the words left my mouth, I knew what had happened. "Crap."

"What?"

I had their undivided attention.

"Her knife. She used it to stab that zombie right before she cut herself. She would have gotten blood from the zombie into the cut."

Silence fell as we thought about the implications of what I said. It made sense. Fresh, infected blood coming in contact with

175

an open wound would surely spread the infection. Why hadn't we seen it before?

"But that zombie at the camp scratched me, and I practically showered in its blood. I didn't get sick." Shawn brought up a good point.

"Wait. You were scratched?" Fallon asked the question that it looked like everyone else was thinking.

Shawn nodded. "Yeah. If it wasn't for Bri, I'd have gotten bitten for sure too." He pulled his shirt aside to show everyone the mostly healed scratches.

"We wondered if it was transferred through a scratch or not." Maya glanced at Bill. "I guess we have our answer."

I thought about the scratches that I had cleaned like a crazy person not so long ago. "You had zombie blood everywhere, except those scratches."

He nodded slowly. "Yeah. I think you are right. I think that shoulder stayed clean somehow. You also insisted on treating it right away." He didn't add what we all were thinking. Carrie had been cut for a while before we were able to treat her hand.

"What do we do now?" Devon asked the tough question.

"If she is infected, there's only one way it will end." Maya's voice cracked on the last word. Bill reached over to rub her back soothingly.

I had forgotten for a minute that Carrie and the couple had been friends before all this went down. It wouldn't be easy for any of us to watch our friend die, but for them, it would be worse.

Bill spoke up, "We don't have to make any decisions right now. Let's let her rest for a while and see. Maybe she won't get any worse."

CHAPTER THIRTY-EIGHT
Day Twenty-One

The moon had tracked its way past the halfway point in the sky. Leaning against each other, Shawn and I watched its progress through the big windows at the front of the gas station. Neither of us had been able to sleep. Instead, we sat on the tiled floor and waited to find out if we were going to lose a friend today.

Rex lay with his head propped on my knee. Absentmindedly running my fingers through the dog's fur, I turned to look at Carrie who was still asleep across the room.

I felt guilt gnaw at me though it wasn't for the first time that night. I wished fervently that I could take back being mad at Carrie for the past couple of days.

When I stitched up her hand earlier, that had been the first time I said more than two words to her since my own close call with a zombie. Now, it felt petty of me to have been so upset with her for something so simple.

Carrie was the only one sleeping. The rest of us had been keeping a grim vigil, hoping for a miracle, but as the hours wore on, it became more and more apparent that our fears were coming true.

Carrie was infected.

She had shivered her way through most of the night, despite the warm temperature. Her hair stuck to her clammy skin— skin that had taken on an unhealthy color that could be seen even

177

in the dim light. Now, her breathing had become labored, and she tossed restlessly upon the pile of blankets.

Fallon and Devon also sat together, not far from where Shawn and I were. Maya had been pacing the length of the room while Bill leaned against the door jam and watched outside, but all of us had spent most of the night tracking Carrie's illness with increasingly grim expressions.

When Maya looked at Carrie one last time and walked resolutely toward her husband, I knew something was about to happen. Nudging Shawn, I jumped to my feet and went to join them by the door. In a matter of seconds, we had all gathered.

"She's infected." Maya's voice sounded hollow.

I felt myself nodding in agreement. "I don't know what the right thing to do is."

We stared at each other. No one knew the answer. How could we have prepared to have to make such a decision?

"I know I'm sick." Rustling fabric and a raspy voice from Carrie herself put us out of our misery. Struggling to prop herself upright on shaky arms, she let us know that she had woken up.

"Carrie, don't wear yourself out." Maya hurried to help her friend.

Carrie waved her away weakly. "Don't touch me. You shouldn't touch me." She finally managed to get herself upright.

"How are you feeling?" I edged closer to her.

"Like someone shattered every bone in my body." She grimaced at me. "I know I'm infected. I saw it happen to someone back at the start. I know the signs."

Abruptly, she started coughing violently. Hunched over, she rode out the wracking coughs while we watched helplessly from just feet away. When the fit finally ended, she sat back up even more slowly than the first time. Blood covered her lips and chin. More of it formed a puddle on the blankets.

Maya whimpered and grabbed Bill's hand.

Wheezing, Carrie looked at her friends. "I need to borrow your gun. Just for a few minutes."

Maya objected to her request, but in the end, Carrie won the argument between herself and her worried friend. She knew she was going to die soon. She insisted on doing it on her own terms. At least.

While I didn't blame her—I watched Evie die from the virus and it was brutal—I couldn't stay and watch. I said my goodbyes and let myself and Rex out of the building.

The stretch of the highway that we had been traveling was desolate. There were very few people around the area before the outbreak, and we hadn't seen a single zombie since stopping there the day before. I felt comfortable enough going outside with just Rex and my machete for protection. I didn't plan to go far, but I was feeling the need for a few minutes alone.

A hint of the sunrise was just starting to show over the horizon when the single gunshot suddenly rang out. Kneeling down, I wrapped my arms around the dog and held on. Patient as could be, the dog sat and let me grieve on his shoulder for a long time.

The tears had finally dried up when another shot tore through the morning air.

I jumped to my feet and whirled to face back the way I had come. I had walked farther than I originally intended and was surprised to find that I couldn't see the gas station anymore. A bunch of trees was blocking my view.

There shouldn't have been a second shot. If everything had gone to plan, the only shot needed would have been the first one.

I started running back toward my friends. Rex stayed by my side as I sprinted. Some instinct that I couldn't explain caused me to stop just before I rounded the trees that would bring the building back into view. Warning bells screamed in my head and an uncomfortable feeling settled in the pit of my stomach. Ducking behind a wide tree, I peered out at the gas station.

A black pickup was pulling into the parking lot. As I watched, a burly man climbed from the driver's seat and walked back to open the tailgate.

The front door of the building stood open—something that no one in my group would have done. Open doors made it too easy for a zombie to get inside. The door being wide open confirmed that something had gone terribly awry while I walked alone.

Rex began to growl and I shushed him. We were still far enough away from the stranger that I doubted he could hear, but I didn't want to take that chance.

"Stay." I hoped the dog would listen.

Movement in the doorway proved to be another strange man. Flaming orange hair and beard concealed most of his features. What I noticed most about the man, however, was the rifle he held in front of him.

The bearded man walked to the back of the truck. He and the other stranger laughed together over something the bearded guy said, but I couldn't make out the words.

Then my friends started to leave the building.

My hand went to my face in horror. Bill came outside first. His hands had been tied behind him, and blood flowed steadily from a wound to his shoulder. The rest filed out behind Bill, all with tied hands. Fallon was crying. Behind them, two more men walked out with their own guns trained on my friends.

The strangers herded my group to the back of the pickup and unceremoniously into the bed. One of the men shoved Shawn down in the truck and delivered a nasty kick to his side. The men all laughed again before two of them settled into the truck bed with guns ready.

Part of me wanted to run from my hiding place and try to do something, but even in my panic, I knew that that was a terrible idea. All by myself, I stood no chance against the four men, at least three of whom were armed with guns. My group was in no shape to help me help them.

So I held my ground behind the tree and watched as the driver climbed back behind the wheel of the truck. The bearded guy walked to our van and got inside. The two vehicles turned away from the highway and drove deeper into the mountains around us.

I waited for several long minutes before cautiously coming out from behind the tree. The open ground between myself and the building felt dangerous, like someone was out there still, waiting for me to reveal myself. I rushed for the cover of the building but stopped dead just inside the door.

In all the chaos, I had neglected to realize that Carrie's body would still be inside. Someone had draped one of our blankets over her. Blood soaked through the material over her head. I shuddered and turned away. Carrie's troubles were over, but the rest of my group still needed me.

Our few belongings that we brought inside with us were scattered around the room. Someone had ransacked the bags and taken what they wanted. A small pool of blood on the floor had been smeared by booted feet. One of the shelves that stood in the middle of the room was knocked over. There had been an obvious struggle.

When I found my backpack with the zombie-bitten strap, I picked it up and began filling it back up with anything left that might be useful. If I was going to track down my people, I was going to need supplies.

With a last look around the gas station, I went outside and hurried across the parking lot. The truck carrying my group, including Shawn, had gone right, so that was the way I was going too.

I had seen his eyes scanning the area as the pickup drove away, looking for any sign of me. If it was the last thing I did, I was going to get my family back.

CHAPTER THIRTY-NINE
Day Twenty-One

The zombie ambled out from behind the thorn bushes and onto the dusty, dirt road. It hadn't seen me yet, and I froze in my tracks, hoping that it would keep on going.

Luck was not on my side as Rex let out a ferocious snarl that turned the zombie our way. It was too late to hush the dog, so I focused instead on not getting bitten.

The zombie wasn't one of the ultra-fast ones, but my heart rate still skyrocketed at the thought of having to kill one completely on my own. I hadn't realized until that moment just how much I had come to rely on the others to always have my back.

It was another humid day, and the sun had climbed high into the sky. The smell of week-old roadkill coming off the zombie made me want to gag as the creature bared broken teeth to hiss at me.

That hiss was apparently too much for Rex to take sitting down. Baring his own sharp teeth, the dog launched himself at the zombie. Colliding mid-leap, the zombie was knocked over by the dog, who began biting viciously into the rotting flesh.

"Rex, no!"

I tried to move closer, to find room to use the machete, but Rex was on top of the zombie. Any movement I made would have been sure to hit the dog first. I yelled at him to stop again, but he kept up the furious assault like he hadn't heard me.

The zombie's grasping hands tugged at the dog's sides, ripping out handfuls of fur. Releasing his hold on its neck, Rex snapped down on one arm. The crack of the bones was clear, even over the sounds of the dog and zombie snarling at each other.

Crunching down on the arm harder, Rex refused to let go of the flailing limb. When the zombie managed to sling him partially off itself, I finally found an opportunity.

The machete sunk into the zombie's skull much easier than a knife did.

Even after the zombie had slumped to the ground and stopped moving, Rex held onto its arm. Bending over to rest my hands on my knees, I tried to calm my racing heart.

"Rex."

This time he listened to me. Dropping the mangled arm, he trotted to my side and grinned up at me with zombie blood splattered all over his fur and coating his teeth.

The dog was inordinately pleased with himself, but I was horrified. Could dogs contract the virus? I knew that some viruses, like rabies, crossed species all the time. I also knew that many other illnesses did not jump from human to dog or vice versa. And I had no way of knowing which way the zombie virus would go.

"Why'd you have to do that, boy?" I patted his head, ignoring the gore.

There wasn't anything I could do about it now. What was done was done, so I straightened up with a final pat to his head and continued trudging along the dusty road. Panting from the heat and the exertion, Rex trotted ahead a few yards, tail held high in the air.

The faint tracks that the two vehicles had left in the packed dirt were becoming harder to see. Hours had passed, and the tracks were disappearing with the breeze. I was certainly no hunter. Even more so, worried that the trail would disappear before I found where my friends had been taken, I picked up my pace.

These little back roads were like a maze as they wound their way through the trees.

"Right, straight, left, left," I chanted to myself as I took a right.

If I couldn't remember the way I came in, we could end up lost out here for days when we tried to get back to the highway.

I was studiously ignoring the thought that we may not be coming back out. If I let myself think that way, I was going to curl up alongside the road and give in to panic. I didn't have time for panic. Whatever the reason behind the strangers' attack and mass kidnapping of my group, it couldn't have been good. I needed to find my friends and figure out a plan to free them as soon as possible.

The skin on my nose felt like it was burned to a crisp by the time I had my first hint that I had reached my destination. Rex's ears perked up, and he stopped in the middle of the road, listening to something ahead of us.

Darting into the trees on the side of the road, I crept forward slowly, listening for any sign of people. We hadn't gone far when I heard something.

There were goats ahead. At least, I thought it sounded like goats. Maybe it was sheep. Either way, live livestock probably meant that people were caring for them.

A little further and I got my first glimpse of humanity. A chain link fence, at least six feet tall topped with barbed wire, appeared. The fence ran to the left and the right from me. Just on the other side, a dozen goats grazed on tall grass. I inched further toward the fence. The grassy field, roughly the size of a football field, led to the compound.

There really was no other way to describe it.

Several low buildings surrounded an area of dirt where the grass had all been worn away. The buildings were utilitarian—ugly grey cinder block affairs that had been built for function instead of form. A line of vehicles was parked nearby. The black pickup and our van were parked at the end of the line.

Two men had the doors to the van open and were pulling our things out and laid them around on the ground. Past the parked cars, what looked like a giant garden had two women and several young kids working at pulling weeds.

The whole picture was one of the most bizarre things I had seen. That was saying a lot considering the fact that the dead now roamed the earth. It reminded me of that TV show I used to watch when there was nothing else on. The one where groups of people, convinced that the end of the world was near, retreated into the mountains and hoarded food and guns.

With a start, I realized that those crazy people on TV had been onto something after all. The thought did nothing to make me feel better. If these people were like those people, then they were organized and well-armed.

No sooner did I think that when I heard male voices. Scrambling behind a tree, I held onto Rex and prayed he stayed still and silent.

What sounded like two men approaching, I found them walking together along the inside of the fence, rifles propped casually over their shoulders. I hid again and listened as they got close enough for me to make out what they were saying.

". . . wonder when Mack is gonna decide what to do with them."

"I bet he keeps them locked up for at least another day. You know how he gets, he's really mad that that one got the jump on his brother." The second voice chuckled. "Did you get a look at Tom's black eye?"

The voices faded as the men moved too far away for me to hear them. Stepping back out from behind the tree, I looked in the direction that they had gone. Soon, the men were out of sight.

Following them seemed like a bad idea, so I began to work my way around the fence, going in the opposite direction. I still had no idea exactly what I was going to do to help my friends, but at

least now I knew that they were somewhere inside that fence . . .
and still alive.

CHAPTER FORTY
Day Twenty-One

A short distance through the trees, I came across a way into the stranger's camp. There was just one problem. The gate was closed and guarded by yet another armed man.

I stayed hidden for what felt like a really long time, waiting and watching for the guard to slip up and give me some opportunity to get inside. But that never happened.

After a while, the two guards who had walked by me before came around again. They laughed with the guard at the gate about something that one of them must have said on an earlier pass before doing another round.

When the guard posted at the gate looked up to talk with the other two, I got a good look at his face. One eye was swollen almost shut, a nasty-looking bruise surrounding it and spreading across his cheek. Unless this group had more than one man sporting a black eye at this time, this could only be one of the men who had directly attacked my friends. The pair of guards had called him Tom. A hint of satisfaction crept through me. Whichever of my friends had managed to fight back, they hit this guy really hard.

I crouched under some bushes and watched. By the fourth time the men walked by, a pattern had emerged. As close as I could estimate, it took roughly twenty minutes for the walking guards to complete one circuit. In all the time I stayed there, Tom never left his post. He wasn't exactly the most attentive to his task; none of them were, really. The walking guards seemed to be spending more time talking than looking outside the fence. And Tom was alternately digging the toe of his boot into the dirt and watching birds flit from tree to tree. But I doubted any of them would miss a strange woman and her dog if we didn't keep ourselves carefully hidden.

Easing back deeper into the forest, I gave the gate a wide berth as I continued my circuit of the fence. After spending the past couple of hours watching the security for this place, I doubted I would get lucky enough to find a conveniently open and unguarded gate elsewhere, but I still needed to check.

There was also still the matter of my friends being inside somewhere. I hadn't gotten any hints of exactly where they might be from the front of the compound, but I was hoping I might be able to find out something useful if I kept looking.

The mosquito bites that I had been picking up from the relentless little bloodsuckers ever since stepping foot into the trees were starting to itch. Scratching at a particularly nasty bump on my neck, I found the fence again and circled the perimeter slowly. I had rounded a corner, bringing me finally to the opposite side from where I first started, when I found exactly what I had been looking for.

The largest of the buildings had been blocking my view of another smaller chain-link fence within the perimeter fence. This second fence was also taller than I was by far and topped with more razor wire. And inside it, everyone in my group sat huddled together.

Back here, the fence wasn't nearly as far away from the buildings as it had been on the other side. I was close enough that I knew they would hear me if I called out to them, but I didn't dare for fear that someone else would hear me too. Finding Shawn sitting between Maya and Devon, I was relieved when he seemed to be sitting upright and looking alertly around.

My eyes flew over the group, looking for any signs that any of them were hurt. My heart sank when I got to Bill.

He was an unhealthy shade of grey. Leaning sideways to rest up against the fence, the big man looked exhausted. The blood that had drenched the front of his shirt dried, so at least he didn't seem to be bleeding any longer, but the damage had already been done. I had been hoping that his injury wouldn't be as bad as my first sight of it had seemed to indicate, but it seemed like that was not the case.

Maya sat next to her husband, leaning toward him, and it looked like she was whispering something to him. Worry clouded her features. The odd way that she was holding herself baffled me for a few seconds until I figured out why. Maya's hands were still bound behind her back.

I looked closer and saw that they all still seemed to be tied. Looking alarmingly sickly himself, Devon was leaning up against the fence with his eyes closed. Fallon had stopped crying, and now, she just looked mad. I could see that she was working at whatever had been used to bind their hands, twisting this way and that in what I assumed was an effort to loosen the ties, but she didn't seem to be having much luck.

I was so engrossed in checking over my friends that I almost missed the walking guard as they came around. A low growl from Rex warned me in time, and I crouched back down until they had passed. It was a close call, and I resolved to be more careful. I was probably the only hope my friends had of getting away from these people, and if I got caught too, there would be no one left on the outside to get us away.

Reluctantly, I finished my circuit of the fence. I hated to leave my group, even for just a little while, but I needed to be sure that there weren't any surprises waiting for us around the next corner. Like I had figured, nothing about our situation changed. There was a second, smaller gate that was also guarded. Other than that, the chain-link continued in an unbroken line that led me back to where I had first found the fence.

By the time that I had made my way back to my position within sight of my people, I had hoped to have come up with some plan to get them free. That was not the case. As I stared at them, I was still as clueless as I had been an hour before. Left out in the open like they were, all of them had started to look a little worse. Exposed patches of skin looked sunburnt, and they all looked like they were too hot.

Even protected from the worst of the sun by the trees, it was hot. My growling stomach reminded me that I had not eaten anything since the day before. I had thrown anything that I thought would come in handy into my backpack, but there had not been much left in the way of food. The strangers had taken most of our stuff with them when they left. Looking at my friends, I was reluctant to use any of the remaining supplies without them, but reason prevailed. If I was going to save them, I needed to not be dehydrated and dizzy with hunger.

Rex had lapped thirstily at a small stream that we had encountered on our walk around the fence. Breaking off a small piece of my granola bar, I handed it to the dog before settling down to finish off the rest myself. I was sipping from a half-full bottle of water when movement inside the fence caught my attention.

Swaggering, the man with orange hair approached the cage that held my friends. In his hands, he twirled a bottle of water. With keen interest, I watched as he opened the latch on the door and let himself in. I hadn't noticed him use any sort of key. He stood over my friends, still twirling the water bottle for several long seconds.

"It's hot out here today, ain't it?" He paused, like he was waiting for a reply, but when he got nothing in return, he continued on unperturbed. "My name is Mack, and you all have found yourselves in a bit of a jam. This is my territory, the things that you took in the gas station are mine, and I can't just let people come in and help themselves to the things that are meant for my group. You see where I'm going with this, don't ya? What kind of a leader would I be if I allowed actions like yours to go unpunished?"

Pacing back and forth the short distance between sides of the fence, he seemed to be deliberating something. Eyeing him like the viper that he was, my group held their silence.

"Now, you all brought this on yourselves, but we're not bad people. We understand, times are tough and you have to do what you have to, to survive. So we are prepared to offer immunity for your actions, if you decide to join our group. To one of you." Mack brandished the bottle of water. "All the perks of being a part of our community can be yours. You just have to say so."

Waggling the water in front of him, he waited.

CHAPTER FORTY-ONE
Day Twenty-Two

Yet another mosquito whined in my ear, but this time, I didn't swat it away. The roving guards were approaching in the night, their flashlights cutting through the dark. It was unlikely that they would notice my movement outside of the beams of light, but I wasn't taking that chance.

A sting on my forehead let me know where the insect had decided to bite. My fingers twitched with the urge to squash the tiny parasite. Finally, the guards passed, and I was able to kill the bug.

The compound was still and silent. Everyone had gone inside hours earlier, with the exception of the four guards who were now on duty. From my hiding place, I watched as one man headed toward the back gate, another toward the front, and two more started walking the fence line.

That had been just before dark.

Hours later, everyone besides the guards seemed to have gone to bed. It was nearly time to make my move. If I was going to get my friends free, it would have to be before dawn.

The orange-haired man, Mack, had been very clear. When my group continued to stare at him in silence, despite his offer to join them, his oddly pleasant expression had morphed. I had no problem hearing his loud proclamation that he would give them the night to think it over before stomping out of the cage.

When the sun came up, I had no doubt that Mack would be back, and nothing good was going to happen.

The plan I managed to concoct was rather simple. The pattern of the guards' activities had been well-established as I crouched behind trees all day. If I could get through the fence quietly enough without attracting attention, I had a good idea of how much time we would have to make our escape.

The chain-link of the fence wasn't impossible to get through if one had the proper tools. Unfortunately, I did not happen to have tools stuffed into my backpack. Likewise, going over the fence wasn't going to work. The sharp wire used to top the chain-link would slice anyone who tried to ribbons. That left only one option: we were going to have to go under the fence.

Digging a hole under the fence sounded easy in theory, but I had a feeling it was going to prove more difficult than I was hoping. I only had about twenty minutes between rounds by the guards. It was not a lot of time considering the hole would have to be big enough for a person to fit through. And if I failed to finish on time, the guards weren't going to miss a giant, partially dug hole under their fence, even in the dark.

Sipping the last few swallows of water from the bottle I had been nursing all day, I zipped the empty container back into my bag. Resolutely ignoring the hunger clawing at my stomach, I swung the backpack over one shoulder. There were only two bottles of water and a couple of smashed pastries left in the bag, and I was saving those for my friends. They hadn't been given anything to eat or drink all day.

The guards came back around and strolled by. As soon as they had melted into the darkness, I climbed to my feet.

The ground was full of stones and packed down hard. Tree roots tangled together in the dirt. It took me mere seconds to know that my half-baked rescue attempt was in trouble. Pulling out my knife, I dug it deep into the soil and attempted to use it to loosen anything in my way.

Standing next to my shoulder, Rex whined softly and I shushed him. Batting a stray piece of hair out of my face, I renewed my attack on the ground. I felt a fingernail snap and the tips of my fingers grew raw, but the pile of loose dirt steadily grew beside me.

Glancing up, I tried in vain to see where the flashlights of the guards were located, trying to gauge how much time I had left. They were too far away, but I could feel time racing by with every fast beat of my heart.

The hole was finally big enough for me to wiggle my shoulders through. I was halfway under the fence when I realized that it needed to be bigger. I was the smallest person in the group. If I could just fit, most of the rest of them would not be getting out that hole. Dragging myself backward hurriedly, I failed to stay low enough. The sharp metal ends of the chain link dug into my shoulder blades.

Hissing, I ducked down and pulled myself the rest of the way out of the hole.

Precious minutes passed as I clawed the hole bigger. Ignoring the stinging on my back, I crawled through to the other side. Reaching back out, I snagged the strap of my bag and pulled it through. It didn't have much of value in there, but I wanted to keep it within reach anyway. Whining, Rex paced on the other side of the fence before stopping at the hole.

I didn't have time to coax the dog through, nor could I afford the noise. With a last glance back at him, I turned and jogged the short distance to the cage.

Their huddled shapes formed ahead of me in the darkness. Too stressed to sleep, they were sitting together, slumped with exhaustion but still alert. When they caught sight of something running their way in the dark, they snapped to attention as much as their condition allowed.

I heard someone whisper zombie as I was taking the last few steps to them.

"That's the second time someone's thought I was dead. Should I be offended?" I tried to joke as I reached the gate.

"Bri!"

"How'd you get here?"

"What are you doing? Get out of here!"

Everyone started talking at once, but I ignored them and reached for the latch. Holding my breath, I hoped that I hadn't been wrong about there being no lock. If the door was locked, I had no idea what I was going to do.

I released the breath I was holding when the latch lifted easily. The screech of the hinges made me cringe as I pushed the door open.

"You didn't think I'd let a bunch of crazy people take you and do nothing, did you?" I dropped to the ground next to Fallon and began cutting at the plastic tie used to bind her. "We have to hurry. The guards will be coming back soon."

The ties had been put on tight, and I ended up cutting her as I tried to get the knife through them in the dark. I mumbled an apology, but she told me to just get them off any way I could. Her wrists were already bloody from struggling to get free.

I finally cut through the tie, and when Fallon didn't immediately get up, I realized her ankles were tied too. I was starting to see why the strangers had been confident enough to leave the door unlocked.

Moving on to Devon, I gave the teen a tight-lipped smile as I worked to free his feet. By the time I freed his hands, I figured out the best way to cut through the ties and was able to pick up the pace. Our dwindling time was an oppressive weight trying to crush me as I tried to keep calm enough to function.

When I cut through the tie around Shawn's wrists, he pulled me into a hard hug. "You should have run the other way."

I stole a second to lean into the embrace. I hadn't missed the fact that his nose was just a little crooked and a nasty cut marred his cheek. Blood from both had dried on his face, making

195

him look even worse. I had come far too close to losing the most important person in my life, and the reality was just now starting to sink in.

Steadying myself, I kept going, and within a few seconds, the last of the group was climbing unsteadily to their feet.

"We have to go now." I started for the gate but pulled up abruptly.

The guard's flashlights were working their way along the fence, far too near to the hole.

"What's wrong?" Shawn leaned close to my back.

"They're too close. We aren't all going to make it out in time. They are going to find the hole."

Whirling around, I tried to come up with another way out of the compound. My eyes went to the vague shapes of the vehicles lined up not too far away. "This way." I darted toward the van.

If we were lucky, the keys would still be in it. And if not, maybe we could hide there until we had a chance to run for the fence.

CHAPTER FORTY-TWO
Day Twenty-Two

"What's that over there?"

I heard the words that I had been dreading as I darted around the end of the van. Scooting along its familiar side, I made room for the others. Shawn and Fallon were right behind me, but it was several long seconds before Devon limped around the end of the van. Behind him, Maya stayed behind with Bill, who was listing sideways and having obvious difficulty staying upright.

"Something's dug a hole under the fence!"

"What?" There was a moment of silence as the second guard must have walked closer to investigate. "What the hell?"

Crouching behind the van, we stayed still and silent. In what was becoming a habit, I sent a quick prayer to whoever might be listening, asking for the time we needed to escape back under the fence.

"Something's moving out there," the first guard said, sounding worried. "I think I heard a growl."

It struck me that Rex was still out there somewhere, at the same time that the second guard exclaimed, "It's a dog!"

"I didn't think there'd be anything like a dog left alive out there. What's it doing?"

"I think he wants in—" A pause. "Do you think that dog dug this hole?"

197

I turned my head to the left and found Shawn next to me, watching me intently. I stared back, suddenly wishing that we had time for me to say a few things that had been on my mind lately, but I had kept to myself. So we sat there, listening to the pair of guards try to decide if they needed to wake Mack up or if they thought that a dog could have created the hole under the fence.

"We have to tell him. He'll have both of our heads if he finds out we found something like this and didn't wake him up."

"You're right." The second guard sounded less than thrilled at the prospect of waking up their leader. "I'll go get him. You stay here and keep an eye out for trouble."

Footsteps swished through the taller grass, coming our way. I did my best to shrink down behind the van. I had to bite back a noise when I rubbed the cuts to my back on the filthy side of the vehicle, but the guard walked right on past where the six of us hid.

"We have to get out of here before that maniac finds us," Devon whispered.

He had a point. Two armed guards were beyond us to fight in our current condition, and the entire camp was about to be woken up. For now, all they knew was that there was a hole under the fence that may, or may not, have been made by a dog. But as soon as someone thought to check the cage, they were going to know for sure that the dog didn't do it. Steeling my nerves, I eased up to look into the front seat of the van.

I watched earlier as a pair of men systematically emptied our van of our belongings. I was hoping that, like with the door on the cage, they had been lax with security regarding the vehicles.

Someone seemed to be smiling down on us at that moment because the moonlight glinted off a familiar set of keys, lying on the front seat.

"The keys are in the van," I whispered excitedly.

I had everyone's attention.

"Let's go then. That gate didn't look like it would stop a car if you hit it hard enough," Bill groaned as he hauled himself back to his feet.

The door slid open, and everyone began piling into the van, but I held back. Looking over the hood, I tried to make out the fence in the dark, but it was too far away. "I can't go yet."

"What?" Shawn hesitated with one foot still on the grass.

"Rex is still on the other side of the fence. He wouldn't come through the hole with me."

"Bri, he's a dog. We have to get out of here before they all wake up." Maya looked out at me from where she had taken the driver's seat.

"I can't." I tried to convey with my eyes just how serious I was. "I might not have even made it here to get you out if it wasn't for him. I can't just leave him."

Five pairs of eyes looked at me like I was crazy, but the one person who I learned I would always be able to count on came through once again.

"Okay. Let's go get the dog," Shawn finally agreed.

Maya sighed, "We will wait for you as long as we can."

Sneaking back through the night toward the remaining guard seemed like a foolish thing to be doing. Sweat trickled down my neck, and I struggled to keep my breath from turning into loud gasps. I switched my knife for the machete, and the handle felt like it was going to slip through my sweaty grasp. Creeping along next to me, Shawn now held the knife with a look of determination.

We hadn't really had time to come up with a plan. He had hurriedly whispered that we would split up before we reached the guard—one approaching from one side and the other from behind him. Hopefully, we would catch the guy off guard and be able to get the gun away from him before either of us got shot, then I would get Rex through the hole by whatever means necessary, and we would run for the van.

In theory, it should work, but there were a lot of variables we had no control over. Just before we made it close enough to begin to make out the guard in the dark, we split. Going right, I swung in a wide arc, staying out of view, until I finally encountered the fence. I had lost sight of Shawn and worried that I was not moving through the dark as fast as he was. If one of us made it to the guard too far before the other, that person was going to be in real trouble. After all, we were bringing knives to a gun fight.

I picked up my pace a fraction.

"Dog, what are you looking at?"

I froze. It hadn't occurred to me that Rex was going to give our approach away. Of course, he was going to know that we were out there and was going to react. I just hoped that he was looking at me instead of Shawn. If anyone was going to get shot over our bid to rescue Rex, I did not want it to be him.

A strange sense of both relief and adrenaline-fueled anxiety hit me as Rex melted out of the darkness, just on the other side of the fence. The guard was going to be looking my way.

I took one step forward and was stopped again.

"Stop! Who's out there?" The guard's outline appeared as he moved toward me.

I threw my hands up, machete still clutched in a death grip and hoped that I wasn't about to find out what it felt like to get shot.

"Stop! Stay where you are."

The guard advanced. On the other side of the chain-link, Rex started barking viciously and jumping at the fence. I kept my focus on the gun, trying to decipher if he was going to shoot.

The guard had come within a few feet of me when movement behind him in the darkness turned into a familiar face. The guard crumpled to the ground, leaving me facing Shawn, who was holding a good-sized rock that he had just used to hit the guard.

"Get the dog and let's get out of here."

He didn't have to tell me twice. Sprinting the short distance to the hole, I bent down and coaxed, "Rex. Come on, boy. Come here, through the hole."

Rex whined and crouched just on the other side, obviously thinking about crawling through. A commotion behind me had me looking away from the dog and over my shoulder. I couldn't see what was going on, and I jumped to my feet.

Someone came barreling out of the shadows and ran headlong into me, sending the both of us to the ground in a heap. I yelped as my back made contact with the ground hard but didn't have time to think about the pain because the man who had jumped me immediately started trying to pin my hands with his own.

"It's a girl. Not one of the ones from the cage," the guy called over his shoulder. He managed to get a hold of my hand with the machete before I could swing the weapon at him.

Over my own panicked breathing, I registered the sound of fighting not far away. Rex was barking frantically, and the fence rattled as he threw himself against it.

From out of the darkness, a voice that I recognized as Mack's said, "Tom, stop fooling around and get her under control."

"I'm trying."

I looked at the face of my attacker for the first time and saw the swollen eye and bruised face of the guard who had been on the front gate during the day. Grappling with me for control of the machete, he dug a knee into my abdomen, driving all the air out of my lungs. My vision swam and I almost missed when someone grabbed Tom and ripped him off me.

I lay there, semi-stunned, and listened to someone cursing colorfully.

I heard a voice yell, "Just shoot him!"

I forced myself to move. Struggling upright, I found Shawn on top of Tom, his hands wrapped around his throat.

Two more men, Mack and the other guard, appeared. The guard aimed his gun at Shawn but seemed to be having trouble finding an angle that wouldn't be likely to hit Tom. I lurched to my feet.

I took one drunken step toward the guard. Seeing that I was up, he swung his aim my way.

A flash of dark fur sprinted past me and straight into the guard. Snarling, the dog latched onto his arm and refused to let go.

Mack cursed again when he saw the dog hanging from the guard's arm. Turning, he kicked at Rex, but I knew by now that nothing was going to get that dog to let go before he was ready.

Distracted by his attempt to kick the dog, Mack missed my lunge in his direction. I didn't think, just acted.

The machete cut deep into his arm. A warm spray of blood covered my neck and chest as I pulled the weapon free. The shocked look in his eyes as he stared first at me, then the wound that was pouring blood with every pulse of his heart, almost made me feel bad for him. Almost.

"We've gotta go!" Shawn grabbed for my arm as he ran past me, toward where Maya had just started the van. Drawn by the noise, more people were coming out of the buildings, their flashlights giving them away.

"Rex!" I shrieked at the dog as we ran.

The van started to roll slowly through the grass, angling toward the gate. Someone inside threw open the sliding door and we ran for it.

Rex jumped into the van, and I threw myself inside after him. Diving in behind me, Shawn jerked the door closed just as the first of the bullets hit the vehicle.

CHAPTER FORTY-THREE
Day Twenty-Two

The sound of a window shattering had me diving for the floor of the van. Maya floored it, and the tires spun on the grass before biting hold. The vehicle lurched forward and bounced roughly over the uneven ground.

More gunfire and shouting followed us. I kept my head down in fear of catching a bullet. When spider cracks appeared on the windshield from a bullet coming from ahead of us, I knew the guard posted at the gate had started to fire. Maya kept her foot pressed to the floor, and we flew past the guard and through the gate. The chain-link fence didn't even slow the van down.

Gravel pinged off the underside of the van. When several seconds passed without the sound of bullets flying through the air, I dared to sit cautiously upright again.

The trees flew by in the darkness. Maya hadn't turned on the headlights, and it seemed she was keeping the vehicle on the road by sheer force of will. Nothing else explained how we didn't end up in a fiery crash as we flew along the dark unfamiliar road. At the last second, I thought I recognized where we were.

"Turn here! Left!"

She wrenched the wheel, and we somehow made the turn, tires sliding in the dirt. Turning around in my seat, I checked for the pursuit that I was sure couldn't be far behind, but the road behind us remained dark and empty.

My eyes traveled to the two people in the back seat. Fallon and Devon sat up and looked shell-shocked, huddled in the back seat. Sunburned, filthy, and exhausted, they looked okay other than the obvious paleness of Devon's face. I turned back around.

"Is everyone okay?"

Next to me, Shawn was sitting upright, watching behind us for any sign of the strange group. It was shadowy inside the van, but I could still see that his face, which already looked like he had been hit a few too many times, was worse after our fight with the guards. But he was alert, and I didn't see any signs of the kind of injury that time wouldn't take care of.

"I'm good," Maya answered me briefly as she concentrated on getting us out of there in one piece.

"I'm okay." Bill's voice was weak. From what I had seen of his condition before, he looked like he lost a lot of blood. When we were far enough away, I was going to have to see what I could do for him, but without our medical bag, I didn't begin to know what I could do.

When I told him my plan, Bill replied, "Don't worry about me. We just need to get as far away from here as fast as we can."

The van never slowed down as we dashed for freedom. I did my best to recognize the turns and guide us back to the highway, but I didn't heave a sigh of relief until I caught sight of the gas station. My fear that we would be lost in the winding back roads did not come to pass.

We flew on by, and I felt a twinge of remorse for Carrie. She deserved better than to be left lying in that building, but we couldn't stop. It would take time to bury her body—time that we didn't have.

A zombie was wandering on the on-ramp that we took to get back to the highway. Swerving slightly, Maya clipped it with the side of the van. I watched behind us as the zombie spun and rolled along the pavement. That was when I recognized that the sun was starting to come up. I could see the zombie tumbling through the gloom just before dawn.

Everyone was silent. The cuts to my back burned, and I flexed my shoulders, trying to find a more comfortable position. All I succeeded in doing was send pain shooting down my back. Giving up, I leaned slightly forward to keep from touching the back of my seat. When we stopped, I was going to have to ask someone to take a look, but for now, I didn't want to cause anyone more worry. There were two other members of our little group who were more in need of care than me.

When the engine of the van started to make alarming noises, probably in protest of the speed that it was being pushed, Maya finally allowed our speed to drop a little. I didn't know why the other group was not following us, but it seemed like we had actually managed to make our escape. Nothing but the occasional zombie moved on the deserted stretch of highway that we had been driving.

A hand eased itself into my own, interrupting me from staring out the window blankly while my mind raced. Looking over, I smiled weakly at Shawn. He had finally relaxed into his seat, and I wondered for how long he had been watching me.

The sun climbed completely into the sky. It looked like it was going to be another blisteringly hot, sunny day. I could finally get a clear view of his face and I held back a cringe. Black bruises circled his eyes, his nose was still a little off center, and the cut to his cheek probably could have used a stitch or two if going to the ER was still a possibility. But he was alive, and the small smile that turned up one corner of his mouth never looked better.

I opened my own lips to tell him so when a shout from the front seat cut me off.

"Bill!"

Maya brought the van to a screeching halt and practically threw herself toward her husband. Mass confusion reigned as everyone began trying to figure out what was going on at the same time. Lurching forward, I leaned over the front seats to try to get a look.

It was hard to see over Maya as her body blocked my view. I was shouting for her to tell me what was happening, but she ignored my questions. Frantically talking to her husband, she did something that I couldn't see because of the angles.

Climbing across a confused Shawn, I slid open the side door and jumped from the van. Whatever was going on up front, it was bad, and I needed to see. Ignoring Shawn's exclamation to stay inside, I hit the pavement with the sounds of more feet and the click of dog paws following me.

Flinging open the passenger door, I looked at Bill.

The first thing I saw was blood. It had run down the side of the seat and soaked the carpet of the vehicle. Following the trail with my eyes, I found Maya's hands pressing against his shirt—a shirt that was stained bright red with fresh blood.

CHAPTER FORTY-FOUR
Day Twenty-Two

Blood coated my hands, rising up my forearms, and dried on my shirt. Completely spent, I sat with my knees drawn up, uncaring that the hard pavement was unforgiving on my backside. Resting my arms on my knees, I couldn't tear my gaze away from the blood that had dried on my hands.

"Let me take a look at this."

Shawn's fingers passed lightly over my skin, just above the gouges into my shoulders. Without the strength left in me to do anything but obey, I woodenly reached for the tail of my shirt and pulled it up around my neck.

I dimly registered his sharp inhale, but my mind was elsewhere.

"Maya, let me see! You have to let me look at the wound so I know how bad it is."

I already knew it was bad. The amount of blood that had pooled in the van wouldn't have been good coming from a healthy person. Bill had already been in bad shape from the first gunshot.

Finally managing to move her hands, I saw exactly where the second bullet had hit him: the right side of his chest, lower than the first shot that had hit him in the shoulder.

"Okay, let's get him out of the van. I need to check for an exit wound. Fallon, bring me anything that we have that may be remotely useful."

My back stung as I felt Shawn doing the best he could to clean it up. A trickle of water ran down and soaked into the waistband of my jeans. I knew that we were down to our last half a bottle of clean water, and I wanted to tell him to save it, but it seemed like too much effort.

Rolling Bill over slightly, I searched his back. There was only one hole back there. The second bullet was still inside him. Trying not to panic, I eased him back down. Blood was still trickling from his wounds and was already starting to stain the pavement, but the flow was slowing. I wasn't altogether sure that that was a good thing.

"This is it. They cleaned everything else out of the van." Fallon dropped my nearly empty backpack next to me and held out the small first aid kit that had been in the glove box.

"I think these need stitches, but this will have to do for now." The burning increased as he wiped antibacterial ointment from the first aid kit into the wounds.

Rex hadn't left my side since I climbed out of the van. My crimson-stained hands were again resting in front of my eyes. Moving in front of me, he nudged my hand with his nose.

Using my knife, I cut the remnants of his shirt away. The wound to his shoulder was no longer bleeding, but it looked angry. A circle of red was growing around it.

The shot to his chest, however, was still bleeding. It took precedence. I wasn't sure how much more blood he could lose. Clamping a hand holding his waded-up shirt to the wound, I handed my knife to Shawn.

"There's water in my bag. Clean this off as well as you can."

"What are you going to do?" Maya looked up from where she was crouched over her husband's head. I could read the anguish in her eyes as they pleaded with me to do something.

"I, uh, I'm going to have to get the bullet out and stop the bleeding." My voice shook at the thought of what I was about to do.

"Wait. You're going to use your knife to cut into him? Is that safe? It's been used on zombies." Fallon looked from the knife in question to where I knelt next to Bill.

"I don't have a choice."

The paper wrappers off the Band-Aids crinkled. Meticulously placing a row of them down my back, Shawn covered the wounds the best he could.

He tugged my shirt back down and scooted around to sit next to me.

My hands were shaking. Bill had only been semi-conscious since we pulled him from the van, but he was completely passed out now. The pain from me digging around in his wound with a finger, looking for the bullet, had been the last straw.

I hadn't found the offending piece of metal, and now, I was poised to use the knife on my friend.

The blood began to flow again as I cut. Suppressing a curse, I tried to work faster.

"Here, let me see your hand."

I allowed him to use the damp material to scrub at the drying blood. My eyes began to wander.

Still lying in the same place on the pavement, Bill was unmoving. Sitting with his head on her lap, Maya leaned brokenly over him. Her shoulders shook as she cried.

Standing a few feet away, Fallon and Devon stood to watch over our group.

"I think I found it."

My muttered sentence was more for my own benefit than anything else. I had been starting to worry that I wouldn't find the bullet, but the tip of my knife had just scraped across something hard. I was fairly sure it wasn't bone.

Carefully working the knife, I pried the hard object free. The mangled metal popped out of the wound.

Such a small object but one that had caused so much damage.

"Bri. You did the best you could, better than any of us could have done."

I slowly turned to meet Shawn's eyes. I had done the best I could, but I was frightened that my best wasn't going to be good enough.

It seemed to take forever to get the bleeding to slow down again. The wound was ragged and ugly now that I had dug around inside it. I smeared a generous glob of our one tube of antibacterial ointment inside and then taped the largest pad of gauze on top.

With a sigh, I noted that a tinge of red began to bleed through the white in seconds.

There wasn't a lot I could do with the limited supplies on hand. Not that I was a real doctor anyhow.

I moved to do what I could for the first gunshot.

Needing comfort, I leaned slowly sideways until my shoulder rested against Shawn's.

"What if he doesn't make it?" I whispered my fears out loud.

The shoulder supporting me lifted in a sigh. "Then we will deal with it. That's all we can do."

"He hasn't woken up yet."

"No, but maybe that's a blessing. When he does wake up, he's going to be in a lot of pain."

I felt a hot tear run down my face and drip from my chin.

"Bri, listen to me. We would all be dead by now if it wasn't for you. Those people were not going to let us go. We all owe you our lives. Maybe Bill won't ever wake up, but you need to know that if he doesn't, it will not be because of you."

CHAPTER FORTY-FIVE
Day Twenty-Two

The bone-chilling scream from not so far away caused all of us to leap to our feet. An answering shriek followed, even closer than the first.

It had been stupid of us to sit out there, exposed like we were, was my first thought when the pair of zombies bolted out of the trees beyond the far side of the highway. They're definitely the fast ones.

My second thought was prompted by Rex as he began running to meet the zombie in the lead.

I had been so preoccupied for the last few days that I had completely forgotten to worry if zombie blood was dangerous to dogs. The answer seemed to be no, but that was of little comfort at the moment as I watched the dog run toward danger.

I grabbed the machete and bolted after him. Fallon had been hanging on to my knife. She picked it up after I discarded it, unwilling to hang on to its bloodied handle for another second. As the only two people in our group with weapons, we were going to be on the front line for this one.

"Bri, wait!"

I ignored the call. Ahead of me, Rex leaped to collide with the first zombie.

This time, the zombie was much fresher, and it stayed on its feet. The dog latched onto its arm with a death grip, but the zombie seemed more irritated than pained by his bite. The creature cocked its head sideways and studied the dog for a fraction of a second, then it snapped its teeth his way and reached for him with its free hand.

My sneakers pounded onto the second wide strip of the highway as the second zombie reached the fight. Rex had his hands full tangling with the first one, and I took the last few steps as fast as I could to push myself. A little wildly, I swung the machete. My aim was off, and I sliced into the second zombie's neck instead of its head.

The machete cut deep but not deep enough. The zombie's head stayed attached to its body, and the creature turned from its assault on the dog to me. Hissing like some sort of demonic, enraged feline, it lunged my way. My second strike with the machete was worse than the first, and it sank into its shoulder. I cringed, expecting the zombie to run into me full force, but instead, I heard it collapse onto the pavement.

Fallon stood over the corpse, my knife sticking out of its skull, panting like she had run a marathon. With one zombie down, I turned my attention back to the one that Rex had effectively detained.

Still hanging onto its arm, he jerked his head back and forth, shredding the muscle between his teeth. Hissing and spitting, the zombie had gone on the defensive and seemed to just want to escape the dog's grasp.

My aim was better the third time and the zombie stood little chance at getting out of my way while anchored by the dog.

I turned to run back to the van—we needed to get out of there before we found out if the noise had drawn unwanted attention—and almost ran into Shawn.

Holding a tire iron, he skidded to a stop next to me. "We've got to go."

Nodding, I started running with the others, back toward the van. Maya and Devon were standing guard nervously over Bill's

212

prone form. Their conspicuous lack of weapons reminded me just how bad our situation really was. "Let's get Bill in the van and get out of here."

It wasn't an easy task moving the biggest member of the group. Trying our best not to jar Bill's wounds any more than we had to, we somehow managed to lay him across the back seat. He was too tall, and we ended up letting his legs dangle off the seat and resting his feet on the floor.

Maya squeezed herself into the remaining floor space in the back of the car. Devon and Fallon climbed into the middle seat, which left Shawn and me in the front. I tried not to think about the sticky stains all over the seat and floor as I got in.

Rex insisted on climbing into my foot space despite the mess and the fact that he was too big to really fit there, but I didn't want to waste time trying to convince the dog to move to the back. Some zombie gore and blood were spattered all over his body from tangling with the zombies.

I saw Shawn dart his eyes at Rex, specifically at the bloody teeth the dog exposed when it panted. I knew that he was wondering the same things I was. I was sure of it.

"It's okay. He's attacked a zombie before. This isn't the first time this has happened." I tried to reassure everyone.

Nodding, Shawn started the van, and we continued our flight south.

*   *   *

The van was running on fumes, but we didn't dare stop and try to find more gas because the number of zombies we were seeing had dramatically increased.

The signs along the side of the road bore somewhat familiar names as we drove by. The towns that we had been passing for a while now were large enough for someone not from this area to have heard of them. It explained the rise in numbers of zombies, and it didn't solve our problem.

It was only a matter of time before we would have to stop, or we would run out of gas completely.

I peered over my shoulder anxiously for what felt like the hundredth time, but the far back of the van was still silent. We had been driving for hours, but Bill hadn't moved at all.

"I'm going to take the next exit that is reasonably empty of zombies." Shawn glanced my way with worried eyes. "We are going to be stopping soon, no matter what, and I don't want to run out of gas while we're surrounded with nowhere to go." His voice sounded rough, like his throat had been sandblasted.

Nodding, I looked back at the pair in the middle seats. My friends were going on two days now without rest, food, or even any water.

We needed to find a place with water.

Licking my own sunburned and chapped lips, I answered, "There has to be a place we can hide that hasn't been cleaned out yet."

Barely a mile later, an exit appeared. We dodged the couple of zombies that were in our way. One of them bounced off my door as it tried to get inside, but I didn't even flinch. Zombie collisions had become an all-too-common occurrence in the last hour. It was almost funny when I thought back to the very first zombie that had tried to get through a car window at me, back at the start. I had been terrified.

I sat up straight in my seat as we coasted down the ramp and turned toward a small city.

We had begun to pass the city a few miles ago. From the highway, I had been able to see the large burned-out section where a fire had obviously raged uncontrollably. The buildings had been reduced to charred skeletons where the only thing moving were the zombies.

Now, a few miles later, we traveled past where the fire had consumed everything, but the view of the city from the higher ground of the highway had still been desolate. The roads became harder to navigate as we skirted around the edges of town, and there were zombies—a lot of them. No one was going to lose sleep over running the creatures over, but the van wasn't exactly an all-terrain vehicle. If too many of them piled up under the wheels, it may be enough to get us stuck.

I saw cars everywhere—parked along the curb, standing abandoned in the middle of the streets, and I even saw one buried up to the hind wheels in the side of the house that it had driven into. Add to the chaos the general trash that was lying around, and more than one partially eaten body, and this city could hardly be mistaken for any kind of haven.

I was watching out the window with growing dread. The atmosphere in the van was becoming bleaker by the minute, if that was even possible. It was obvious to anyone who cared to look that the city belonged to the dead now. In fact, a growing horde of them was falling in line behind our vehicle. With the van dangerously low on fuel, the situation was a disaster in the making.

When my frayed nerves couldn't take any more, I opened my mouth to give my opinion that we should get back on the highway and get as far away as we could before we ran out of gas. But a sign caught my eye. A sign that—as long as some of the supplies inside remained—could mean the difference between life and death.

"There!" I pointed. "There's an Urgent Care building ahead. We need to go there."

When no one agreed with me right away, I knew that I was going to have to convince them. Twisting sideways in my seat, I did my best to do just that.

"Look, I know we already agreed hospitals are too dangerous. They would have been full of people who died of the virus, but an Urgent Care building would have sent all their worst

215

cases to the ER. There may not be any zombies at all inside. And we need medical supplies." I glanced back to where Maya was watching me over the seat in front of her. "Bill needs fluids to start building his blood back up. If he doesn't wake up soon, an IV may be the only thing that can save him."

Then I turned to Devon. "And, you, I haven't missed that you're getting worse again. We need more antibiotics."

Silence fell as they thought over my words.

I looked over to Shawn. He disagreed with me, I could see it in the way he frowned slightly and kept his eyes fixed ahead. Slumping back into my seat, I kept my mouth shut. This had to be a decision made by the group, not just me. If they didn't want to try for the medical supplies, then that was that.

"Please." Maya's voice cracked from dehydration and her grief. "Please, if there is any chance, we have to try."

CHAPTER FORTY-SIX
Day Twenty-Two

Our destination came into view. The front of the one-story building was made almost entirely of glass. Posters depicting white-coated doctors smiling brightly at their patients covered a lot of the windows but not all.

As far as I could tell from my admittedly compromised vantage point in the van, the seating area appeared to be empty.

A thud to the back of the van was followed by the sound of someone scrabbling at the window. One of the more mobile zombies had caught up to us while we idled out front of the building, and that brought up a good point. I stared at the glass windows.

The last time we had relied on a glass wall to keep zombies out, we had lost someone, and Shawn and I had barely managed to escape.

There was a growing sea of zombies trailing along behind us. Even if we did manage to move the entire group safely from the van into that building, it wouldn't take long for the zombies to break through.

My heart sank. "We can't stop there."

"We're going to have to stop somewhere really soon," Shawn reminded me needlessly.

Everyone watched as we passed the building with somber expressions. Now that our need for medical care had been dragged out into the open, it was harder to pretend that everything was going to be okay.

"Maybe we can find somewhere nearby to stop, and we can sneak back for the things we need once the zombies have cleared." Fallon sounded hopeful.

Pressing my forehead to the side window, I sighed. If only it were that simple. There were a lot of zombies here. The odds of enough of them going somewhere else to make that play anything besides suicide were not high.

"The warning light has been on for a while. We need to make a decision."

I knew what Shawn was saying. We either had to get as far away from this city as we could before the van died, or we needed to find a place here to try to stop.

"We have to go." It sounded like Maya was crying again. "There's too many of them. We have to get out of here."

When no one objected, Shawn nodded and began following signs back to the highway. We were going painfully slow as we tried to keep from becoming swarmed. I kept looking at the needle of the gas gauge. The little piece of white plastic rested firmly on E.

We finally spotted the way out, but it brought no relief. We still had our zombie entourage, and the van was still dangerously low on gas. When a clear path opened up in front of us, Shawn sped up to try to gain us some distance from the horde.

A box truck that had been abandoned halfway up the on-ramp caught my eye, specifically the writing that had been hastily spray-painted across its back.

"Stop!"

Any message that had been important enough for someone to risk their lives to leave here was worth slowing down to read. I hoped.

The van halted abruptly. Shawn looked my way, alarmed by my sudden outburst. Murmurs from behind me let me know that none of the others noticed the sign.

I pointed.

The writing had been sprayed quickly. Some areas had too much paint; others had too little. But it was still easy enough to make out.

Safe haven. South. Five miles.

Another zombie bounced off the back of the van, causing Shawn to step on the gas again. But we had enough time to read the words.

"What do you think?"

"Can we trust it?"

We were all thinking the same way. After our last interaction with strangers, we were reluctant to trust anymore, but looking around the van, I realized that all the people present were strangers to me less than a month ago. I looked behind me, at Devon's pale face and then past him to the top of Maya's head.

"What if they have a real doctor? And medicine? I think we should go. We can stay back and take a look around. If we don't like what we see, we'll get out of there." I tried to justify my intention once again.

We were already traveling south along the highway. I looked at Shawn who looked thoughtful. As if feeling me looking at him, he turned to meet my stare.

"Yeah, okay."

More answers on the affirmative made the decision unanimous.

"Okay," Shawn said again. As the numbers of zombies dwindled, he was able to drive faster.

The landscape changed a bit over the next mile or two. We left the city behind, and the view from the highway became more rural. There were still occasional zombies wandering along the road

219

but not enough to slow us down. We were driving past what used to be some sort of farm when the engine began to sputter.

"Not now. Come on." Coaxing the van along, he was able to drive us another hundred yards down the road before the engine died ultimately.

The silence was deafening as we coasted to a stop in the middle of the road. We had known this was coming, but the reality of the situation was much worse. Bill was still unconscious, and there was no way we would be carrying him very far.

Then a zombie crashed into the side of the van. The only sounds from inside were harsh breathing as we all contemplated the newest hurdle in front of us. Outside, the zombie snarled as it clawed at the windows with bloodied fingers. The glass squeaked as it worked its way along the left-hand side of the van.

"Now what?" Devon's voice was troubling, like he had given up.

"We stick to the plan." I heard Shawn assert.

Surprised, I looked to my left.

"We can't be more than two, maybe three miles from wherever that place is. Someone should still go check it out. If there really are people there who can help, they can help us get Bill to safety," he continued.

He was right. We couldn't just stay in the van indefinitely.

"Okay." I turned around to look behind me. "Shawn and I will go find this place and see if they can help us. Maya, Fallon, and Devon, you guys stay here and keep an eye on Bill."

I didn't say that I doubted Devon could walk that far without stopping, and I didn't want him to feel bad, so I lumped him in with the other two as Bill's protectors.

I handed the knife that Fallon had given me earlier back to her. She looked solemn as she took it.

"Ready?" I gripped the machete and turned back around.

"Yeah, let me get rid of the zombie." Shawn picked up the tire iron from where he left it on the floor.

The zombie worked its way around and was now growling at me through my window. Rex watched it alertly from his spot by my feet as the creature fixed its bloodshot eyes on me. Shawn's door opened, and the zombie immediately switched its focus to the person who had just become an easier target. The zombie was older, and it tottered around the front of the van unsteadily.

As soon as my door was clear, I jumped out too, but Shawn had already taken care of the zombie with a hard whack to the head.

"We will be back as soon as we can." I ducked my head back inside the van. Three pairs of eyes watched me. They all looked scared, and I couldn't blame them. To be honest, I was terrified of walking miles through unfamiliar, zombie-infested territory, but I didn't see any other options.

I shut the door firmly and met Shawn in front of the van. The only sound we made as we walked away, south along the highway, was the click of the dog's nails on the pavement.

CHAPTER FORTY-SEVEN
Day Twenty-Three

Sticking my head around the corner, I stifled another groan. "They're still out there."

I ducked back out of sight. It felt like much longer than the approximately twelve hours that passed since Shawn and I left our friends, but then, so much had happened in that time.

Making progress was a lot harder than I had anticipated. There were enough zombies around that we never made it far without running into another one. The first mile down the highway had been hard fought for both of us, and we ended up covered in zombie gore.

The machete was starting to feel more like a large chunk of lead in my tired hands by the time we saw the next sign.

Safe haven. One mile.

The words had been sprayed over the top of the sign for the exit to our right. A semi-circle of badly decayed zombies lay not far from the bottom of the sign. I hoped that whoever had painted the words escaped without being bitten.

Trudging down the off-ramp, we noticed that an arrow pointing right had been painted on the stop sign. Looking that way showed what looked like a strip mall just visible in the growing darkness.

A zombie shuffled our way from the middle of the intersection. A growl rumbled through its torn-out throat as it moved at a snail's pace on mangled limbs. It was almost a relief to encounter one of them that was a minimal threat after the struggle of the last couple of hours.

When Shawn used the now filthy tire iron on it, the zombie's head caved in like an overripe melon. Slinging the clinging bits of rot off the weapon with a grimace, he joined Rex and me back under the stop sign.

According to the painted directions, we had to be near the "safe haven." The plan was to find the place, stay back, and watch for a while. If we got a creepy, murderous cult vibe, we would leave and not come back.

That had been the plan anyhow, but the best thought-out plans sometimes failed. We barely walked another hundred yards before someone shouted from within a small group of trees, "Stop! You are entering a restricted area. Identify yourselves!"

I couldn't find the source of the voice no matter how hard I stared at the trees. It was weird because they weren't that thick. I should have been able to see whoever was speaking.

Beside me, Shawn shifted from foot to foot, also unable to see the source of the voice. It made us both nervous.

Movement from higher up, probably ten feet off the ground, was what finally gave the speaker away. There, perched on top of a small metal contraption fixed to one of the trees, stood a man . . . with a rifle casually trained in our direction.

Seeing the person whom the voice belonged to made me feel a little better, but the gun immediately negated those feelings. "Um, we followed the signs . . ."

The man stood watching us for a few seconds before he spoke again, "Is it just the two of you?"

I looked sideways at Shawn. I was reluctant to reveal our friends, especially in the compromised position they were in.

He took over. "Yeah, it's just us."

I wasn't the only one who felt the need to protect our friends.

"Either of you bitten?"

"No."

"You sure about that?"

Looking at us, I wasn't surprised that the guy felt like he needed to ask again. We were a mess. Even the dog's hair was clumped and matted together with dried zombie blood. Good boy that he was, Rex hadn't hesitated to tear his way through the zombies.

"We're not bitten. I'm sure." I raised my voice to be heard clearly.

Darkness was falling rapidly now, and the man was becoming harder to see.

"Alright then. My shift here is about over. Just have to wait for Charlie to replace me. I'll walk you in if you wait."

The man swung over the side of his perch and began descending using a ladder that I had missed until that moment. He jumped to the ground and began walking toward us.

I didn't miss that Shawn took a step, putting himself partially in front of me, but the concern seemed to be unnecessary as the guy stopped a few feet away and held out a friendly hand. "I'm Colton."

He probably wasn't any older than me. Dressed in hunting camouflage, he looked at ease in his surroundings and us.

Shawn took his hand. "I'm Shawn. This is Bri."

The smile that Colton directed my way looked genuine. "Nice to meet you two. We don't get too many new arrivals anymore." He looked down at the dog who was watching him intently. "And who's this guy?" He started to reach toward Rex but thought better of his actions when a low rumble rolled up the dog's throat.

"This is Rex." I reached down to pat the dog.

"Everyone will be happy to see him. I can't tell you how long it's been since I saw a dog."

Just then, a woman's raspy voice called out, "Whatcha got, Colton?"

Swinging around, I saw a short form approaching through the gloom. As she got closer, I saw a middle-aged woman, also dressed in camouflage and armed. She moved with a pronounced limp.

"Charlie, this is Shawn and Bri. And Rex. They followed the signs in."

"Either of you bitten?" Her pack-a-day-for-thirty-years voice was oddly soothing. Maybe because it reminded me of my grandmother.

"No." I couldn't help but smile a little at the woman.

"Well, okay then. Nice to meet you, but I need to get on watch. You can follow Colton in, and he'll get you set up for the night." Turning away, she limped to the cluster of trees.

"Ready? It's not far, just to the strip mall up ahead." Colton gestured with his hand.

Eyeing Shawn, I moved to follow. Other than running in the opposite direction, we didn't have much choice. They hadn't given us any reason not to trust them so far.

The walk had been nerve-wracking. I kept second guessing our choice to go with this stranger.

If Colton noticed, he didn't say anything and just kept up a steady stream of chatter the whole way.

As we walked across the parking lot to the strip mall, I noticed a few more people on guard, even one on the roof. They all called out greetings to Colton but didn't seem alarmed by two new faces. I wasn't sure if that should make me feel better or not.

Stepping up onto the wide sidewalk that ran in front of the stores, Colton led us right to the front door of an outdoor store near the middle of the row of stores. The windows and glass door had been covered on the inside, blocking any view of what was going on inside.

Colton knocked on the door lightly, waited for a second and then pulled the door opened.

A man and woman eyed us as we hesitated just inside the door.

"This is Shawn and Bri. Is Maggie around?" Colton leaned his rifle next to the door as he addressed the pair.

The man nodded at us. "I think she's in the back. I'll go get her." He turned around and disappeared into the dark store.

Here and there, lanterns had been lit, casting circles of light that seemed to strategically show the way through the maze of shelves. A couple of people watched us but stayed back. I caught a glimpse of a little girl's head peeking around a corner before she smiled and waved—I think at the dog.

"Maggie is in charge around here. She'll want to meet you and explain how things work herself." Colton flashed us a reassuring smile.

I moved a little closer to Shawn. So many people staring at us was making me more nervous.

"I hear we have newcomers."

"Hey, Maggie, this is Bri and Shawn. They found our signs."

The woman walked through a circle of light, briefly showing brunette hair and a blank expression before coming to stand a few feet away from us. "Hi. I'm glad you made it. We just have a few questions and then we'll settle you in for the night."

Maggie asked the expected questions, showed interest in the fact that we still had a dog and then explained that all new people were quarantined for twelve hours. Just to be safe.

Everything seemed to be going smoothly, until she mentioned the quarantine. We had already left our friends for too long on the highway. We couldn't leave them there all night. But the lie we told that we were alone had made it impossible to say so. Instead, we found ourselves herded into an office at the back of the

226

store. They shut us in, leaving several bottles of water and more food than either of us had seen in a while.

The night had been long. I felt guilty as I ate too much and guzzled an entire bottle of water without taking a breath. The ones that we left behind needed us, but the guards that had been posted in front of the office door were armed. We weren't sure how they would react if we tried to leave the office before Maggie said so. I could guess that it wouldn't be pretty.

So we spent a mostly sleepless night leaning up against each other, sitting on the office carpet when morning finally came. The small window high on the back wall of the office let in the light. I hoped that the rest of our group didn't think that anything bad happened to us.

I wasn't sure yet if it had or not.

"I don't know. This group doesn't feel like the other one," Shawn said for the first time in a while. "The other group came in with guns drawn and shouting orders."

"I don't like being shut in here," I grumbled.

"Me either, but I get it. I've been thinking; they have to protect themselves too. I saw a kid. It's not unreasonable for them to want new people to stay separate until they're sure that they aren't sick. Yeah, they kinda hustled us in here in a hurry, but I don't blame them."

"They don't know about the others waiting for us," I added the thought that had weighed on my mind all night. "We're going to have to tell them as soon as we can. If we're going to stay."

He thought for a minute before answering, "I think we should stay at least for a while. They have food, maybe they'll have the meds we need too. I think we can trust them as much as we can trust anyone we don't know."

"Yeah. Okay." I didn't really see any other choice. If our friends were still okay, they wouldn't be for much longer. While these people had hurried to lock us up, they had been polite and provided us a safe place to spend the night and plenty of food.

I entertained myself for the next hour by feeding bites of a granola bar to Rex. When that was gone, I tried to figure out how to fold the wrapper into an origami bird. I failed miserably.

I had just chucked the wrapper into a corner in agitation when I heard Maggie's voice outside the door.

CHAPTER FORTY-EIGHT
Day Twenty-Three

"I'm sorry to have locked you in here so quickly, but it's necessary. I hope the night wasn't too uncomfortable," Maggie addressed us from just inside the door.

An unfamiliar man watched us with interest from over her shoulder.

"We're fine," Shawn answered her a little abruptly. We still couldn't be completely sure that this group was safe.

"And you're both still feeling okay?" Maggie searched us for any indication that we may be infected. Covered in dried gore like we were, it would have been difficult to be sure at first, but enough time had passed by now that we would have been visibly ill if we were infected. "You seem okay."

"We're fine," I repeated Shawn's words.

The first smile that I'd seen from Maggie spread across her face. "That's good news. You are free to leave quarantine. Let's get you cleaned up and I will show you around." Stepping to the side, she indicated toward the open door.

Glancing to the side, I shared a meaningful glance with Shawn. It was time. We needed to make a final decision. He nodded almost imperceptibly.

I inhaled to steady my nerves and hoped that we were making the right choice. "We haven't been completely honest with you."

When suspicion bloomed on Maggie's face, I hurried to explain, "There are more of us. We left them up on the highway, and we really need to get back to them. Several of them need medical attention."

Maggie was quiet for a few seconds as she seemed to be thinking through what I had just told her. Finally, she said, "Why did you feel the need to hide this?"

Shawn stepped in to answer, "Not everyone left alive out there can be trusted, you know? A couple of our group are in bad shape. We weren't sure if we wanted to tell you about them. The plan was for the two of us to find you and decide if you could be trusted first."

Maggie nodded slowly. "I understand. That's smart. How many are in your group?"

"There are four more. Two aren't in any shape to walk."

Maggie looked to the man who had been silently looming through the conversation. "Gather a group to go out, two trucks." She turned back to us. "Let's go get your friends."

*   *   *

The metal bed of the pickup was nearly hot enough to burn my skin. Crouching in the back, I did my best to come into as little contact with the metal as possible; however, it was no easy task as the truck dodged a small group of zombies.

The sun was already brutal, and I could feel my hastily scrubbed face and hands trying to burn. Beside me, Shawn shielded his eyes with one hand, and Rex panted heavily, eyeing our companion warily. Colton was also in the bed of the truck with a rifle nearby.

Maggie was behind the wheel. She slid open the back window to better able to hear our directions. Following us was another pickup with three armed men watching alertly from its bed.

230

The trip that had taken us hours to make the day before was flying by in minutes under the humming tires of the vehicles. I knew we had to be getting close to where the van had finally given out on us. I could only hope that our friends were still waiting for us.

"Hey, we got trouble," Maggie called back.

Switching my gaze from watching the disappearing group of zombies running after us, I looked ahead. I sucked in a breath in horror.

The straight stretch of highway ahead was all too familiar. It was where we had left the van, but I couldn't see the van because dozens of zombies crowded it from every angle. You could hear their distant shrieks even over the sound of the engine.

"That's the rest of our group."

Maggie nodded and slowed down to allow the second truck to catch up with us. When the other driver pulled even, she indicated the swarm of zombies ahead.

"This is good news." Colton moved to stand just behind the cab of the truck. When I eyed him with an expression that said he was crazy, he elaborated, "The zombies wouldn't be so interested in that van if there wasn't anyone inside."

He was right, but I didn't have much time to think that over because the truck was slowing to a stop. Less than fifty yards from the van, both trucks swung around to face back the way we had come and stopped completely. The zombies at the edges of the swarm noticed us, and some immediately broke free of their group to attack easier prey.

I jumped to my feet as several of the freshest zombies sprinted full tilt, snarling. It would only take a matter of seconds for them to cross the space between us. Shawn and Rex had also lunged to their feet, and I grabbed hold of the dog's collar to keep him in the truck.

"Fire at will," Maggie ordered as she climbed into the back of the truck. The men in the second truck had already taken aim, and the first of the charging zombies fell. My ears started ringing as the rifle Colton seemed to always have nearby fired too close, but that was fine by me because the zombie nearest to our truck fell in a spray of its brains.

The gunfire drew the attention of more of the zombies. A second wave of them—this one mostly made up of older and slower creatures—began working their way toward us. They didn't come as fast, but there were more of them, and my heart pounded in my chest as the mindless predators came closer to the trucks. By then, the armed members of the new group had fired a lot of rounds. More than one of them was reloading.

One rotting zombie managed to dodge enough bullets to make it to the side of our truck. Grabbing my machete, Shawn brought it down square on the zombie's forehead as the creature swiped over the side at him.

Heat waves shimmered off the road. The stench was nearly overwhelming. A few more shots and the last of the zombies shuffling through their fallen brethren went down. There was only one of the creatures left—a single zombie who paid no attention to its own kind running off. It still snarled and clawed at the van's windows.

As I watched, the opposite door of the van swung open and Maya climbed out. She stumbled a bit before straightening up and striding around the van determinedly. The zombie crumpled to the ground as she stabbed it.

I missed what happened next because I was climbing down from the back of the truck. As soon as my feet hit the pavement, I started sprinting.

CHAPTER FORTY-NINE
Day Twenty-Three

I tripped over the body of a zombie and nearly landed facedown onto the pavement. Jerking back upright, I slowed down to a more reasonable pace. The ground was littered with corpses in varying stages of decay, but I barely noticed them. My entire focus was on the van.

Its original color was unrecognizable with the thick layers of dirt and zombie blood covering it. Maya leaned up against the side, just in front of where the sliding door now stood open. As I got closer, I could see just how bad she really looked. Her hair was plastered to her skull from sweating in what must have been unbearable temperatures inside the van. Already too thin, stress and dehydration had done nothing to improve her sunken features, worsening them until she resembled some of the zombies that I was carefully stepping over.

"You have impeccable timing." Her voice was raspy.

"We couldn't get back any sooner. Bill?" I skidded to a stop next to her, afraid of her answer.

Relief nearly brought me to my knees when a hint of a smile tried to form on her cracked lips.

"He's been in and out of consciousness. He's a little confused, but I think if we can find a place for him to recover. He'll be alright."

A full-blown grin stretched across my face. I indicated the group that was approaching, carefully driving the trucks closer over the piles of zombies. "I think we've found just the place. They have plenty of supplies, and someone said they even have a nurse."

Maya grinned back at me. Knowing that Bill was not only still alive but he had improved a bit too galvanized me into stepping closer to look in the open door.

"Took you long enough." Devon waved at me without lifting his head from where it rested on the back of his seat. Frankly, he looked too sick and exhausted to lift his head. Fallon hovered next to him. The look she sent me was full of things that she didn't want to say out loud.

"Hey, guys. I am glad to see you." I leaned in the door and peered into the back seat. Bill wasn't awake, and he still looked awful, but the steady rise and fall of his chest proved that he was still alive.

The first of the pickups stopped with its lowered tailgate about ten feet from the front of the van. Shawn and Colton jumped down, and Maggie stepped from behind the wheel.

"How's Bill?" Shawn looked from me to Maya.

"He's alive. I think he's going to make it." Maggie smiled again upon saying those words.

"That's good." Shawn broke out in a smile of his own. It occurred to me that we all were smiling more right then than any of us had in a while. "Guys, this is Maggie and Colton." He introduced the two who had stopped a few feet away from us.

"Hi." Maggie stepped forward. "Looks like you folks could use some help."

Maya glanced sideways at me. When I nodded slightly to her, she held out her hand in greeting. "I'm Maya. We're really glad you all came along."

Moving our group from the van into the back of the two trucks didn't take long. We had essentially zero belongings. The hardest part was helping Devon and Bill. Despite doing his best to

234

hide the amount of pain he was in, Devon's condition deteriorated badly since we last saw him. He needed help to move, and once we settled him in the truck, he leaned over in an obvious effort to control his dizziness.

Bill started out asleep, but there was no way to move him without jostling him around. By the time the four guys lifted him into a truck, his eyes were open. Climbing into the truck after him, Maya shushed his efforts to speak with assurances that everything was okay.

The addition of the rest of our group had filled the trucks. Colton still rode with us, but this time, he climbed into the cab next to Maggie. He rolled his window down and kept an eye out for dangerous zombies that way.

Between Bill lying flat out back there and Devon having to keep one long leg stretched out in front of him, the rest of us crowded into what felt like a sliver of the truck bed. I leaned tiredly up against Shawn and let my head rest on his shoulder. It had been days since I really slept.

The adrenaline from trying to survive had kept me going, but now it was starting to feel like we had the chance to breathe even just a little. This new group had supplies and weapons. They even had the next best thing to a doctor. And they had proven helpful instead of insane. It became increasingly difficult to keep my eyes open as the realization hit me that we were finally safe or, at least, as safe as a person could be during an apocalypse.

I must have dozed off because the next thing I knew, Shawn was shaking my shoulder lightly. The truck had stopped in front of the door to the shelter, and a man and a woman were already helping Devon down.

"We require that all new people go into quarantine for twelve hours. But don't worry, you will be provided food and water, and I'm going to go get our medical people to come take a look at your wounded right away," Maggie told them before she began issuing orders to her people. They scurried to follow orders.

"It's okay," Shawn answered the questioning look Fallon sent us. "Bri and I had to be quarantined overnight too."

It felt like I was walking through a fog as I trailed behind my group. When we reached the same room that Shawn, Rex, and I had spent the previous night in, I noticed with bare interest that it had been converted quickly into a hospital of sorts. Medical supplies, including a bag of IV fluids that managed to perk up my interest, waited, along with an entire case of new water bottles. A pile of blankets lay in one corner, and a couple of people hurried to make a makeshift bed for Bill to be placed on.

The room quickly became crowded with all the people trying to fit inside at once.

"You two don't need to be quarantined again. Why don't you let Colton show you some place you can rest? You look dead on your feet. We will take care of your friends." When she noticed my reluctance to go, Maggie added, "It's too crowded in here. We need room to be able to treat their injuries. And it won't do anyone any good to be cramped for the next twelve hours."

"Bri, that makes sense. Let's get some rest. We can come check on them in a few hours." In the end, it was Shawn who convinced me to be led out from the group. The others were so busy drinking water while watching the guy who must be the nurse checking over Bill, that they paid no attention as we left the room.

Back out in the main dark area of the store, we passed at least a dozen new faces who watched us go with varying degrees of friendliness. I was too tired at that point to really care or do more than half-heartedly respond to anyone who greeted us. The shelving in the store was like a maze as we followed Colton into the interior.

"This will be your area," he indicated a cleared-out space with four cots standing inside. "I'll send someone by with some basic supplies for you. When you're ready, I'll take you around and you can pick up anything else you need. All these beds are empty, so feel free to take your pick." Reaching down, he turned on a

236

battery-powered lantern and handed it to Shawn. "Get some sleep, guys." Colton turned and disappeared back into the dark store.

The bed closest to me was calling my name. I had never been so tired in my entire life. I was actually feeling physically ill. I was that exhausted. Without a backward glance, I took the two steps needed to get close enough and collapsed facedown on the cot.

CHAPTER FIFTY
Day Twenty-Four

A low murmur of voices was what finally woke me up. Blinking my eyes open, all I saw was black. In my disorientation, it took several seconds for me to figure out where I was: in Maggie's group's safe haven, on a cot, and apparently under a blanket that I didn't remember covering myself with. With a groan, I pulled the blanket off my face.

The area around me was illuminated softly by the lantern. Now that I wasn't nearly dead on my feet with exhaustion, I was able to look around and actually see.

The space was slightly rectangular, with just enough room for the four cots lined up in it. The walls had been made from the store's shelves. Though most of them were empty, one shelf had a few items on it. The trusty backpack that had saved me in more ways than one lay on the floor at the foot of my bed.

I tumbled onto the cot on the far left of the space. The one right next to mine had a rumpled blanket on it, but whoever had slept there was no longer on the cot.

Swinging my feet to the floor, I stood up. Stuck in the perpetual darkness of the converted store, it was difficult to tell exactly how much time had passed, but it felt like I had been asleep for a long time. Right now, all I wanted was to find the rest of my group and check that they were doing okay.

Moving to the doorway, I peered out into the mazelike walkway. Lanterns lit up the space well enough. I could see that more cubicle type spaces had been formed along the hall. Not knowing which direction to try, I took a guess and turned to my left. I silently kicked myself for not paying better attention when Colton first led us to our space.

As I passed the doorways to other rooms, it was obvious that a few of them had been home to someone for a while. Belongings lined the shelves. A few cots had someone sleeping in them. I continued down the dark walkway.

Ahead, the path split. I stopped, looking both ways. The path to the right was dark and quiet. The one to the left had a light showing at the end, and I was pretty sure that the voices I heard were coming from that direction. I walked toward the light.

The narrow path opened up, and I was relieved to have run into people. I hadn't noticed just how tense I was at being alone and in the dark until I wasn't anymore. Even better, I recognized Shawn's back as he bent over the struggling dog, trying to briskly dry him with a towel. Two more people—one of them slightly familiar—were talking together to the side. They waved a greeting when they saw me.

Catching sight of me, Rex doubled his efforts to escape and managed to pull free. Flashing a toothy canine smile, the dog bounded across the open space and leaped up on me.

"Hey, buddy." I rubbed the dog's wet ears. He smelled like wet dog, which was a marked improvement from smelling like a rotten zombie. "You got a bath."

"Yeah, I thought everyone would be happier if he weren't covered in zombie." Shawn tossed the damp towel over one shoulder as he reached us. "Speaking of being covered in zombie . . ." He reached out and pinched a piece of my filthy hair between two fingers.

I grimaced. "Getting clean would be good, yeah."

239

"You are not going to believe it, but they have showers here."

I felt my eyes lit up. I never thought I would see anything like a shower again. "Lead the way."

Bumping my shoulder good-naturedly with his, Shawn turned and started in a direction I hadn't been yet. "I managed to convince Maya to take a break. She's in there now. I think Fallon too."

Startled, I looked at him. "Maya and Fallon are out of quarantine? How long did I sleep?"

He glanced over his shoulder. "A day. Both of us. I haven't been up for too long either."

I fell silent as I thought that over. I had never slept for so long before, but then, I had never been so desperately tired before either.

"So Bill's doing okay? He must be if Maya left his side."

"Yeah. He's awake. He's not moving around much yet, but he's talking. Now that they've got the dehydration under control, he's making sense again."

A weight lifted off my shoulders, but Bill wasn't the only one who had been in bad shape. "And how's Devon's leg?"

Shawn stopped to turn my way. "That's not going as well." He frowned. "The nurse is doing everything he can. He says the infection is spreading."

That had been my fear ever since the first time I saw the cut on Devon's leg. It had been bad from the start, and we had been on the move through wet, filthy conditions almost nonstop. The look on my face must have matched the stricken feelings I was having because Shawn pulled me close for a hug.

"They are doing the best they can. It's not over yet."

"I knew this was a possibility."

"We all did. Bri, you have kept all of us alive in more ways than one. We would all have been gone a long time ago without you. Don't you blame yourself, no matter what happens."

240

I let myself relax into the hug, needing the comfort. I knew that he was right, but a part of me couldn't help but think that I could have done more. That there was always more that could be done, no matter what.

"Alright, no offense, but you need that shower." He eased back and smiled at me.

I sighed and smiled back. I did stink.

Shawn led me through a back hallway that seemed to connect this store to the rest of them in the mall. We passed a few doors before he gestured to an open one.

I stepped inside and was surprised to find myself in a gym. Amazingly, there were actually a couple of people there using the weight machines. The highest windows had been left uncovered, and the light felt bright after the darkness of the store I woke up in.

"It's this way." Shawn led me toward the locker rooms. Water was dripping from inside the girl's room. "I'll wait out here if you want me to."

"Yeah, that'd be good. Thanks." I wasn't super excited about walking back to the main store through the dark alone.

Rex balked at following me into the locker room. He was probably afraid I would give him another bath, so I entered the room alone. It looked just like any other gym locker room, except lanterns provided the light. The whole effect was kind of creepy, so I hurried to get clean and get out of there.

I immediately heard the sound of water coming from the shower room. When I peered around the corner, I found Maya with a towel wrapped around her. She looked tired but better than the last time I saw her. Fallon was at the far wall, rinsing her hair under a bucket-looking contraption.

"Hi, guys," I announced my presence.

"Bri!" they greeted me at the same time.

"This place is great!" Fallon gushed.

I smiled at her exuberance. It was the most animated she had been in a while. "It kinda is, isn't it?"

241

Maya startled me when she hugged me suddenly, uncaring that she was clean and I was far from it.

"Thank you," Maya said. The raw emotion in her voice brought an answering lump to my own throat.

I squeezed her back.

Clearing her throat, she backed up. "I need to get back to Bill. I don't want to leave him alone for too long."

"I'll stop by to see him once I'm cleaned up."

"He'd like that." She smiled at me and disappeared around the corner.

"Well, the water's cold, but it's a shower. Want me to show you how this thing works?" Fallon chirped from where she was using a towel to dry her hair.

"That would be great."

CHAPTER FIFTY-ONE
Day Twenty-Four

I managed to find a pair of jeans and a shirt that almost fit me in the pile of clean clothes that had been left in the locker room for that purpose. Dressing quickly, I did the best I could to get the tangles out of my hair and got out of there. Once Fallon and Maya left the locker room, my earlier feelings that the room was too creepy returned with a vengeance.

Back out in the gym, I found Shawn talking to one of the men who had gone with us to rescue our friends the day before.

"Bri, this is Mark."

I said hello and waited while the two guys went back to talking about whatever they had been talking about. Although I didn't understand everything—working out had never been even a blip on my radar—but I was easily able to tell that they were talking about—the gym. It reminded me that Shawn liked to go to the gym regularly before the zombies ended the world.

I looked around the open room with a little more interest. Being in the gym, in the middle of the night, was probably what had saved Shawn during the initial outbreak. And if it hadn't been for my roommate trapping me in our bathroom, I would have probably been dead too.

The testosterone-fueled manly bonding session seemed to be winding down. Mark invited Shawn to use the gym whenever he wanted, and Shawn turned to me. "Ready?"

I nodded and waved goodbye to Mark. The walk back to the main area was every bit as creepy as the first time—maybe worse. My eyes had adjusted to having more light while standing in the gym. I was definitely glad that I had asked Shawn to wait for me. Walking beside him—and Rex on the other side—helped. The zombie apocalypse seemed to be making me more scared of the dark than I had been as a kid.

Back in the main store, we twisted and turned our way through the dark walkways. Whoever had been responsible for moving things around in here deserved some sort of award. I was lost, but luckily, my companion seemed to have it figured out. Somehow, we emerged right next to the front door, in the large open space there.

"Hey, guys. I see you found the showers." Colton nodded to the guy he had been talking to and walked our way, pushing his slightly too long hair out of his face.

"Yeah. I ran into Charlie earlier, and she told me how to find them," Shawn answered.

"Good. Has anyone given you the tour yet?"

"Not yet. I did explore on my own a bit. Bri hasn't seen anything but the showers yet."

Colton grinned at us. "I have about an hour until I need to take my shift on watch. Why don't I show you around?"

"That would be great," I chimed in.

I didn't like feeling so disoriented. Hopefully, a tour would solve that problem. And maybe we would find something to eat. Now that I was wide awake, I was starving.

I discovered really quickly that the layout inside the store wasn't too confusing once it was explained. Along with the open area near the door, the quarantine room, and the bunch of cubicle-like sleeping spaces, there was an even larger open area at the center of the store. There, everyone tended to gather whenever they weren't sleeping or carrying out their assigned jobs.

There were about a dozen people hanging around when we arrived, and I was pleased to notice that most of them were starting to look familiar. Likewise, they seemed to be getting used to us, and a variety of greetings came our way.

Colton was just starting to tell us the schedule to come get something to eat when a girly squeal pierced through the silence.

"Doggie!" A little girl with tangled hair darted toward us.

Tensing up, I tried to step in between her and Rex. I had no idea how he would react to an overzealous kid, but I did know that he took some time to warm up to strangers. To my dismay, Rex wandered further into the space than we had, and there was no way I would reach the dog before the kid did.

The girl launched herself at him and wrapped thin arms around his neck, burying her face in his fur. Rex's tail began to wag.

I reached him a second later, but by then, I could already see that I need not have worried. I wasn't great at guessing people's age, but my guess was this girl could be five or six years old.

Happily, she tugged the dog closer. The lantern light wasn't bright, but it gleamed off her hair, highlighting her red curls. Pulling slightly away from Rex, the girl smiled up at me with a face full of freckles.

"What's your dog's name?"

"Luna, you know better than to run up to a strange animal," Colton lightly chided her, interrupting me before I could answer.

When I realized that the quiet conversations around us had gone silent, I looked up. Every adult present was watching the little girl hug the big dog with concern. I couldn't blame them, but I did find it strange that no one seemed to be stepping forward to take charge of the kid.

Colton answered my unasked question, "Bri and Shawn, this is Luna. She's the only kid we have living here with us. We found her hiding in her school in the first week, and we all watch out for her now."

245

"Mommy didn't make it to my school to pick me up, but that's okay because I'm just going to wait here for her." She gripped the dog's fur tighter and looked up at me with an almost defiant expression.

I couldn't imagine how hard it must have been for someone so young to comprehend just what had happened. I sank down to her level and reached out to pet Rex with her. "That sounds like a good plan." Her riot of red hair and demeanor reminded me so much of Evie that I had to clear my throat before I could continue. "This is Rex. Is it okay if he and I, and our friends, stay here too?"

When she realized that I wasn't going to challenge her statement, the tension left her small shoulders. Smiling at me with a missing tooth, she answered, "Yep. But only if I get to pet Rex sometimes."

"Deal." I stood back up.

Enough time had passed that I was sure Colton would have to go soon. I was hoping that he could direct me to wherever the rest of my friends were staying. I had a promised visit to keep.

"Colton, can you tell me where I will find Bill and Devon? I'd like to check up on them."

"Sure, follow me." He turned to walk back into the sleeping area. "We cleared out a space next to where Alex sleeps. He's our nurse here. The rest of your group is probably all there."

CHAPTER FIFTY-TWO
Day Twenty-Four

The guy who I assumed was the resident nurse was standing in the walkway, talking quietly with Maggie. He had a faint accent, almost nonexistent, that reminded me of a woman I used to work with. That woman was likely dead by now. I wondered—not for the first time—if there was anyone left alive from my old life.

Colton waved a greeting to the pair and then sauntered off into the darkness, leaving Shawn and me standing there somewhat awkwardly.

"Hey." I attempted to cover up the feeling.

"Bri, Shawn, this is Alex. He's been working around the clock to try to help your friends."

I managed a half-smile at Maggie before turning to Alex. "How are they doing?"

"I was just telling Maggie here that there's good news and bad. Bill is already recovering remarkably well. I hear he has you to thank for that."

I shrugged, uncomfortable with the attention.

Alex rubbed his eyes that were so bleary I could see just how bloodshot they were even in the low light and continued, "I could sometimes really use some help around here. I'd appreciate it if you'd consider being my backup."

When I nodded reluctantly, he went on, "Bill's healing. There's no sign of infection, and he's already asking when he can get out of bed. As long as nothing unexpected happens, I expect him to be back on his feet in another day or two."

When he stopped there, I shifted from one foot to the other. I was glad to hear that Bill was going to be okay, but from what I had heard, Devon was the one in trouble at the moment. Alex's pause seemed to confirm that. Shawn had shuffled closer while we listened to the nurse talking, and I leaned lightly back into the warmth of his chest, seeking some sort of shield against the bad news.

Alex sighed. "Devon is the one I'm worried about. That wound has been infected for days, and the infection is spreading. I've been giving him the best antibiotics that we have, but it is getting worse. I'm not sure what exactly to do."

"What do you mean?"

"The thing is, I know what the options would be for him if we were in a hospital—as fast and as far as the infection is spreading—I would be talking about amputation at this point. But right now, I'm not sure if there's any other option for him."

Heavy silence fell between the four of us.

Amputation. How would we do such a thing safely in these conditions? And even if he survived the procedure, how would Devon make it with only one leg? I wasn't naive enough to think that we would never have to run for our lives again, no matter how nice this place seemed to be.

"Does he know?" I breathed.

"No, but it's time that I'm going to have to tell him." Alex sounded like it was the last thing he wanted to do.

After another pause, we ended up talking for several minutes about just how we would break the news to Devon. In the end, there really was only one way to do it. He deserved to know what was going on and to have a say in the matter. After all, it was his leg we're talking about here.

We were just about to go talk to him when Shawn stopped me. "After this, you should have Alex take a look at your back."

Maggie and Alex turned to look at me, forcing me to reply, "It's fine, really. I hardly even notice the scratches anymore."

That was a lie. They pulled unpleasantly whenever I moved wrong, and they burned like fire during my shower, but I felt like there were more important issues to worry about at the moment.

Seeing that I was going to be stubborn, Shawn went ahead and told on me. "She cut her back on a fence a few days ago. We cleaned them up, but one, in particular, was pretty deep."

I glowered at him, but the three of them ignored me. "I'll check you out when we are done here. Come on over to my bunk whenever you're ready."

I grumbled my displeasure at Shawn. "They are just scratches. Yours were way worse, and you're fine."

"Mine was not worse. You can't see your back, but I have." When he noticed that the attention had shifted to him, Shawn elaborated. "Back toward the beginning, a zombie scratched me." He pulled his shirt aside to show the healed marks. "They're fine now."

"Wait, you were scratched by a zombie?" Alex moved closer to look at Shawn's exposed skin with interest.

"Yeah."

"And you didn't get sick at all?"

"Nope. We were worried for a while, but I guess scratches aren't dangerous." He released his shirt.

The look on the nurse's face was starting to make me uncomfortable again.

"That's just it." Alex looked rapidly back and forth between Shawn and me. "I was in an ER at the start of all this. I saw patients with plenty of bites and scratches. They all were infected. If blood was drawn, fatality seemed to be a hundred percent." He looked like he was lost in thought, and his tone suggested that he was talking more to himself than anyone else.

"The scratch itself isn't deadly. Or so we thought. But the zombies are all filthy and covered in blood. Blood from under their

249

nails introduced into an open wound was all it took. You would have to be the luckiest person alive to be scratched and not get infected. Unless you did, and you were somehow immune." Alex looked speculatively at Shawn. "I wish there was some way for us to know. If there were actually a person who was immune, that could maybe be a start to a vaccine."

Listening to the nurse ramble on was making me uncomfortable. I had watched my share of TV in the past. This was always about the time a crazed scientist would decide to experiment on some unlucky person.

I felt myself glaring at Alex and couldn't seem to stop it. Anyone who messed with my family was going to get on my bad side in a hurry.

"Well, that's a talk for another day." Maggie was watching me with interest. She appeared to be the only one who picked up on my body language. "Right now, I think it's time we tell Devon the truth. He needs to have some time to decide what he wants to do."

Her words were the wet blanket I needed to put out the slow anger that had started in my veins at the mere thought of anyone hurting Shawn. Maggie was right. Devon needed us right now. He needed me calm, not freaking out over something that hadn't even actually happened.

I attempted to shake off my bad mood and turned to Alex. "Lead the way."

CHAPTER FIFTY-THREE
Day Twenty-Four

He cried.

Devon tried to hide the tear that slid down his cheek, but I saw it. That tiny bit of moisture dragged an answering tear from my own eye. It wasn't fair. Devon was barely an adult, and he was faced with an impossible decision.

I held back my gasp when Alex pulled the blanket up to expose his leg. The entire lower part of his limb was swollen grotesquely, and the area around the wound was black.

Pulling out a sharpie, Alex drew a line where the infection met the paler color of healthy flesh. The mark was at least an inch higher than a similar sharpie line already on his leg and above his knee.

"The infection is spreading too fast. Whatever you decide, it needs to be soon." Alex pulled the blanket back down to cover his leg.

I shifted uncomfortably. I didn't know what to say to Devon. Around me, the others seemed to be having the same problem. Maggie hovered just inside the door. Shawn and I had stopped near the end of the bed Devon was laying on. Fallon was sitting cross-legged on the cot next to his. Bill and Maya took the other two cots in the room.

I was glad to see that Bill looked as good as he did, but that had been tempered by the knowledge of what we were about to hear. Now, everyone in the room looked equally grim. We all knew that there was no good solution to this problem.

"Um, I need some time. Could you guys leave me alone for a while?"

"I'll just be at the door. Call for me when you're ready to talk." Alex flashed a tight smile at Devon before gesturing for me to follow him.

I spared a backward look at Devon—more than anything, he looked like he was in shock—before allowing Shawn to lightly direct me after Alex. Over in the next sleeping cubicle, I found the nurse rummaging through the well-stocked contents of his shelves.

There were only two cots in this space. The rest of the floor was taken up by a variety of medical things. One cot was obviously in use, but the other seemed like it hadn't seen a body in a while. Alex pointed to the empty cot.

"You can have a seat there and pull the back of your shirt up."

I eyed the cot with distaste but walked to it and plopped down. Shawn was still hovering. I think he was making sure I didn't make a break for it before Alex got a look at my scratches.

Making a face at him, I reached back and gingerly worked my shirt up high enough.

"You hardly even notice them, huh?" Shawn hadn't missed how carefully I was moving my shoulders.

I wasn't going to win that argument, so I just sighed and kept quiet. Alex was pulling on a pair of latex gloves anyway.

"Okay, let's see what's going on back here."

The rubber gloves felt cold as they brushed against my skin. Alex moved my shirt a little higher, and I felt him gently poking around the wounds. They were already sore, and whatever he was doing wasn't helping any.

I had never been a good patient, and I knew it, so I grit my teeth and let the nurse do his job.

After a minute, he spoke, "Bri, these actually don't look too bad. This one probably should have had a couple of stitches, but it's healing without them. I think if you keep them clean and take it easy with how you move for a few more days, they should heal up fine."

"That's great. Thanks." I waited less than patiently while I felt him smear ointment over the scratches and plaster some kind of bandage over the whole mess.

He stood up, and I heard the rubber snap of the gloves coming off. "All finished. Come back tomorrow, and I'll have a check on it again, but don't worry, I think you're fine."

I jumped to my feet and pulled my shirt back into place. "Will do. Thanks." I had no intention of coming back tomorrow.

I started to make my escape, but what Alex said next stopped me in my tracks. "Shawn, would you mind if I took a closer look at your scratches?"

"Sure." Shawn shrugged and moved closer to him.

He didn't seem to mind the nurse's interest, but I felt myself getting defensive all over again. I crowded closer to the two of them and watched skeptically. I had no idea what Alex could hope to learn by looking at already healed wounds.

Alex pursed his lips in thought and studied the marks on Shawn's shoulder with dark eyes. He didn't touch, but he looked like he really wanted to.

"You are positive that they were caused by the zombie?"

"Yeah, I mean, I don't think it could have been anything else. I didn't actually feel it when it happened, just noticed them after."

"And they didn't get infected at all. Or you didn't have any symptoms?"

"No, nothing. But Bri hauled me inside and spent a lot of time cleaning them right away."

"Interesting." Alex flashed a look my way. "I don't honestly know what to think. Maybe you just lucked out and were scratched by a freakishly clean zombie. Or maybe having the wounds cleaned so quickly made a difference. Or, maybe, you have some sort of immunity."

Shawn frowned a little. "Is there any way to find out for sure?"

Alex finally backed up a step, making me feel like I could breathe again. I had half-expected him to go all mad scientist on us. "No, I'm afraid not. At least, not here. Some place with a functioning lab would be able to run tests and give you answers, but we aren't capable of anything like that."

It made me perversely glad to hear those words. If they were less capable here than my overactive imagination had feared, then maybe there wouldn't be any reason to worry. Then again, being in any way less capable during the zombie apocalypse was not a great thing.

Confused by my own inner monologue, I reached down to scratch behind Rex's ears. I needed to get a grip.

The empty growling from my stomach turned into an embarrassing snarl by then. Fortunately, it was time to go eat, so Shawn and I worked our way back to the larger community area. Fallon and Maya were already there, having left too when Devon asked for privacy. Bill was the only who stayed with him, although he wasn't supposed to be getting up just yet.

I slid onto a bench next to Fallon. "How you holding up?"

Her voice was quiet when she answered, "Not good."

"Yeah. Me either."

No one really knew what to say after that, so we ate a subdued lunch with the people from the group and waited to find out what was going to happen next.

I had just finished shoving the last of the stew down in a very unladylike fashion when Maggie walked out of the shadows.

She walked right up to our little group. "Alex just informed me that your friend has made his decision. He's decided that he doesn't want to amputate."

CHAPTER FIFTY-FOUR
Day Twenty-Five

It wasn't until after I learned that Devon was choosing to not have his leg amputated, that I realized that I did have an opinion on the subject. A rather strong one, in fact. Hearing that he was essentially giving up, I suddenly knew what choice I would have made in his situation. This was one thing that we did not see eye to eye on.

No matter what, I knew that I could never stop trying. Not just for myself but for the rest of our little group. We had become something of a family as the weeks went by. I guess you couldn't really expect anything less when your life literally depended on those around you. We were all going to feel the loss keenly but no one more than Fallon.

The two of them had grown close. It seemed to be more of a best friends or brother-and-sister kind of thing, and that maybe made what was inevitably going to happen all the worse. Fallon was only a couple of years younger than me, Devon only a couple of years younger than her, but they both seemed so young to me. The kind of young that still needed a family around, and I knew that Fallon was going to be wrecked if we lost him.

The whole situation made me mad. I was mad that the world had gone to hell, making it a possibility to die from a cut. I was mad that Devon was giving up without a fight. And I was mad that I hadn't been able to fix the situation before it got to this point.

We spent most of the previous day hanging out with the group. The mood had been subdued at best. The conversation had been stilted. Alex continued to do his best to treat Devon, but the sharpie lines steadily advanced higher up his leg no matter what the nurse tried.

I had come to a conclusion, in the night, that I did not want to spend another day sitting around and watching a friend slowly die. That was how Shawn and I ended up joining the group of scavengers who were spending the day searching for anything useful that might still be in the nearby buildings.

"We've already been through most of this area. There's a small grocery store that we skipped at first because we could see a lot of zombies inside, but the last time anyone went by it, they reported that the zombies seem to have gotten out. Today's goal is to check it out. If the zombies were there from the beginning, there is probably still a lot of usable food inside." It turned out that Mark, the gym guy, was in charge of scavenging.

"Alright." I checked my knife that was strapped to my belt and gripped the machete that had become my favorite weapon. Someone had offered me a gun, but I hadn't the first clue what to do with it. I'd be just as likely to shoot a friend as a zombie. Better to stick with what I knew, for now.

"You know how to handle yourself with that?" The throaty voice could only belong to one person.

"Yeah." I turned to face Charlie, who was eyeing the machete. "I'm better off with this than anything else."

"Okay. Just checking. We had a guy cut his own thumb off with one of those once." She grinned at me.

It felt good to think about something other than Devon and his leg, just for a while. I smiled back at her.

"You have everything you need?" Shawn walked up to the group gathering by the front door. He picked up a knife from somewhere and was carrying the tire iron. It had turned out to be an effective zombie killing weapon.

"Yeah, I'm ready to go. I just need to get out of here for a day." I felt like I needed to explain myself.

"It's alright, Bri. Sitting around doing nothing won't change anything. If we can go out and help bring back food, we will be doing something good for the whole group."

I shouldn't have been surprised that he understood so well. That was just one of the many reasons that I had become so attached to him. Despite the tough guy exterior, Shawn was actually very observant of those around him.

"Luna is having a good time with that dog of yours," Charlie interrupted my thoughts.

I had decided not to take Rex out with us. There were too many things that could go wrong, and if I could keep him safe, that's what I wanted to do. The problem had been figuring out who to leave him with. The rest of my friends were too busy and then inspiration struck. Leaving him with the little girl would keep both of them occupied for a while. "Good. Maybe they will tire each other out."

"Right!" She chuckled. "That child needs another kid to play with."

"Let's go!" Mark called the group and ended the conversation.

The same two trucks that we used before stood waiting outside. Charlie, Shawn, and I climbed into the back of one, as a woman I hadn't met yet got behind the wheel. Mark and two other guys I'd seen around took the other. Before long, we were winding our way down roads clogged with abandoned vehicles. Zombies, mostly of the slower variety, bounced off the sides of the trucks. Most of them stood no chance of getting inside at us. The few who came too close were dealt with easily.

The edges of the town looked like every other place we had seen since coming back out of the mountains. Fires had burned a few buildings. Cars, trash, and zombies littered the streets. A tabby cat darted in front of our truck and into some bushes along the side of a house. It was going to be another hot day, and the smell in the air was decay with hints of the fires that had burned.

Despite it all, the wind felt good on my skin as we drove along. The strip mall was too dark and enclosed, and with emotions running so high, I was feeling trapped.

Within a couple of minutes, the trucks pulled into the parking lot of the grocery store. The front wall was made mostly of glass, and we could easily see a lot of the interior of the small building. A zombie was roaming up and down the aisles, but one glass pane had broken out, and the rest of them must have gotten out that way.

Driving slowly, the trucks came to a stop not far from the front doors. We had attracted a small group of zombies. One of them was a runner. It shrieked as it sprinted toward us, making me cringe. That call would attract more unwelcome attention.

Beside me, Charlie nonchalantly took aim and the running zombie immediately dropped. Remind me not to get on that particular woman's bad side.

"Nice shot." Mark jumped out of the other truck.

Shrugging, Charlie jumped down. She didn't seem to overthink, one way or the other, of her own ability with that gun. I had been drawn to the older woman from the first time I met her. After that little display, I was starting to wonder if maybe she wouldn't mind teaching me.

"Okay, guys. Here's the plan. Sara and Ed will stay out here and keep watch. If anything too bad comes our way, they will honk the horn once. The rest of us are going in. We will sweep the store first. Once it's cleared, we'll load anything that's left up and get out of here. I don't want to stay any longer than absolutely necessary. You know how it is: the longer we stay out here, the more zombies will find us."

CHAPTER FIFTY-FIVE
Day Twenty-Five

The inside of the grocery store smelled like long rotten produce and death. We had walked across a dried pool of blood with bits of torn jeans and bone right inside the front door. Overturned shopping carts had spilled their contents across the floor. It looked like when this building was overrun, there had still been more than a few shoppers inside.

I got a flashback to the day before the start of all this when I stood in a checkout line in another grocery store and contemplated getting that flu shot. If not for the crowds of people getting on my nerves, I would likely be one of the zombies right now—eternally trapped inside our apartment with Evie and maybe Austin.

I wondered if the little girl with the snotty nose was alive out there somewhere. I hoped she was, but the odds weren't good. Other than those couple of kids living in murderous Mack's compound, Luna was the only child anyone seemed to have seen in weeks.

That was the thing about the end of the world. Only the strong, and maybe a bit evil, survived. Humanity's most important resource stood little chance.

Deeper in the store, something kicked a can, sending it rolling out into the main aisle with a clatter.

"Stay alert." Mark walked in the lead. Charlie was next, with Shawn and me fanning out behind them. The guy whose name I hadn't caught yet was last, keeping an eye on our backs.

A half a dozen aisles away, a badly decomposed zombie shuffled into view. The long, stringy hair was the only feature left that hinted what gender it had been. The creature shuffled toward the can that had rolled, oblivious to us watching it just feet away. While the fresher zombies were frighteningly fast and smarter than was comforting, these older ones were both slow and stupid. Thankfully, there seemed to be more of the latter than the former.

Sticking together, our group moved toward the zombie. Mark pulled a knife just as the creature finally noticed us. Swinging stiffly around, it let a low growl and lurched our way. Using one hand, Mark was able to easily hold it back while he stabbed it in the head. The zombie slumped to the floor with a disgustingly wet sound.

Grimacing, Mark tried to shake the zombie body fluids off his hand. He ended up wiping it the best he could on the equally dirty floor, which didn't help much.

The store turned out to be just as small on the inside as the outside had made it look. Working together, we swept up and down all the aisles, checked in the bathrooms, and wandered around the warehouse. In the back, dragging itself along, we found the only other zombie still in the store. Whoever the guy had been, both of his legs were gone below the knees, nothing but ragged looking stumps were left. Shawn's tire iron made short work of the pitiful thing.

The warehouse turned out to be the perfect place to start taking food. Most everything back there was already in boxes. It was an easy task to read the labels and choose nonperishables. With so many helping hands, the trucks filled up quickly. There were still entire skids of unopened boxes, plus the shelves out in the store that hadn't been completely empty. It was going to take more than one trip to empty the store of supplies.

261

We were walking back through the store, arms loaded down with boxes of canned peaches and pasta when a short blast from one of the trucks outside roared.

Picking up speed, we jogged back out into the parking lot, fully expecting to see distant zombies. A few had been showing up in low numbers while we went back and forth carrying boxes, and the two who had been left outside had taken care of them.

Maybe a couple of dozen bodies were now slumped around on the pavement, but we had all been operating with the understanding that, sooner or later, too many to safely face would show up, and we would need to make a hasty retreat.

So when we emerged from the gloomy store and stepped into the sun, I was surprised when I didn't see any threatening zombies. Instead, a third pickup had appeared and was parked maybe a dozen yards from our own vehicles. Two men sat tensely inside the cab. Two more heavily armed men stood in the bed, eyeing our group with expressions that set off all sorts of warning bells.

Charlie and Mark both dropped their boxes right on the spot and took defensive-looking holds on their guns. Standing behind either of our trucks, both Sara and Ed also had their guns in hand. The situation was turning into a tense-looking standoff, and no one had even said a word yet. I shuffled sideways, putting a vehicle in between myself and the strangers, and wished that I had already learned how to handle a gun.

Finally, Mark spoke up, "Can I help you gentlemen with something?"

It took several seconds, but the one driving their truck seemed to make a decision. Slowly, he opened his door and got out. "Looks like we weren't the only ones who wanted to check the store."

Something about the man set me on edge. It was more than his aggressive body language and the guns pointed our way, but I couldn't put my finger on it.

262

"Yeah, there's still a good amount of food inside. Plenty to share. We were just getting ready to move out." Mark made a gesture that I interpreted that we should get the last of the boxes in the truck. He seemed to be going cautiously friendly but wanted to get out of there in a hurry.

"That so?" The man looked to his own group meaningfully before turning to look back at us. His focus shifted away from Mark as he evaluated the rest of our group.

We outnumbered them, something that I was fervently thankful for. These strangers were barely concealing their hostility. As I slid my box into the back of our truck, I was hoping that fact would keep them from trying anything.

Watching him suspiciously, I saw as he dismissed our group one after another as unimportant. He nearly scoffed at both Sara and Charlie, his eyes flicking to their weapons like he found it humorous that they were aiming guns his way. He looked over Ed a second longer before dismissing me with barely a second glance.

But then his eyes lit up as his gaze landed on Shawn. It was the moment I saw recognition in their flat depths that I knew why I was so aware of this person as dangerous.

It was the man that Rex had bitten as we escaped from Mack's stronghold.

I must have made some sort of sound of distress because I felt Shawn step closer behind me. The action brought the guy's focus back to me, and I saw that this time he recognized me too.

A flush started to work its way up to his dirty neck.

A calculating look crossed his face. "Well, if there's that much still inside, I don't see any harm in sharing. If you all are finished, we'll head on in and take what we need."

I could see that Mark knew that something had just happened, but he didn't know what. One minute, the strangers had been clearly deciding if they should take our food, the next they were playing nice. Either way, he wasn't about to waste the chance to leave.

"Sounds like a plan. You fellas have a safe trip home." He looked around at us. "Get in the trucks."

My arms were shaking so hard that I almost fell climbing into the back of the truck. Shawn caught me and practically lifted me into the back. I could tell that he was unclear about what had suddenly set me off, but we trusted each other enough to know that if one of us was upset, there was a reason.

Swinging around, I kept the others in view, not about to turn my back on them. Charlie and Shawn were both crowded into the back of the loaded truck bed next to me. Slamming doors and starting engines were cold comforts because the man was watching us intently.

His earlier dismissal of me was long gone. With glinting eyes, he watched us as we started to pull away. Before we got too far away for me to have missed the expression, he sent a feral smile directly at me.

CHAPTER FIFTY-SIX
Day Twenty-Eight

My eyes burned with exhaustion. I barely managed to sleep for three days. Between worrying about the group of insane people finding us and watching a friend slowly succumb to his illness, I was mentally tapped out.

"Hey."

"Hey." I glanced over my shoulder to where Shawn was walking toward me through the darkened building. He walked up to stand right behind me and looked me over. When a hint of a frown twitched at the corners of his mouth, I knew he wasn't thrilled with what he saw.

"You haven't gotten any sleep yet, have you?"

"Not really." I turned back to look out the sliver of cleared glass. I spent way too much time over the past few days peeling back tiny sections of the newspaper that had been used to cover the windows so I could see outside. "With everything that's going on, I just can't."

"Yeah." He moved closer and wrapped both arms around me. I settled back into the embrace but kept watching outside. "But it's not going to do anybody any good if you run yourself into the ground."

I sighed. "Something bad is coming. I feel it."

He didn't respond, so I kept going.

"Those people are dangerous. I don't know how we managed to run into them twice, but we barely got away the first time. What if they're still out there?"

"What if they're not?" I stiffened at the question, so he hurried to go on. "It's been days. If they were going to try anything, I'd think they would have by now. Maybe all they really wanted was the food in that store. Besides, Maggie took your warning seriously. The extra lookout is still up on the roof."

I sighed again and covered the window back up. The only thing moving out there was a trio of slow zombies. If they came too close, someone on watch would take care of them. I turned in Shawn's arms and wrapped my own around his waist.

He propped his chin on top of my head. "Are you sure that all this isn't because of what's happening to Devon?"

I winced at the reminder.

We had all spent a lot of time with Devon these last few days. Someone was always with him, but he had fallen unconscious in the middle of last night. I hadn't been able to bring myself to stay with him after that. Alex had quietly told us that he probably wouldn't wake up again.

"I'm on my way to go sit with everyone. You should come too. It would mean a lot to them."

He was right. I knew it. I had simply been stalling as I stared out the window. Devon was going to die, probably today, and we should all be there to support each other.

I didn't know if I could watch someone die though. We had all done so many things that none of us would have thought ourselves capable of. We lost so much of ourselves somewhere along the way, but the one thing I hadn't had to endure yet was actually watching a friend die. At least, not since I knew what was going on.

Deep down, I feared that that would be the one thing that would change me into someone I no longer recognized.

We had lost friends along the way, and I, of course, knew that it would happen again and again, but actually seeing it, comprehending what was really at stake, would somehow make it too real.

Death was inevitable in our new world, but I knew that the death of one person, in particular, had the potential to break me. And that was what ultimately scared the heck out of me.

"Okay." My voice came out as a whisper.

"Okay." Taking one of my hands in his, he led the way through the maze. While we were on the move, Rex came out of the shadows to follow us. The dog had been spending a lot of time following Luna around, and the two of them were becoming fast friends. Maggie didn't seem to mind him roaming freely, and he had stopped growling suspiciously at all the new people, so I was happy to let him go play. Right now, the little girl was better company than me anyhow.

I mentally steadied myself as we approached Devon's room. I needed it.

Someone had thought to move several folding chairs into the space. Already cramped, it was downright claustrophobic now.

I was a little surprised to find Maggie sitting in one of the chairs. Shawn and I took the two empty ones. Bill had been given the all clear to get out of bed, and he was sitting in the other chair. He had jokingly said that he never wanted to lie down again. Maya and Fallon sat next to each other on one of the cots.

Finally, I couldn't put it off any longer. I looked at Devon. His breathing was rapid and shallow, but that wasn't new. He had been having difficulty breathing for at least a full day. More shocking was the swelling. The infection had spread throughout his system. Under the light blanket he was covered with, I could make out just how distorted his leg had become.

His face and neck, which were the only parts of him uncovered, were swollen and discolored. Broken blood vessels were visible across his cheeks. His eyes were closed, but an almost

267

distasteful-looking expression was on his face, as if he was uncomfortable.

The smell of sickness shrouded the room, despite having great air flow. I shifted uncomfortably in my seat and looked away. Next to me, Shawn reached out. I took his hand gratefully.

My eyes traveled to Maggie. "Hi." I kept my voice soft. It seemed wrong not to.

"Hey, Bri. Hanging in there?" Her eyes were warm with genuine concern. I knew that she knew about my obsessive new hobby of peeling back the newspaper.

"Not much of a choice really. So, yeah."

"This will never get any easier, and that's a good thing. As long as death isn't easy, we keep that bit of our humanity." She smiled softly and stood up. "I need to go check on a few things. I'll be back around after a while."

After Maggie left, strained silence returned to our group. Fallon looked even worse than I felt. Her skin was blotchy from crying, and she was now staring vacantly into the distance. She hadn't spoken since Devon fell unconscious.

I was glad when Alex shuffled into the room despite my lingering mistrust of him. His comings and goings gave me something to focus on.

Squeezing his way to Devon's bedside, Alex went through his usual routine of checks. Pulling a syringe from his pocket, he gave a dose to Devon.

"Morphine," he explained, looking at Maya. "We don't have a lot of the stuff, but I'll do what I can to keep him comfortable."

After that, there wasn't much left for the nurse to try. We were long past the point of no return. Smoothing the blanket back down, he quietly left the room.

Others came and went for the next few hours. Most didn't stay, just offered their condolences, but I found that I appreciated the gesture. Maggie's group had embraced us as one of their own, and it was starting to feel like we belonged here, instead of feeling like guests.

If my growling stomach was anything to go by, it was around lunchtime when we first noticed the change. Devon started to wheeze. When the sound didn't go away, Maya jumped up to go find Alex. Fallon finally broke from her trance and moved closer to his cot. I was still hanging on to Shawn's hand, and I squeezed it tighter, my own breathing ratcheting up.

Alex came quickly, but after another look at Devon, he straightened up with a grim look on his face. I realized then that I wasn't the only one blaming themselves for not being able to save Devon. The nurse was too. He sat in the empty chair and joined our vigil.

Devon deteriorated rapidly after that. Within minutes, he choked out one last stuttering breath and fell completely still. Kneeling on the floor next to him, I saw tears begin to slide down Fallon's cheeks.

Bill moved to sit next to his wife, and he rubbed her back reassuringly as the two of them soberly watched on. Beside me, Alex let his head fall toward his chest for just a second before he straightened up with a sigh and went to the cot.

I realized that I was squeezing all the blood out of Shawn's fingers and forced myself to relax my grip. He gave my hand a light squeeze back as we watched the nurse.

"I'm sorry. He's gone." Alex tucked the wrist he had been checking for a pulse back under the blanket. He looked around at all of us and spoke before leaving the room. "He was a fighter. He held on for a long time. I, uh, I just thought you all should know that."

CHAPTER FIFTY-SEVEN
Day Twenty-Eight

Shawn went outside with a couple of other men to dig a grave. Maggie told us that they had started a graveyard on a grassy hill just behind the mall. They had been lucky so far—only a half a dozen people had been buried on that hill.

I had been clutching his hand nonstop, and not having that anchor to keep me grounded had left me feeling oddly bereft.

Looking for a way to keep busy, I wandered toward the community area. If I had to watch those silent tears track down Fallon's face for another second, I was going to end up screaming my frustration for the world to hear.

Luna was playing with a doll in the corner. Rex jogged away from me to go sit next to the girl, his big ears perked up in interest as he watched her talk with the doll.

A pair of fire rings—the kind that stood on short metal legs and was topped with grates for cooking—was where the group heated food. Sara and a woman I hadn't met yet were watching strips of some sort of meat sizzle over top of the coals.

I wandered their way. "Mind if I join you?"

Sara looked up at me. "Sure. Bri, this is Sasha." The tone of her voice changed. "I'm sorry. We heard about Devon."

That lump was back in my throat. I swallowed hard. "Yeah, thanks."

The three of us looked at each other uncomfortably for a second before Sara cleared her throat. "Um, so Charlie came back with a deer earlier. She said it ran right by her while she was up in the stand. It's strange. We don't usually see deer here, but I'll take it."

I knew what she meant. For the last month, any meat that we ate was of the canned variety. Along with the meat, fresh fruits, and veggies were long ago spoiled. It was a detail that I knew weighed on everyone's mind. What would we do when the cans ran out?

The simple answer was to farm, but I certainly didn't know the first thing about growing my own food. I once tried to grow basil in my windowsill. The instructions on the box said for ages six and up, so I thought for sure I could handle it. I was wrong.

Shaking off those depressing thoughts, I pulled a camp chair over and sat with the two other women. No one said much as they kept an eye on the cooking meat. Seeing that a bunch of it looked almost ready to take off, I got up and went in search of a plate to pile it on. After handing the platter over, I sat back down.

The pile of cooked meat grew. When Rex came to investigate, Sara told me to go ahead and give him some. The dog took the strip of venison carefully, impressing me with his self-control. I knew he was still too hungry. We all were more days than not. Despite my best efforts to put weight back on him, there just wasn't enough food a dog could eat most of the time.

"Bri?"

I turned around when I heard Maggie's voice.

"They're almost finished digging. We're going to take Devon outside now. It's better if we don't wait."

I nodded my understanding and stood, handing the giant plate of meat to Sara before following Maggie.

I wasn't ready to see the body again, and I exhaled with relief when I turned into the room. Someone had wrapped Devon

271

in a sheet, sparing me that at least. Bill, Maya, and Alex were all standing quietly there. Fallon was missing.

Maya noticed me looking around and correctly guessed who I was looking for. "She said she needed some air, and she'll meet us on the hill. I think she wants to be left alone for now."

That wasn't surprising really. Of all of us, Fallon had been closest with Devon.

Alex flat out forbade Bill to help us, so he joined Maya, Maggie, and me when we carefully picked the body up. As we walked through the building, heading toward the back, we gathered a small group who trailed along behind us. By the time Bill held open the door leading outside, nearly a dozen others were with us.

The sun was high in the sky, and I squinted at the brightness after days spent inside the dark stores. When my eyes finally adjusted, I saw the gradual incline of the grassy hill just ahead. Near the top, the group of gravediggers had a mound of freshly dug earth piled waist high.

The physical burden of carrying Devon was nothing compared to the emotional one. Every step was harder than the last. By the time we passed his body over to Shawn and Mark, who were standing in the grave, I was glad to let someone else take over the burden.

They carefully laid him at the bottom of the grave and climbed back out to stand with the rest of us. Shawn was muddy, the sweat and dirt mixing on his skin, but I didn't care. When he moved to stand next to me, I grabbed his hand again. He must have needed the contact, too, because he held on tighter than usual.

Fallon swished through the tall grass as she joined us. She had stopped crying, but she avoided looking at anyone as she paused near the hole. I watched as she looked down at the shrouded body for a few seconds before dropping a wildflower onto the body. Looking around, she met my gaze for a second before slowly walking away back down the hill.

After Fallon left, there wasn't a reason to delay any longer. Maggie and Mark each picked up a shovel and began to slowly fill the hole back in. They were halfway done when the walkie talkie that Maggie always had nearby crackled to life.

I recognized the scratchy voice as Colton's. "Maggie?" Even through the tiny device, I could hear that he sounded like something was wrong.

She immediately grabbed the radio. "Yeah, Colton. What is it?"

"I don't know what I'm looking at exactly. I'm up in the stand, and I started to hear a strange noise. It's coming from the highway."

"Colton, what's going on?" When he hesitated, Maggie prompted him.

"This is going to sound crazy, but there's a pickup driving along real slow. And there are a lot of zombies behind it. Maggie, it's a whole lot of zombies."

Maggie took a second before she responded. I could see her thinking, trying to figure out what was going on. "Does it seem like it's people who need help?"

"No, I don't think so. They speed up if the zombies get too close, but slow back down when they are clear. It's like they are leading them."

My heart started to pound. Somehow, I just knew that it was finally happening. The disaster that I had felt was coming, was here.

"Maggie," I choked out her name. "Maggie, it's them."

She frowned at me before pressing the button to talk again. "Colton, stay in the stand and keep an eye on them, but stay hidden. Don't let them know you are up there. Keep me informed."

"Okay."

She turned to look at us with wide eyes. "I think it's time we all go inside."

CHAPTER FIFTY-EIGHT
Day Twenty-Eight

The waiting was the worst.

Anyone who wasn't currently on duty outside was gathered in the central space in the main store. With a few dozen people there, it was crowded. Low murmurs could be heard here and there, but everyone mostly kept quiet. No one wanted to miss the radio updates that Colton was sending every few minutes.

The strip of venison that I was attempting to get down my throat felt like it was going to choke me. I wasn't the only one. Sara had passed out the meat to everyone, but more than a few of them looked too sick to eat.

Sitting in the corner, leaning up against the wall, Shawn and I watched the people around us. They all looked worried, and they had a good reason to be. Colton's last update had given us the news that we were dreading.

The pickup had started to slowly roll down the exit, leading the horde of zombies our way. He estimated that there was at least a hundred of the undead stumbling along behind the truck.

I was worried about Colton. He had stayed to be our eyes, but now that the danger was coming down the ramp, he was trapped. At least he was up high enough that he would be beyond the reach of even the tallest zombie, which was the whole point of that tree stand. None of the lookouts were on the ground.

I caught the occasional glimpse of familiar faces in the crowd. Here, Bill and Maya were talking with another couple. There, Mark and Charlie were standing with Maggie, listening for the next update. Over by the fire pits, Luna was sneaking a piece of meat to Rex. All around us, the people were waiting tensely to find out just how bad things were going to get.

The horde of zombies was shuffling along at their slow speed. Colton had reported that there were a few runners in the group. They banged and screamed at the sides of the truck, but the two men in the cab just ignored them. But even at a zombie shuffle, they had covered ground in the hour since we came inside. If they were down the off-ramp now, they would be able to be at our door in less than half an hour.

I was starting to wonder if we should have ran instead of trying to stay here. I wasn't the first to think that way, but Maggie had convinced the crowd that it was safer to stay. If we stayed quiet, the zombies would move on. The men in the truck would have to keep going themselves or risk becoming trapped by the horde. The potential for something like this was exactly the reason they had covered the windows. If we didn't give them a reason to stick around, the zombies should keep following that truck.

From our position on the floor, we watched the group mill around nervously. Most of the lanterns had been turned down until they barely cast any light at all. The shadows blanketed our corner, giving me the illusion of some much-needed privacy. It felt like everyone in the group was looking our way more often than usual. The feeling was probably just my frazzled nerves and lack of sleep talking, but it was making me jumpy either way.

Time passed by tediously slowly. I wished for a way to tell time because I was sure that my inner clock was off. It seemed like it was too long since we last heard an update from Colton.

Then again, maybe I wasn't crazy because Charlie spoke up, "Maggie, how long has it been since we heard from Colton?"

I honed in on the conversation.

Maggie frowned at the radio in her hand. "It's been too long." She looked around herself a little helplessly.

I wanted to be sure I didn't miss anything they were saying. Glancing at Shawn, I climbed to my feet and wove through the crowd toward them. "What can we do?"

"I don't know. We need to stay quiet in here. And I don't want to radio Colton first, just in case."

It was my turn to frown. I didn't like that thought. If Colton wasn't able to talk without giving himself away, that meant the danger was too close to him for comfort.

Others around us picked up on the new tension from their leader. The quiet talk died down as more and more people crowded around, trying to hear what was going on. For her part, Maggie looked torn, like she wasn't sure what she should do.

When the radio crackled to life, I think just about every person in the room held their breath.

"Hello, in the store. I'd like to speak to the person in charge."

My blood ran cold at the voice. As long as I lived, I doubted I'd ever be able to forget that voice.

Warily, Maggie raised her radio and pushed the button. "How did you get this radio?"

A chuckle came through the static. "Sweetheart, I think you can probably guess."

"Where's Colton?" Maggie sounded furious.

"Is that his name? I didn't ask, and now he's not talking."

Chatter started up around me as everyone started talking at once. My stomach dropped at the thought of something bad happening to Colton.

Keeping it together, somehow, Maggie asked, "Who are you? What do you want?"

"Right to business then. I like it." His voice sounded mocking. "A couple of my men told me that you have some people in there that I've been looking for. Here's how this is going to work. You send them out to my guys in the lead truck, and they will keep on going and lead the zombies right on by your place. They don't come out, and things are going to get real messy real fast."

Maggie looked over at Shawn and me. "How do I know who you want? I can't send my people outside. It's too dangerous."

"You have a lot of murderers in there? Because I'm looking for the POS who killed my brother and his friends. One of them owes me an arm. You have two minutes. After that, we go to plan B."

Wide-eyed, I stared at Shawn. I wondered about the damage we had caused that night. If Mack was to be believed, Shawn had killed his brother after he yanked him off me. He stared back at me, clearly anxious, worried how the knowledge would affect me.

In that second, I realized that I didn't care. The old me would have been horrified. The new me was just glad that the other guy was the one who ended up dead. I wasn't innocent either. I hacked a guy with a machete. I reached for his hand to show him that we were okay.

I turned back to Maggie. She already knew most of the story of our encounter with Mack. I told her everything, trying to make her understand how bad those people were. "You are not going anywhere." She raised her voice to be heard by the people at the back of the group. "We will not negotiate with people who would terrorize us. We will not send some of our own to their deaths. That's not who we are."

I exhaled. A small part of me had worried that Maggie would send us outside to save the rest of her people.

Distracted as we had been, it wasn't until then that I noticed the sounds coming from outside.

A zombie screamed. Another one answered, and a chorus of groans and growls was audible.

The radio crackled. "Thirty seconds."

"What do you think they are going to do?"

277

"We should run out the back!"

"Maggie, what do we do now?"

Everyone started panicking. No one knew what was coming exactly, but we knew that it was going to be bad.

CHAPTER FIFTY-NINE
Day Twenty-Eight

Tires squealed as a vehicle came to a hard stop right out front. There was a second of silence, then the pair of guys standing watch from the roof started to fire. Maggie had instructed everyone not to make any noise unless they had no other choice, so I immediately knew that whatever was going on out front was very bad.

The rifles rang out a few more times and then the world exploded around us.

Automatic gunfire shattered the large windows on the front of the store. People started screaming as they ran for cover from the few bullets that made it that far into the store. Some of them didn't move fast enough. Sasha, the woman I just spent the afternoon with cooking, fell to the ground at my feet. My arm was nearly yanked from its socket as Shawn dragged me behind a heavy shelf.

The hail of bullets stopped, but barely a second later, a small explosion rocked the front of the store. Thick smoke immediately started to cloud the air, and I could see the orange flicker of flames.

"We have to get out of here!" Tires squealed again as the truck sped away.

"Stay close!" Keeping his head down, Shawn started to lead the way through the chaos.

It was already dark in the store, but the rapidly growing smoke made it worse. Someone slammed into me in their panic, sending me careening into a shelf. By the time I got back to my feet, I lost sight of Shawn.

He could have been nearby, but it was impossible to tell. Bodies ran in and out of my sight, obscured by smoke. Coughing, I pulled my shirt up to cover my mouth and nose. It didn't really help.

A zombie shrieked from somewhere inside the store.

Breathing was getting harder, and my eyes started to water. I had to find my friends, and we had to get out of the store. Making it into the maze of the sleeping area, I tried to avoid being run over again. People dashed blindly from their rooms with hastily gathered belongings. They gave me an idea. Maya and Bill had a habit of always keeping bags packed and ready to go, just in case. They would probably try to get to their things before they left the building.

Someone started screaming, a terrified sound that caused the hair on the back of my neck to rise. It sounded like a little girl.

Abandoning my first course of action, I tried to find the source of the screams. If it was Luna who was in trouble, I couldn't just leave her alone.

Turning a corner, movement ahead swirled in the smoke. I was very glad that I had my machete in hand when I drew close enough to see what it was.

Crouched in a corner, Luna held her hands over her head as she shrieked again. Standing in front of her with teeth bared, Rex snarled warningly at a zombie. The zombie hissed back at him as it weaved back and forth, looking for an opening to attack.

My heart plummeted. This zombie was very fresh.

I had become adept at killing the older ones, but I had not faced one that could still think by myself before; however, the time for doubts was over. A harsh cough tore its way up my burning throat, alerting the zombie to my presence. The creature spun around and bared its teeth at me. Calculation flickered in its dead eyes as the zombie decided to set its sights on easier prey.

It lunged my way. Hacking with the machete, partially blinded by my tearing eyes, I managed to hit the zombie's arm before it could get a hold of me. The deadly machete severed the limb almost completely, leaving its hand dangling by a strip of flesh. The zombie hissed and reeled back.

I'd become familiar with the damage that Rex could inflict upon flesh with his own sharp teeth. Now that the zombie was closer, I could see that its remaining arm had come out the loser already in a fight with the dog. With one arm now useless and the other shredded, the zombie changed its tactic.

It shrieked as it began trying to circle behind me. An answering shriek came from somewhere in the smoke-filled store. I had to kill the creature and get Luna out of there before another fast zombie found us. I knew that there was zero chance of me fighting off multiple of them without someone getting bit or worse.

As the zombie circled, it moved away from its original target. I took the opportunity to move closer to the little girl. Keeping my eyes locked on the zombie, ready for its next move, I tried to talk to her. "Luna. Luna, it's Bri. I'm going to get you out of here."

The zombie reacted to my words, and with a snarl, it flung itself at me a second time. Aiming to kill, I swung the machete with all my strength. The tip of the machete caught the zombie in the face. The smoke had made me miscalculate, swinging too soon, but luck was on my side anyhow. The machete sliced through the zombie's brow before lodging into its eye.

There was no time to stop and think. The world was on fire around us. Fire crawled across the ceiling, the heat stinging my bare skin. The moans of the zombies and the shouts of horror from the survivors were dying down. By now, most of the people had fled this part of the store.

Coughing harshly again, I reached for the little girl still hiding in the corner. "Luna! We have to go now!" Grabbing her by the arm, I hauled her along behind me as I bolted for the back of the store. Seeming to snap out of her stupor, she began running along behind me.

I couldn't see. The smoke was too thick. The light appeared in the darkness, approaching from my right. I almost didn't have time to register the flaming zombie as it stumbled toward us.

Running on pure adrenaline, I shouldered the zombie, dashing past it, still dragging Luna behind me.

Part of the ceiling crashed down somewhere behind us. Looking around desperately, I tried to figure out where the door that led into that long back hallway was.

"That way," she squeaked out between coughs. Luna pointed into the darkness. I tripped over Rex. I couldn't even see my own feet anymore but took off in the direction she had pointed.

The back wall loomed suddenly through the smoke. Just to our left, I thought I saw the blurry outline of the door. Dashing toward it, I couldn't stop the shriek that left me when the door suddenly flew open.

A large figure loomed in the doorway for a second. My already hammering heart beat harder with the terrible possibilities of who, or what, it could be before a voice soothed those fears.

"Bri! Jesus, I've been looking all over for you. Come on!" Shawn said.

The flood of relief made me want to sob, but I clamped down hard on the emotions. Moving again, I swept into the hall with the others close on my heels.

The darkness back here was complete, but the air felt just a little easier to breathe. I jumped when a large hand found my arm in the dark and started pulling me rapidly down the hall. Within seconds, the crackle and roar of the flames died down, and I started to hear voices and shuffling feet just ahead.

"It's okay. It's a bunch of people from the group." Shawn must have felt me tense up. "They're waiting to try to gather as many people as possible before leaving the building. We're gonna try to stay together."

"Bill and Maya? Fallon?" I croaked out.

"Bill and Maya are there. Maggie, too, I think. I haven't heard anything from Fallon."

I sensed rather than saw when we were nearing the group.

"It's me. I found Bri," Shawn said out loud.

I realized that not only could I not see any of them, but they couldn't see any of us either.

"I have Luna. She's okay," I croaked. The little girl's small hand was still clutched in my own death grip.

A relieved murmur rose in the dark.

"Thank you." Maggie was to my right, and she sounded relieved to hear that the girl had been found. "I don't think that we can wait any longer. The smoke is getting thick in here."

Compared to back in the main store, the air back here was bliss, but I kept that to myself.

"We need to stay together. Watch out for each other, there will probably be some zombies out back. Does everyone have some kind of weapon?"

A chorus of affirmative answers revealed how many people were standing there in the dark. It sounded like at least a dozen. I picked up Maya's voice in the crowd.

"Okay, be fast and quiet. We will get through this. Let's move."

The distinct sound of the bar on the door being pressed was accompanied by a flood of bright light. Shielding my eyes, I looked ahead to see a familiar outline pushing the door open. Still blinking rapidly, I thought for a second that my eyes were playing tricks on me when the back of his head exploded all over those crowded behind him.

283

CHAPTER SIXTY
Day Twenty-Eight

"No!"

I watched in horror as Mark crumpled to the ground. More screams echoed down the hallway as the people nearest to his body backpedaled frantically. I was shoved and only maintained my grip on both of the hands I held by sheer force of will. I wasn't about to lose Shawn again. Becoming aware of something wet on my forehead, I tried to wipe it off on the shoulder of my shirt without the benefit of hands.

The door slammed shut, leaving us trapped in the dark once again. Maggie's voice tried to rise above the chaos, trying to bring the group back under control. I heard her voice shake for the first time since I met her.

"Are you okay?" Shawn pulled me closer to talk directly in my ear.

"Yeah. Luna, you doing okay?" I wished I could actually see them.

"I'm okay. What's going on?"

Thank goodness for small favors. I was glad that the girl hadn't gotten a good view of what had just happened.

"It's going to be okay. We'll figure something out." I turned back to Shawn. "How about you?"

"I'm fine."

"People, please calm down!" Maggie was still trying to get the crowd under control.

"There has to be another way out. One where we don't get shot as soon as we open the door!" The voice sounded like Sara's.

A couple of voices agreed with her.

"I'm going back. We'll find a way out one of the other stores. They can't be watching every door," Sara yelled.

Someone bumped into me as they felt their way along the wall. Another body brushed mine as they followed.

"Please! We need to stay together!" Maggie sounded desperate, but it didn't do any good. Another body brushed by.

"Shawn? Bri?" Bill's voice was close to my ear.

"Yeah, Bill? We're here."

"Okay, just checking."

The shouting died down as the group split. As far as I could tell, more than half of the group was still standing at the end of the hall.

"Maggie, what should we do now?" That was Charlie. I was relieved to hear from the woman.

"Um, Charlie. Let me think a second."

The smoke in the hallway was building. It was only a matter of time before the fire consumed the entire mall. We couldn't stay here.

A bang at the far end of the hallway made me jump. Everyone froze, listening for a clue as to what had caused the noise.

A faint orange glow flickered way down there. The fire.

Movement, highlighted by that glow, made my blood run cold. Someone was down there. Someone who moved in startling fits and starts.

An inhuman howl echoed through the corridor.

"Zombie," I whispered, like any of the others could have missed the new arrival.

It was hard to see, but I thought that the zombie hesitated for one long second before starting down the hall. Midway between us, something clattered to the floor.

Everything happened fast after that. Someone from the group that had split off cursed and the zombie screamed. Footsteps began pounding the hard floor as the people who had left us started to run.

"We have to go now!" Maggie yelled. I looked back up the hall, but other than that flickering glow clear at the other end, it was an endless pit of darkness, then I saw another zombie amble through the door.

Tightening my grip, I started pushing toward where I knew the way out was. "We don't have a choice."

Too close for comfort now, there was the sound of a scuffle, and someone cried out. Ignoring the call for help, I pushed toward the door.

"Stay together!" Maggie practically shouted in my ear and then she pushed the door open again.

The light appeared just in time to keep me from stepping on Mark's body. I was numb. The day had been too much, and I merely stepped over him and into the light. Ahead of me, Maggie was the first one out. She ducked and started running. A bullet whizzed by her and hit the next person in the door. He staggered but stayed on his feet.

Shawn let go of my hand, and I started to protest but stopped when he reached to pick up Luna. Looking at me with wide eyes, he bolted out the door.

I was the next one out. It was a surreal feeling—being sure that you were running straight into the arms of your own death. I was shocked when I realized that I was still alive despite the bullets that were raining down all around.

Already tortured by the smoke and heat, my throat screamed as I panted. My breath was racing in and out. I focused on Shawn's back and just kept running.

Zombies were milling around everywhere. Those that hadn't been drawn into the store by the fire were now roaming the area. I raced past the guy who had been hit by the bullet meant for

286

Maggie, two decomposing zombies digging their rotting hands into his flesh.

Running next to me, Rex snarled at anything that looked like it was going to get in my way.

Focused solely on not losing sight of Shawn, I didn't take note of where we were going. My only thought was to keep him in sight. When my upper arm started to sting, I ignored it.

Rounding the far corner of the mall finally put an end to the bullets. There were fewer zombies on this side too. Ahead of me, Maggie was swinging a hatchet at a zombie that tried to go for her. Shawn still carried Luna, and I sent a quick thanks to whoever may be listening that neither of them appeared to have been hit.

A throb from my own arm reminded me that I had not escaped completely unharmed. The arm still seemed to work okay, and I was glad for that. Blood dripped steadily off my fingers, but it could have been worse.

Gasping breath behind me made me look back, and I almost smiled. I was so happy with what I saw. Bill looked like he was in a lot of pain, but he and Maya rounded the corner and looked okay. On their heels came Charlie, a guy whose name I had never learned on our ill-fated grocery run, and a limping Alex.

I kept glancing back, expecting more people to round the corner, but they never came. I gave up watching for them when my inattention almost made me run straight into a zombie. Slashing at it with the machete, I dodged and put on an extra burst of speed to catch up with Shawn.

We must have ran for more than a mile before Maggie swerved toward a house.

"In here," she panted as she threw open the front door.

Diving inside, I looked around a little wildly. Running headlong into a building wasn't a very smart idea anymore.

Seeing the look on my face, Maggie whispered as she pulled the door shut behind the stragglers. "We cleared this one already. It's our rendezvous."

I sagged against the wall. A few feet away, Shawn set a very shaken-looking Luna on her feet. To her credit, the little girl hadn't made a sound. But then, maybe I shouldn't be surprised. She managed to survive on her own for a while before the group found her in her school.

"How bad is it?"

The question pulled me from my contemplation of the girl. I almost forgot the fact that I had been shot. Apparently, I was still more numb than anything. I looked at my arm.

"I don't think it's too bad." I wiggled my fingers as blood dripped onto the floor.

"Let me see." Alex pushed in between Shawn and me, earning himself a dirty look. The nurse ignored him and reached for my arm.

He poked around at the wound, making it start throbbing to the beat of my heart. "You're right. It's not bad, but we should clean it up and cover it." Alex walked away down the hall. "Maggie, you guys left a medical kit here, right?"

"Yeah." She was busy looking out the window, back the way we had come.

Most of us moved into the living room. Maggie and Charlie paced from window to window, keeping an eye out for anyone else who may have made it out alive. Shawn sat next to me on the couch as Alex treated my arm. Next, he wanted to look at Bill, much to the big man's displeasure. Bill was in luck. He had endured the physical activities without tearing his wounds open again.

I was concerned about Alex's limp, but he assured me he hadn't been bitten or shot. He quietly murmured that he tripped on Mark's body and twisted an ankle, all the while watching to be sure Luna wasn't listening.

The afternoon wound into the evening, and there was no sign of Mack or his crazy group, but there also was no sign of any of our people. I worried about Fallon. I hadn't known about the

288

rendezvous, so I doubted she did either. I wasn't sure how we were going to find her again.

Maggie became more subdued as darkness descended. I knew she had been expecting more of her people to show up, but as the hours passed, that seemed less and less likely. Finally giving up her watch to let Shawn take a turn, Maggie sank into the couch with a defeated sigh.

CHAPTER SIXTY-ONE
Day Twenty-Nine

Rex raised his head from where he had been resting it on his paws and growled lightly. That wasn't all that unusual. Whenever a zombie wandered too close to our hideout, he did the same. It had been going on all night.

Dawn was just starting to lighten the night sky. Dante—I finally figured out the unnamed guy's name—and I were taking a turn keeping watch. I looked out the nearest window, checking for the zombie. There had been plenty of them that went by in the night, but we stayed quiet, and they kept on going. Unscrewing the top of the water bottle I had taken from the stash of supplies, I raised it for a sip.

Over the top of the bottle, movement from outside caught my eye.

Suddenly alert, I craned my neck to get a better look. The figure ducked behind an abandoned van on the curb. It was definitely not a zombie.

"Hey," I hissed lowly. No one was really sleeping, only trying to rest, and I heard shuffling in the next room as someone got to their feet.

A second later, Maggie and Shawn both appeared at my side. A questioning look from Maggie had me jerking my chin toward the window.

"There's someone out there. They just went behind that van."

I stepped aside to make room for her to look out.

"I don't see— Wait." She looked intently out the window for several seconds before bolting for the door.

Glancing at Shawn, I saw he looked as confused as I felt. I followed her through the dark house. I stepped into the hallway just in time to see Maggie swinging open the front door.

My mouth fell open. Standing in the predawn light was Colton. He swayed on his feet a little before coming inside and shutting the door. Snapping my mouth closed, I joined the rapidly growing group at the other end of the hall.

"Colton!"

"You're alive!"

"What happened to you?"

Everyone talking at once was too loud, and Maggie shushed the group.

"You need to sit down." Alex took control of the situation, steering Colton toward a chair.

It was still too dark to see detail, but it was clear that Colton was injured. Blood flowed freely from a cut to the side of his head, soaking his shirt. The whole mess was dry now, so at least the bleeding had stopped. As he sat down in the offered chair, he winced and listed sideways.

"Other than your head, does anything hurt?" Alex was already pulling on a pair of latex gloves.

"No. It's just my head. That orange-haired asshole hit me with a bat." He looked miserable, but to his credit, Colton stayed upright.

Alex had to tell everyone to back up. We had all unconsciously crowded closer, shocked and relieved to see someone we thought was probably dead.

Watching from behind Charlie's back, I cringed as Alex began cleaning the dried blood from the side of his head.

The wound was ugly, swollen, and bruised with a long gash. There was no way Colton had escaped a hit to the head like that without a concussion. It was probably some sort of miracle that he survived at all.

Alex must have agreed with me. I noticed that he kept asking Colton seemingly random questions. To my relief, as far as I could tell, he was getting the answers right. I didn't know a lot about treating a person with a bad concussion, but I knew enough to know that he was going to have to be careful for a while.

"Okay, all finished." Alex sat back and removed his now bloodied gloves.

"Colton, do you think you can answer a few questions?" Maggie moved in closer.

"Yeah, but first, how many of us made it here?" He let his eyes close but was alert for the answer.

Maggie hesitated. "Um, there's Charlie, Dante, Luna, Alex, Bri, Shawn, Maya, and Bill. And you and me."

His eyes popped open. "That's it?"

Maggie nodded.

He closed them again and slumped further in his seat.

"What happened out there?"

Colton sighed. "I was watching and radioing you updates like we planned. When the first truck got too close to the stand, I ducked down and hid. I was afraid the zombies would hear me and surround the tree, but they didn't. They just kept on going toward the mall. I thought it was clear and I could radio you again."

He stopped for a second. He looked a little green and his head had to be killing him. "Then this other truck came flying down the exit. I didn't even know it was coming until it was already there. It drove right up to the stand, and the guy in the back pointed his gun right at me. They already knew I was there."

I cringed again. Mack's group had been watching us all along. They spent the past few days learning about us. I felt guilty.

If Shawn and I hadn't been recognized that day at the store, maybe none of this would have happened.

"They ordered me to come down, and there were three of them, so I did. The big one took my rifle and knife and then he wanted me to radio you, but I refused to say what he wanted me to say. That's when he hit me. I don't really know what happened after that. The truck and men must have left me there because, the next thing I knew, I was sitting in the grass, and my head was killing me. A zombie was coming, and all I knew was that I had to get away from it, so I went back up in the tree."

His voice got quieter. "I, um, I couldn't remember where I was for a while. By the time I could, the mall was completely in flames, and I knew that there was no way anyone was still in there. And then I remembered this place, so I climbed down and started running."

There was silence when Colton finished his story. Maggie rested her hand lightly on his shoulder. No one knew what to say. We had all lost so much in the past hours.

Beside me, Rex had been sitting alertly, his nose working overtime as he smelled the air. The hair on the back of my arms rose when he let out a low, threatening growl.

CHAPTER SIXTY-TWO
Day Twenty-Nine

The radio that had somehow made it to the rendezvous with us crackled to life. Maggie kept it close on the off chance that anyone from the group that couldn't make it to us could use it to make contact.

Swinging around, she grabbed for the plastic device. Pressing the button, she raised it nearer to her face and then hesitated. A sudden expression of concern crossed her face. She lowered the radio without saying anything.

"Maggie? What if it's someone from the group?" Charlie questioned her.

"What if it isn't?" She looked dead serious.

Her look of concern was contagious. It seemed to infect everyone else as her words sank in.

We didn't have to wait for an answer as the voice that came through was loud and clear and sent a cold shiver down my spine. They were somewhere nearby.

"I've been searching through the rubble and rolling over bodies for the past hour. Now, admittedly, it's hard to be sure what some of them used to look like. You know, the fire and the zombies can do a lot of damage, but much to my surprise, I have not found any of the faces I was looking for. Except one." Mack paused dramatically, giving me enough time to wonder who he was talking about.

I was looking right at Shawn, Bill, and Maya. Devon was dead. My eyes popped wide with horror when I figured out who he meant. Fallon was the only one unaccounted for, but as far as I knew, she had not been in the mall when we were attacked. At least, none of us had seen her after she left Devon's burial. I knew we all had been holding on to the hope that she ran and hid when the mall was attacked.

"Thing is, this particular body is still alive and kicking. And after you letting me burn down your cozy little home instead of just giving me what I wanted, I'm guessing you want to keep her that way. Do you see my problem?"

The radio fell silent as we all stared at each other with expressions varying from horror, to anger, to confusion.

Shaking myself, I rushed to the front of the house. The sun had broken over the horizon, and it was becoming easier to see with every passing second. Reaching a window that had a view of the overgrown front lawn and street, I carefully moved the edge of the curtain just enough to see out.

Standing just in front of the abandoned vehicle sitting on the curb—bright morning sun lighting up that almost unnaturally orange hair—stood the man I had last seen when I attempted to chop off his arm with a machete. He was looking right at our hideout. My breath caught in my throat when he raised the radio in his hand in a mock salute.

By now, I could feel other bodies pressing close behind me.

"How did he know where we would be?" Charlie was peering out the other side of the window.

No one answered. While everyone else seemed to be thinking over her question or trying to figure out how we were going to escape this time, I studied the man on the street.

I noticed dispassionately that the arm I hacked was actually gone midway between the shoulder and elbow. While I knew that I had cut him badly, I was fairly sure that arm had still been attached, so they must have had to take it the rest of the way off for some reason. I fervently hoped that he suffered. Judging by how he looked, like he lost a lot of weight in a short amount of time, that seemed to be the case. His face appeared almost gaunt.

"There's at least three of them around the back of the house." Dante slipped back into the room. I hadn't noticed he was gone until he came back.

"Okay, that's not a surprise." Maggie scrubbed her face hard with her hands. "Um, okay. We have the weapons: a rifle, three handguns, and some ammo. There're also about a dozen knives. We need to plan carefully what our move is going to be."

"We can't leave Fallon with him," Maya spoke up for the first time.

Maggie turned to look at her. "We are all getting out of here. Including Fallon."

I backed away from the window. I didn't want to look outside anymore. Drawn by the confusion, Luna woke up from where she had been sound asleep curled up on a chair. She stood with one hand buried in Rex's hair, the other hanging on to Shawn's shirt. Big eyes watched the adults around her solemnly. Taking the few steps needed to reach her, I brushed her riot of hair out of her face.

The little girl wasn't the only one who was scared and confused.

From outside, Mack shouted, no longer bothering to use the radio. "You have five minutes to send out the people I want. Do that, and I'll consider letting the rest of you walk away. Don't send them out, and I'm gonna start taking pieces off the one I do have. Think I'll start with her arm. If my shouting doesn't bring the zombies, I'll bet her screaming will."

"We can't let them do that to Fallon." Shawn shifted uneasily next to me.

"No one else is going to die," Maggie repeated her earlier statement.

"Well, if any of them show themselves, I'm thinking that's what's going to happen." Dante gestured toward us.

Maggie thought for a second. "What if we pretend to comply, buy some time, and get them to show themselves? Charlie, if you can see them, I know you could get at least some of them before they knew what was happening."

Charlie frowned but nodded.

"Get me a good vantage point and a rifle. I'll get it done," she sighed.

"What do you mean when you say pretend to comply?" Bill sounded a bit suspicious.

"We send two people out but not any of you. I'm thinking that may throw them off for just long enough for them to mess up. I'm sure it would be the last thing they expect." She looked around in my direction. "He's looking for two people specifically, so we need a man and a woman that aren't from your group."

"Ticktock." The booming voice from outside carried into the house.

"We don't have time to argue over this. Charlie, get that gun and find your spot. That leaves me as the woman. Does anyone want to volunteer to be the guy?"

"I'll do it," Colton volunteered, wobbling unsteadily into the room. "It's my fault they found us. It has to be. They must have followed me. It was stupid of me to come here. I should have known."

"Colton, no." Maggie shook her head at him. "They've seen you before. Besides, whoever goes out there is likely going to have to run from the crossfire. You aren't in any shape for that."

She had a point. Colton looked progressively worse as I got light enough to really see him. He had taken a serious beating. With a defeated expression, he conceded that she was right.

"I'll go. I'll do it," Dante spoke up.

CHAPTER SIXTY-THREE
Day Twenty-Nine

"Who here knows how to use a gun?" Charlie swept back into the room as fast as her limp allowed. A rifle hung from a strap over her shoulder, and I presumed the lumpy-looking duffel bag contained the rest of the weapons.

"I do." Bill raised his hand slightly.

"Alright." She hastily handed him a small gun from the bag. "That's it? No one else knows?" Frowning, Charlie looked over everyone else. I felt like a kid getting a good scolding when she muttered, "Gonna have to fix that if we survive this."

"Here," she continued. "I know you two know which end the bullets come out of." She thrust the remaining guns at both Maggie and Colton. Still muttering, she pulled a box of ammunition from the bag and stalked toward the stairs.

"Here, you take it." Maggie's words interrupted me watching Charlie's exit. She was handing her gun to Dante.

"You sure?" He looked reluctant to take the weapon.

"Yeah." She looked away from him and to the rest of us. "Is everyone clear on what to do?"

I nodded. The plan was probably completely foolhardy, and we were likely all going to die. I couldn't help feeling relieved that they weren't simply handing Shawn and me over to save themselves, but I also felt guilty for that relief.

If I were really a good person, I wouldn't let others risk their lives for mine.

"Okay. We are out of time. Go."

Maggie's order galvanized me into action. Luna was being left in my dubious protection, and I pulled the frightened girl toward the stairs. It felt wrong to hide when everyone else was going to fight, but someone had to try to keep the kid safe, and I'd been elected. I scowled at Shawn when he made the suggestion.

The upstairs bathroom seemed like the best place, and I ushered Luna in as I heard the front door open. The window in a room just down the hall slid open. Charlie must have found her perch.

I wished that I wasn't blind to what was happening outside. Shooing Rex inside after Luna, I followed but didn't close the door all the way. In the unnatural quiet of the abandoned neighborhood, it wasn't hard to pick up the conversation from outside.

"Who the fuck are you?" Mack's voice rang out in the silence.

"Look, we don't know who you are. We just wanted to be with a group, but we'll go. We don't want any trouble." I heard Maggie, but she pitched her voice higher than it was usually. The sound was startling, as was her apparent ability to act. If I hadn't known better, I would have bought the nervous tremble behind those words completely. Then again, those nerves were probably real.

"Is this some kind of joke?" A long pause had me holding my breath in anticipation of what was going to happen next. "You two are not who I want. Who else is in there?" Now a hint of anger seeped through Mack's voice.

Any reply that Maggie may have been going to make was cut off by a loud shot coming from down the hall. My already pounding heart leaped into my throat when Charlie's gruff voice started cursing colorfully. Another shot followed the first.

299

Outside, chaos had erupted. Someone was returning our fire. Bullets made a dull thwack as they hit the sturdy house, and glass shattered somewhere downstairs. Men's voices were yelling, and I picked out Maggie's voice too. Tires screeched to a stop somewhere nearby. And then I heard the inhuman shriek of a zombie.

Stuffed into the dark bathroom behind me, Luna whimpered, reminding me that I was supposed to be watching out for her. "Luna, get in the tub. Get down and hide."

With bullets flying, I hoped the tub would be enough to protect the girl.

More glass shattered downstairs, and someone began shooting from down there too. Shouts and expletives filled the air. Looking back and forth between the cracked door and Luna huddled in the tub, I didn't know what to do. I was supposed to stay with the girl, but what good would that do if everyone on our side was killed while I hid upstairs?

"Zombie!" Maya's warning shout from downstairs made up my mind. A handful of bad men weren't the only dangerous things coming for us. We were making a whole lot of noise.

"Luna, I'm going to go help our people. You stay in this bathroom. Lock the door behind me and don't open it until someone you know tells you to. Do you understand?"

I waited until her wide eyes met mine before swinging the door open. "It's going to be okay. Just stay here."

I heard Charlie cuss again as I stepped back into the hallway. The door pushed open again just as I was about to close it.

"Rex!" I yelled after him, but his tail was already streaking around the corner toward the stairs. There wasn't time to try to get him back. I closed the door firmly and hoped Luna remembered to lock it behind me.

A strange sort of resolve settled around me as I ran for the steps. People were dying. I wasn't stupid enough to think that everyone was going to come out of this alive. Maybe I would be

300

one of them, but I couldn't just hide and wait to find out which side won.

I gripped my machete as I bounded down the stairs. I had already used it on a living person once before, and in defense of family, I would do it again.

I hit the first floor running and plowed headlong into a complete stranger who had just bolted into the room. The two of us crashed to the floor. I somehow managed to keep ahold of my weapon, and I flipped over and jumped to my feet, turning to face the threat.

I stopped dead in my tracks. The man had kept possession of his weapon too, and it was aimed directly at me as he lay sprawled where I knocked him over. His lips quirked up in a cold, half-smile as he cocked the gun.

A shot from so close that it made my ears ring made me jump. I cringed and waited for the pain, but it didn't come. Disbelieving my own eyes, I watched the man slump back onto the floor.

Bill stepped through the door behind the body, gun in hand. "You okay?"

When I nodded, he kept going toward the back of the house.

The fight was still raging, and I tried to shake off my close call as I ran after Bill. Skidding into the kitchen, I found where the worst of the noise was coming from.

The back door was hanging from broken hinges. Two zombies were already inside, and Shawn and Colton were trying to keep them from getting any further into the house. Barking wildly, Rex circled the zombies, confusing the creatures but also adding to the noise and chaos.

Bill stopped next to the kitchen window and was shooting at someone outside before ducking back to avoid return fire. A picture hung on the wall not far from my head shattered as a bullet hit it. I ducked away from the window and tried to angle my way to help fight the zombies.

Someone started screaming outside just as I swung the machete at the first zombie. I jumped and nearly missed my target. Luckily, a hard enough blow to the neck with a machete did enough damage to take the zombie off its feet. The other one was easier to deal with once it was three against one.

"Bri, where's Luna?" Colton swayed unsteadily. The situation wasn't good for him in his condition.

"She's okay. She's locked in the bathroom upstairs."

He nodded. None of them commented on my sudden appearance, which I was grateful for. I had expected Shawn to yell. Instead, he pulled me close for a quick hug before darting across the room to stand next to Bill.

"What's going on?" I directed my question to Colton.

"There's a lot of them. And the noise is drawing the zombies."

"Maggie?"

"I don't know. She and Dante started to run when Charlie first fired. I lost track of them."

"Why are they still fighting?" I had thought that, without their leader, maybe the other group would back off.

"Charlie missed. Or he moved at the last second. I don't know what happened, but the guy with the orange hair was still alive the last time I saw him."

The revelation stunned me into silence.

Mack was still alive. Our plan to get him first had failed.

CHAPTER SIXTY-FOUR
Day Twenty-Nine

A loud crash back at the front of the house had Colton running from the room.

"How many of them can there possibly be?" Bill muttered to himself as he dodged more bullets.

"Too many," Shawn answered him. "This is taking too long and making too much noise. We have to end it."

Another loud crash rocked the house. Shouting followed. Whatever was happening out there, things sounded like they were going worse than back here. With a last look at the pair of guys trying to guard the back, I bolted back to the front.

I leaped over the pool of blood that spread from the man who had almost shot me and darted into the next room. Or what was left of it. Someone had driven a small car through the front of the house.

The mangled front end of the little red sedan had smoke rolling from under the hood. Maya and Alex were struggling to keep from being slashed by a tall man with a frighteningly large knife. Alex's twisted ankle was slowing him down enough that he was practically defenseless, leaving Maya to try to save him.

Colton was there too, but he had his hands full trying to stop the group of zombies that were crawling their way into the house, around the wreckage of the car. I took a step toward him to help, but he caught my movement out of the corner of his eye.

"Help them!" he hissed, looking over.

Changing direction, I approached the knife fight. The man, who had been looking smug, grew more worried when he realized that someone else was in the room. His attack changed to defense, giving Maya a much-needed breather.

I had never purposefully attacked another human before. Not that I had any qualms over it, I would defend my family, whichever way I needed to, but I didn't know how to go about it. Frowning, I attempted to circle the guy, leaving him in a position where either Maya or I were always at his back.

Seeing what I was doing, he lunged at me with his knife. I barely dodged out of the way, avoiding getting a slice that would have probably killed me slowly. His attack sent Rex, who had been at my heels, charging into the room.

He didn't make a sound as he leaped through the air and bit down hard on the arm holding the knife. The man didn't have time to even react before Maya swept in behind him and stabbed him in the back.

There was no time to stop or contemplate on what just happened. Colton was slowly losing the battle to keep the zombies out. Whirling around, I darted to help him, using the machete on several zombies. By the time the last one had been killed, the hole that the car punched through the wall was partially filled with corpses.

The gunfire was slowing down. I hoped that meant that we were winning and not that we were running out of ammo. The front of the house was quiet for the moment, so I turned around and ran toward the back.

I hadn't made it to the kitchen yet when I knew that something had changed while I was gone. I no longer heard the sound of bullets raining into the kitchen. Instead, there was an ominous silence. Sliding to a stop, I peered around the corner before rushing into the room.

It was empty.

The door still hung open. The dead zombies still lay on the floor, but Shawn and Bill were both missing.

I had a flashback of Shawn's words just before I ran from the room.

"No! They wouldn't be that stupid," I said it out loud. In reality, I knew that leaving the protection of the house was exactly the kind of thing that they would do if they thought they were saving their people.

"What's wrong?" Maya had come in behind me.

"Shawn and Bill were here two minutes ago. Now they're not." I looked at her, distressed.

Her eyes darted around, assessing. "That foolhardy man." She headed for the open door.

Following Maya, I went into the backyard. No one shot at us, so I guessed that was a good sign. Maybe we weren't running out of bullets after all.

A single shot rang from around the side of the house. Trying to be stealthy in the open yard wasn't really happening, so the two of us just ran as fast as we could toward the sound.

Rounding the corner of the house, I almost crashed into Maya's back. She had come to a sudden stop. The reason was easy to figure out. There, in the small stretch of grass between the house and the next, we found Bill and Shawn . . . and Mack, holding a gun to Maggie's side.

"The gang's all here!" he sang mockingly, flashing a predatory smile at us. "That's good news. Things are getting a little too hot here for my comfort, but I didn't want to go without the two of you. Even better, now I've got four."

Maggie looked supremely ticked off, but other than a bruise that was already forming on her cheek, she seemed okay. I eyed the gun, wondering how proficient Mack was with it without his arm. His grip looked steady.

The others must have been wondering the same thing as they all had stopped a wary distance from him.

"Now, I don't know who this lovely lady is, but I don't, as of yet, have any quarrel with her. You, four, on the other hand, well, that ship has sailed. So how about we all walk over to my truck, nice and easy, and you all use the duct tape in the back to tie each other up. Don't give me any problems and I won't have to kill this pretty thing."

There was no way I was going to follow those instructions, but I couldn't just let Maggie die. The others looked as conflicted as I was, and Maggie wasn't giving us any hints on what to do. She stood stiffly, her face blank.

The sickening smirk on Mack's face slipped a little. He jabbed the end of the gun at Maggie. "I don't like repeating myself."

Not sure what else to do, I took a slow step toward the road, my mind racing to come up with a plan. I didn't know how we would rescue Maggie without getting one of us killed in the process.

I took another step when something caught my eye.

Charlie was leaning around the front corner of the house, rifle aimed.

Too busy trying to keep an eye on the four of us, Mack failed to notice the biggest threat of all.

She didn't miss the second time.

"Gotcha this time, asshole." Charlie looked like she had been vindicated. Everyone else looked stunned. They must have missed her approach too.

Wiping the bits of blood that splattered on her face and neck, Maggie sprang back into action. "Is everyone okay?"

"Everyone who was in the house is just fine." Charlie limped her way to our group. "Dante?"

Maggie frowned and shook her head before starting toward the back door. "We need to get everyone and get out of here. Now."

It didn't take long to gather the rest of our group and get out of there.

The sun was higher in the sky than I would have expected. We heard growls from what sounded like at least a dozen zombies coming from a couple of yards over. It wouldn't be long before they made it to us. At least, it seemed, any fast zombies within hearing distance had already reached us and been dealt with. The ones that were showing up now were the slow variety, not that that would be much help if too many of them came at once.

Maggie cautiously edged her way out of the house, in the lead. We were fairly sure that all of Mack's followers were either dead or had run away, but there was no way to know for certain.

Luna was hanging on to the tail of my shirt, and her tight grip was causing my shirt to rub uncomfortably on my neck. I knew the kid had been terrified to be left alone in the dark bathroom. The experience must have brought back her ordeal, trying to survive all alone, waiting for her mother to come for her, so I didn't say anything.

After the noise from the fight, the silence that had now settled over the street was even stranger than it had been before. It seemed heavy and expectant.

We crept down the driveway. I stepped carefully over the body of a zombie and then over another body—this time one of Mack's men. We were near the street when Rex suddenly darted away from the group and toward the black pickup that was parked sideways in the street.

The dog circled the truck fast before jumping up to put his front paws on the side of the bed. Trying to peer over the side, he whined.

Shawn looked over his shoulder at me worriedly. The group shifted uncomfortably before Maggie, Bill, and Shawn started toward the truck. Hanging back a few seconds, morbid curiosity got the best of the rest of us as we followed a few steps behind them.

Bill was the first to see what was inside the truck, naturally. The stricken look on his face alerted the others that they weren't going to like what they see. The next second, Shawn and then Maggie both looked inside.

We were close enough to the truck now that I noticed the steadily dripping red that was escaping from the tailgate end of the truck and pooling in a large puddle on the pavement. I watched it drip for a second before swallowing hard and taking another step.

I stepped right into a hard chest. Eyes finally coming away from that puddle of red, I found Shawn right in front of me.

"Don't." He shook his head at me slightly.

"Who is it?" My voice was steadier than I felt.

"Don't look, okay?" He waited for me to nod before he answered, "Fallon."

I blinked at him, trying to sort through myriad complicated emotions. There was anger and fear and grief, but I was just overwhelmingly tired.

"We need to get out of here before too many zombies show up." Charlie backed away, looking into the back of the truck.

"At least she's been spared the indignity of turning." Maggie gently turned Bill away from the sight. "Charlie's right. We need to get out of this area while we still can."

CHAPTER SIXTY-FIVE
Day Thirty

Being so close to a previously populated area had a few perks. It hadn't been hard to find another house to spend the night in, a few miles away from the scene of the fight. It also hadn't been hard to find a couple of vehicles with full gas tanks and enough food and water to give us a good start.

As soon as the sun was up, we were gone. We didn't have much of a plan except to go south, keeping watch for a place to start over along the way.

We still had more questions than answers, but we were the ones who had survived. That had to count for something.

Ahead of us, a small face surrounded by wild curly hair appeared in the back window of the SUV. Waving, Luna smiled when I waved back at her before disappearing back into their vehicle. Smiling a little, I had no idea how my face was even still capable of that expression. I turned to look at Shawn driving beside me.

Then again, the world as we knew it had ended, but in the chaos, I had found family. That was certainly something to smile over. Shawn felt me staring and looked my way. He smiled a little back at me, not the full-blown grin that I loved. It was too soon for that, but it was enough.

As long as we had each other, it was enough.

"We're going to be okay." He echoed my thoughts.

"Yeah."

"Yes, we are," Maya chimed in from the back seat.

I nodded. "It's not going to be easy. People are only going to get worse."

"We stay together," Shawn quietly said. "No matter what happens next, it's going to be okay so long as we have each other."

Do you like fantasy/horror stories?
Here are samples of other stories
you might enjoy!

THE
FOUR
BARISTAS
OF THE
APOCALYPSE

GEOFF BLACKWELL

CHAPTER ONE

The start of the end of the world should be a pretty hard thing to miss. But in a peaceful Australian paddock, under a moonlit sky, four friends on a camping trip were giving it their best shot.

Two tents were pitched side by side. From one, came the sound of static.

Cora rolled over and regarded the other occupant of her tent with a drowsy glare. "Max, I'm trying to sleep."

"Sorry, won't be long. I really need to check the cricket score, and I can't get a signal on my phone." Max took his cricket very seriously.

Cora could have cared less about cricket but only with a significant effort. Sleep, on the other hand, was something she currently felt very strongly about. "One minute," she muttered, pulling her sleeping bag over her head. "If you're going to drag me out here to the middle of nowhere and make me bushwalk all day, the least you can do is not keep me up all night with your crackly radio."

"It's weird," replied Max as he delicately adjusted a dial. "Every time I find a station, it keeps fading away." Reception in their isolated location was often poor but not usually this bad. And, being in Australia, it normally wasn't too hard to find somebody talking about cricket.

The radio crackled and hissed and then an urgent voice emerged from the static. ". . . defence forces have been overwhelmed. Parliament house has been destroyed, and the prime minister is unaccounted for. Attacks have also been reported in Washington, London, Paris, Beijing and . . . " The voice faded and became white noise yet again.

Cora's head re-emerged and she stared at Max with wide eyes. "Can you get that station back?"

"I'm trying."

Another voice cut through the static. ". . . know where they came from! These big boxes just appeared in the sky, and then things started coming out and shooting . . . " Once again, the transmission died.

Sitting up, Cora hugged her knees to her chest. "What on Earth is going on?"

"Don't know," replied Max, "but it sure as hell doesn't sound good." He hunted for another station, but, when his continued efforts proved to be in vain, he switched the radio off. "Let's wake up Cam and Mel. Maybe their radio can get something."

He stooped and made his way out of the tent, but when Cora tried to follow, she found her way barred by Max's legs.

"Hey, out of the way."

"Cora," he breathed, as he slowly moved aside, "you've got to see this."

"See what?" With the way clear, she slipped out of the tent. "Whoa."

Overhead, the night sky was ablaze. Silent trails of fire streaked in all directions across the firmament, bathing the surrounding countryside in flickering golden light.

"Max, what is this? I've never seen anything like it before in my life."

The unearthly light illuminated Max's upturned face. "That makes two of us. I think this camping trip is over. We need to head for home and find out what the hell is going on."

Cora nodded, her expression grave. "No arguments here. We need some answers." She flinched as a particularly bright streak of fire flamed across the sky. "And I want a roof over my head."

Max strode over to the other tent, which was pitched a few metres from their own, and scratched on the canvas. "Hey, guys." There was no response. "Guys," he repeated, raising his voice. "Wakey, wakey. We need to talk."

Muted rustling came from within the tent, followed by a sleepy voice. "Mate, I don't care what the cricket score was. We can talk about it in the morning."

"Cam, this isn't about cricket. You and Mel need to get out here."

There was a pause. "And it's definitely not about cricket?"

"Yes, you idiot."

"Yes, it's not; or yes, it is?"

"Cam! This is not about the bloody cricket! Right now, I don't give a rat's testicles about cricket! Get your arse out here!"

Cam was so shocked by this statement, he was moving before he even realised it. Anything that made Max rank cricket lower than rodent genitalia had to be serious.

His disheveled head emerged from the tent. "Mate, this better be—"

Few things could make Cam stop talking mid-sentence. The dazzling light show overhead was apparently one of them.

"What the hell . . .?"

"Exactly," replied Max. "Wake up Mel and get packing, dude. We need to head back to town, to find out what's happening."

Blinking sleepily, Cam emerged from the tent and slowly turned, taking in the spectacle above them. "This leaves New Year's Eve for dead. It's like the end of the world or something."

"Yep," agreed Max, "and, judging by the stuff we heard on the radio, it just might be."

Another voice emerged from the tent. "If you losers don't shut up and let me sleep, it's going to be the end of your world."

Cam's face grew anxious. "Er . . . Mel, honey, I think maybe you'd better come out of the tent."

There was a pregnant silence. The streaks of fire continued overhead. Crickets chirped. Cam began to wonder whether he should be more worried about the fireballs or the silence. Or, to be more precise, the end of the silence, whenever it might come. It came.

"You think I'd better come out of the tent? *You* think I'd better come out of the tent!? Do you want to know what *I* think?"

Cam assumed this to be a rhetorical question, at least until the silence that followed became pregnant again. This time, possibly with twins.

"Um, of course, honey." He looked despairingly at Max, who smiled the blissful smile of a person not required to take any part in the conversation. "What do you think?"

"What do I think?" replied Mel in honeyed tones. "What do I think? Do you really want to know?" All traces of honey vanished. "I think you don't really want to know what I think! You might think you want to know what I think or you might think that I should think you think you want to know what I think, but I don't think you know what I think, and I don't think you even want to know what I think! But I'm going to tell you anyway! I think I am sleep-deprived and coffee-deprived and patience-deprived and tonight, I am going to get some sleep, and, tomorrow, I am going to get some coffee and if you're a very, very, lucky little man, I might also get some patience because, right now, I have none and let me make it very clear for you that there is not a thing on this planet or off it that is going to make me get out of this tent, so kindly just SHUT THE HELL UP!" There was a pause, presumably for a breath. "And stop whistling!"

Cam and Max looked at each other. Neither were whistling. Yet, now, in the post-rant silence, they could both very distinctly hear a whistling sound. They glanced over at Cora. No whistling there either. Slowly, as one, they all looked up.

The fireballs continued to streak overhead. All except for one. One fireball hung motionless in the sky above them. Motionless but not unchanging. The fireball grew, and, as it grew, the whistling sound became louder and louder.

"Er, guys," said Max, staring fixedly up at the flaming orb. "I really think we need to get out of here. Really, really. Like now. Like yesterday." He started edging away from the tents and in the direction of their two cars, parked at the edge of the clearing. "C'mon, Cora. Cam, I don't know how you're going to do it, but you need to get Mel up and moving. ASAP."

The fireball now lit up the clearing like a mini-sun, and Cora had to raise her voice to be heard above the whistling. "It's coming in too fast, Max. There's no time for the cars. Everybody, down!"

Diving for the ground, she wrapped her arms around her head, and Max and Cam followed suit as the whistling became a roar and the fireball slammed into the space between the two cars, sending both cartwheeling in opposite directions. In a violent maelstrom of heat, noise, and dirt, the blast wave washed over them.

Gradually, the noise subsided. Three groggy, dirt-encrusted heads looked up. Blinking, Cam wiped his eyes and looked towards his tent. It was gone. Staggering to his feet, he stared at the empty patch of tumbled earth. "Mel!"

Unsteadily, Max and Cora also stood. Wiping his face and brushing the dirt off his clothes, Max looked around. His tent was gone, too. Smoke rose from the area where the fireball had hit, and his car lay on its roof several metres from the point of impact. Of Cam's car, there was no sign. The waters of the river were choppy from the blast wave, and bobbing up and down in the wavelets were two objects, indistinct under the light of the moon and the fireballs still streaking overhead. Swallowing, he tapped Cam's shoulder and pointed. "Mate, I think those might be the tents." He began to take off his shoes. "Come on."

With a groggy blink, Cam looked at the river. "Huh?" Realisation dawned. "Mel! I'm coming, baby!" Ripping off his T-shirt, he attempted to remove one leg from his pants while hopping on the other towards the river, but, after about three hops, he fell flat on his face.

"Guys," said Cora, staring at the spot where Cam and Mel's tent had been. "Keep your pants on." She glanced over at Cam's sprawled figure. "And I mean that literally." She pointed. "I don't think Mel is in the river."

The pile of raw earth moved slightly, and a fourth disheveled head rose up from it. Mel blinked and spat out some dirt. "Okay." She gasped. "Fine. So you got me out of the tent."

If you enjoyed this sample, look for
The Four Baristas of the Apocalypse
on Amazon.

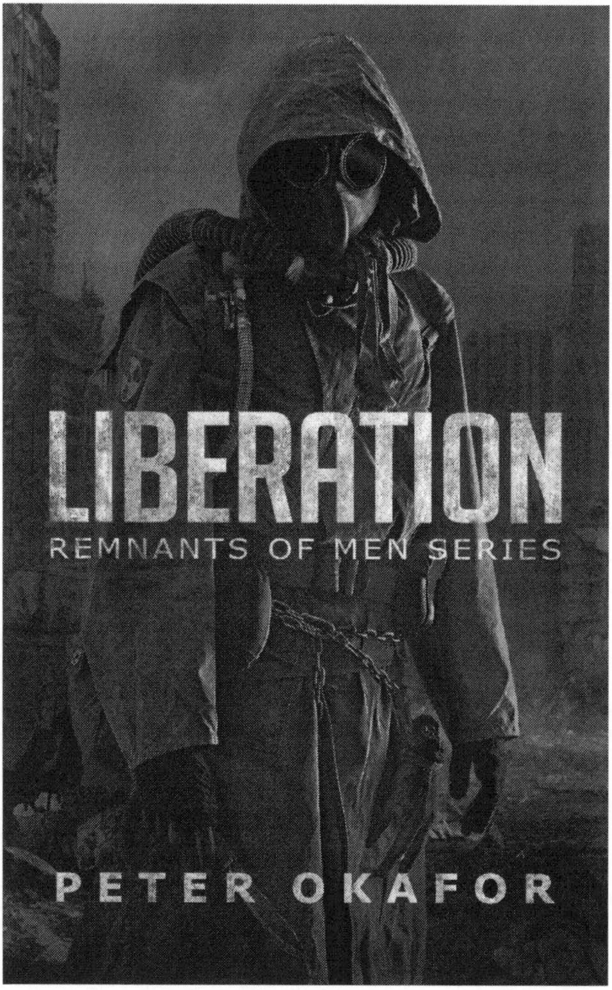
LIBERATION
REMNANTS OF MEN SERIES
PETER OKAFOR

CHAPTER ONE
Runner of Rat Town

There were no clouds in the sky, nothing but a grey mass stretching to ends unknown. The last yellow sunshine was seen twenty years ago. He was not born then, but everyone knew the tales of those wonderful rays that would kiss the skin with great warmth.

Those days were memories to some and nothing but a myth to others like Runner. He did not care much for a large ball of fire. All he wanted was to join the well-paid guards of Section 5, and that was the reason he was standing before the first dead body he had seen since birth.

He stood motionless and squeezed his face, covering his nose with his hands to keep the obnoxious smell away. It was the body of an elderly woman half burnt by a fierce radioactive storm that swept beyond the domed comforts of MegaCityOne at an hour interval. A silver handgun sat on the palm of her right hand, and resting on her body was a dead baby with a bullet hole in his head. There wasn't much investigation to the horrid scene as all connections seemed to be in place.

Runner felt a blunt pain in his heart. He knew that was very much a fate destined for half the poor folks that lived outside the protective dome of MegaCityOne.

His best friend, Troy Decker, hissed. "Come on, Runner. She suffered a better fate than any of us would hope."

Runner tightened the belt that held his gears around his waist. It was hard to be brave when the entire world wanted a piece of him. It was even harder to survive a world where air and water could cost a man his life savings. No thanks to Reinhardt Reddit, the tyrant that left half the planet at the mercy of radiation.

He raised his hand and gazed at an old wristwatch that had all its silver coating worn out by time, but it still displayed time accurately.

"10:30 AM. Oh my god!" He raised his gaze to the sky. "Oh my god! We have less than five minutes. Move, everyone, move."

Dust grew in the air like fumes from an exhaust. He inhaled the air, the sour taste unwelcomed on his tongue. He curved his hands over his brow and looked further. In the distance, a large storm of dust was raging forward. Runner turned around to see how many were behind. He waved his hand and shouted at the top of his voice, signaling a crowd of wayfarers to hasten.

Troy grasped the end of his torn beige jacket. "We've gotta go, man. We-got-to-go." He stressed the last words.

"Where is the cargo?" Runner asked, but Troy gave no answer.

Runner seized him by the neck of his jacket. "Troy, where is the cargo?"

"I don't know . . . I kinda left it behind. You know, the storm and all that shit made me panic." Troy looked woeful.

"What do you mean you left it behind? That's our ticket to never going hungry again, our ticket to Section 5 and then to the comforts of MegaCityOne—the paradise in this damned wasteland. You know there are people in that truck. Human beings, Troy . . . human beings."

Runner took another look at the raging storm. It was like the waves of a restless sea, one of those in the tales of Old Max—his colony's mad mechanic. The old man had told him once that the storms were poisonous radiation that could melt the skin in seconds. He didn't know how true that was, but the melting part of the story—that was definitely certain.

"Give me your cloak." He stretched his arm towards Troy.

Troy pulled his long black cloak and handed it to Runner. "What do you want with it?"

"Just get the others to safety." Runner threw the cloak on and made sure no part of his body was exposed.

He used a dusty turban to wrap his head and then put on dark goggles to protect his vivid brown eyes.

"Are you crazy, Runner? I know for certain you don't have any more stash of Sense pills left. You won't last a heartbeat out there," Troy spoke sternly.

"Just go. I will see you in five."

Runner paused for a moment and inhaled deeply. He ran into the growing storm of hot fog and dust. His feet sank into scattered scraps of bricks and metals as he struggled to push forward. The heat was becoming unbearable, and it stung his flesh with a burning sensation. His goggles protected his eyes, but he could barely see the cargo truck that was a few steps away from him.

He managed through the sinking scraps and reached the window of the truck. Everything was covered by dust. He used his hand to wipe the dust off the window and peeped. There were men, women, and children clustered together at one end, awaiting nature's wrath. Runner slammed his fist on the window, and a man wounded it down.

"What happened?"

"We can't get our truck to move. We are all going to die here!" the man screamed in confusion.

"Calm down." Runner urged. "How many do you carry?"

"Roughly forty," the man answered hysterically.

"Okay . . . okay." Runner opened the door and pulled the man down from the truck. "You see that storm in the distance?"

The man nodded.

"It will be here in two minutes. Gather everyone together. We can make it to the city gate before that storm hits us. Can you do that?"

The man nodded again and turned around, calling everyone out. They were all a bunch of the big city inhabitants, who—for some reason—had gone out of the city. They knew nothing of life outside the comforts of MegaCityOne. Well, it seemed nature had a lesson to teach.

Runner had survived by guiding passengers through the ruins of the barren waste beyond his home. It paid enough to keep him fed. Before, he never did care. Wealthy folks meant big bucks for him, and that was all that really mattered. But staring at their faces, his heart would never free him from torment if he abandoned them to die.

"Move! Move!" Runner bellowed.

The passengers rushed down the vehicles. They moved like a herd in a stampede, running towards the towering gate of the city. Runner felt the discomfort on his skin grow intense. The storm would hit them soon. He could feel it. He needed to push them to press forward with haste, or they would all die horrible deaths.

With each stride, the gates of MegaCityOne grew closer. Troy had already made it into the city with a few others that had left earlier, and he beckoned at Runner to move faster.

A loud thud sounded. Runner stopped and turned quickly to see an elderly man who had stumbled into a pile of rubble. The poor man's right foot was caught in blocks of broken concrete. That moment, Runner's mind was conflicted. He had two choices: help the man and get obliterated or continue onwards to the safety of the domed city.

In a quick decision, he took a step forward. Runner leaned towards him and stretched his hand to reach for the man. The storm was mere inches away.

"Give me your hand," Runner yelled.

The words had barely left his mouth when he found himself dragged backwards by an unknown person.

"Let him go, Runner. You can't help him." He heard Troy's voice.

Troy pulled him through the gate. The storm engulfed the man, melting his flesh quickly into flakes of red-hot ash. The enormous metal gate slammed shut to prevent the storm from passing through.

Runner sank to the ground on both knees and hung his head in disappointment. People die all the time—he knew that—and the fact that mortality rates had really surged was not a fictional account. For some reason, the death of the man seemed to weigh heavy on his heart.

A hand came upon his shoulder. "I don't understand why you feel this need to save everyone in trouble. It is not your fault that a man cannot walk outside the dome without his gas mask. It is not your fault that the skies can only manage acid rains. These folks knew the cost of surviving in this world before they set out."

"Perhaps they shouldn't have." Runner stood to his feet. "A man risks his life on promises of better days for what? To ensure that his children endure a life of shit and piss? Look around you, Troy. Things can never get better than this. A man would have a better time choosing to ingest poison than living in this sewer pit we call home."

Troy put his arm over Runner's shoulder. "It is the life we find ourselves in, my friend. Come, let's go get our pay from the chief enforcer."

Finally, something good that could come out of all the despair he had endured. That pay was the light at the end of a tunnel. He could literally hear his rumbling stomach, how deeply it cried for sustenance.

Runner trailed behind his friend as they ascended the stairs of a towering outpost that overlooked the gates of Rat Town. The slum town was his home and one among ten colonies that had become the slums of MegaCityOne. The lingering smile on Troy's face only proved one thing to be true—the mere thought of a full belly could make a slum dweller happy for weeks. But truth be told, Troy wasn't the only one that bore that joy. Runner was no different; he was only good at concealing his enthusiasm.

"Guys, guys, guysss . . . " a voice called from behind.

Runner missed a step and almost stumbled as he heard that voice. In the entirety of Rat Town and even the MegaCityOne itself, only one person made him so tense—Dope "Skittish" Davies. Nothing good ever came from associating with Dope, literally. He was an only child to the chief enforcer, an ideal role model to any aspiring psychopath.

"Here we go," Troy muttered without turning to look behind.

Runner turned around to face Dope. "What do you want, Skittish?" He had said that, having a good idea what was about to come.

"My father asked me to take care of . . . whatever it is he asked of you," Dope said, waving his arm incessantly.

Unlike Runner who was of average height and lean build, Dope was a short, burly boy, thickly muscular with powerful shoulders that could intimidate anyone. But Runner knew within all that sinew was a pathetic excuse for a boy who found pleasure in mockery and guile.

"Where is the cargo?" Dope asked, looking around.

Runner knew this was coming. He grimaced at the thought of something far worse. "We . . . " He glanced at Troy. "I didn't come with the cargo. I ran into a bit of a situation, and I chose to secure the passengers first."

"Oooh!" Dope raised his gaze to the sky, putting his hands on his waist. "You're so not getting paid today."

If you enjoyed this sample, look for

Liberation
on Amazon.

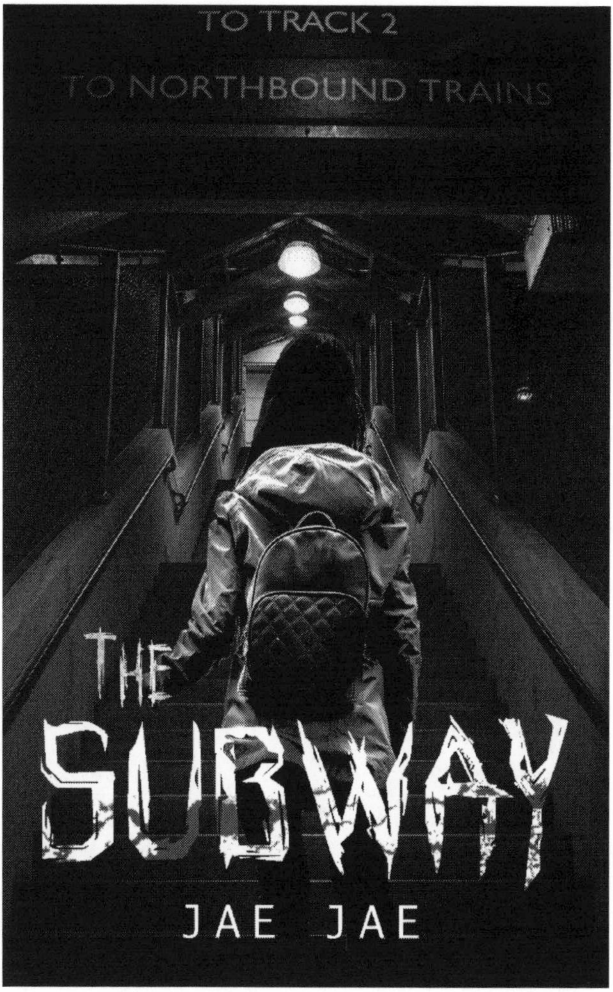
TO TRACK 2
TO NORTHBOUND TRAINS
THE
SUBWAY
JAE JAE

CHAPTER ONE

I hated riding the subway. Not just any subway either. The subways in New York City, to be exact. I hated those things with an unyielding passion. There were no ifs, ands, or buts about it.

Who wanted to ride in an underground train that smelled like stale play dough and old people? Maybe it was just me, maybe I was over exaggerating, or maybe I was losing my sense of smell, but that was definitely the smell that aggressively assaulted my nose whenever I stepped foot in a subway car.

I hated how crowded they were too. I would receive an elbow to the ribs or a hard shove from someone's shoulder almost every time I was forced to ride that thing. At the end of my ride, I always walked out looking like I just went ten rounds with a mildly ferocious ten-year-old.

There was never anywhere to sit. If all the seats were taken by the time I got on—and they usually were—then I would be forced to stand among the crowd of swaying bodies, where perverts would "accidentally" rub up against me. It was like a game of musical chairs where the loser would get felt up by a bunch of strange old men as a punishment.

As if all that wasn't bad enough, the ride itself took at least twenty minutes and I had to ride the damn thing twice.

Why did I have to ride it twice?

Well, that's because I lived right outside my school's district. So *technically*, the school bus couldn't pick me up from my house, but we lived close enough that I could walk to the subway station in the city and get a ride closer to school and walk the rest of the way every single day.

I was eighteen. I should have been riding back and forth in my own car but no. My parents, who were definitely using their parent logic on this, thought it would be better if I rode the subway every day, despite the fact that I kept reminding them that I was bound to be kidnapped, robbed, shot, or a mix of all three by doing so. I did live in New York after all. Worse things had happened.

I made it my job to constantly remind them that when they saw me on the news with the caption "Missing Girl" above my hideous high school ID picture, it was going to be all their fault. With all the money I spent riding the subway, I could have bought my own car by now, but did I? No. Apparently, I wasn't ready for that big of a responsibility yet.

This is where you insert the eye roll and dramatic sigh.

Basically, they trusted me to venture into a crowd of people that could easily be hiding serial killers and knife-wielding maniacs—I really needed to quit watching so much *Law and Order*—but they didn't trust me with my own car.

Parent logic.

However, what happened on that one day I rode the subway, that one day that was supposed to be just like any other, I don't think anyone saw it coming.

Not me, not my parents, not the unsuspecting passengers on the subway.

No one.

The day where I would really be in my very own episode of *Law and Order*, and unfortunately, I'd end up being the victim.

Lucky me.

*   *   *

Whoever decided to make an alarm clock sound like the siren for the end of the world was an idiot. If I didn't die from the small heart attack the stupid thing gave me, then I'd end up smashing Satan's creation against my nightstand.

I'm currently on alarm clock number three.

Lucky for my current alarm clock, I wasn't in a *complete* hostile mood when it abruptly woke me this time.

Groaning, I blindly slammed my hand down, knocking various items off my nightstand until I found the snooze button and rolled out of my warm bed, blankets and all.

I landed on the hardwood floor with a loud *thud*.

My mom's voice rang from downstairs not even two seconds after.

"Gemma, what was that?! You better not have broken anything!"

Yeah, Mom, don't ask if I was the *thing* that fell and possibly broke.

I didn't even bother getting up or untangling myself from my blanket to answer her. I just rolled over to the door like some sort of deformed giant baked potato and yelled, "It was just a shirt!"

"What kind of shirt makes that sound when it falls?!" she yelled back. I could almost picture the deadpan look on her face.

Did I leave out the part where I was *in* the shirt when it fell?

"Well, I'm fine anyway! Thanks for asking!" I yelled back down.

"Just hurry up! You're going to be late!"

There was a slight pause before she added, "Again!"

Groaning again, I sat up and threw off my blanket, making goose bumps instantly rise against my skin as I slowly made my way across the hall to the bathroom.

I even made an extra effort to drag my feet.

Who cared if I was late? Was I really missing out on something important?

Lord forbid I miss out on my science teacher teaching us that the nucleus was the powerhouse of the cell.

Or was it the mitochondria?

See? I couldn't even bother to remember.

And don't even get me started on the whole y=mx+b thing.

I'd *definitely* need that information later in life.

After showering and doing my basic morning routine, I brushed out my hair so it no longer looked like a bird had made a nest in it, and it fell in its usual lifeless sheet down to my shoulders.

I got dressed in a simple white long-sleeved shirt, black zip-up hoodie, and jeans that my mother had bought me for Christmas last year, claiming that they hugged the curves I had, but I was pretty sure they were nonexistent.

I'm sure she only said it to try and make me feel better.

She got an A for effort.

After slipping into a pair of Converse, I did a once-over in the mirror to make sure I passed the 'Acceptable to be seen by society today' test, which really just consisted of me making sure I didn't look like I had been living in a cave for the last three months before I went outside.

Satisfied with my look, I grabbed my backpack off the desk in the corner of my room and bounded down the stairs one at a time. I tried the whole taking two steps at a time thing once, and let's just say my face paid the price.

As soon as I reached the bottom step, the smell of bacon assaulted my nose, making my mouth water. Stepping into the kitchen, I saw my mom—her dark and slightly graying hair pulled into a messy bun—still in her pajamas, leaning over a frying pan full of bacon.

My dad, with his also graying black hair, was sitting in a chair at the kitchen table with a newspaper in one hand and a white "World's #1 Dad" mug—one of the many I had gotten him for three Christmases in a row—filled with coffee in the other. He looked like a dad straight out of a TV series. Who even still reads newspapers these days?

He was dressed in a white button-up shirt and a black tie with purple polka dots—another Christmas gift from me—black slacks, and a pair of glasses was sitting on the bridge of his nose.

Walking over, I plucked two pieces of bacon off his plate and smiled sweetly at him as he looked up from his newspaper with his eyebrows raised.

"You weren't going to eat it anyway," I said in response to his look as I shoved a piece into my mouth.

I walked over to my baby brother, Aiden, who was sitting in his highchair with a bowl full of, for lack of a better word, slop. I hope he hadn't been eating that.

I ruffled his fluffy brown hair before I leaned down and whispered in his ear, making sure I was still loud enough so that my parents could hear me clearly. "If you want live to see three, I wouldn't eat that," I said, gesturing to the unidentifiable contents that I'm pretty sure had just moved in his bowl.

In response to my whispered warning, Aiden smiled up at me like he knew exactly what I was talking about. My dad chuckled and my mom turned around to glare at me.

I shrugged and kissed her on the cheek before heading towards the front door.

Before I opened the front door, I yelled over my shoulder, unable to stop myself, "Only eat the bacon, anything else and you have two options: hospital or the grave!"

I quickly ran out the door before my mom could throw the frying pan at me. I could hear my dad's laughter echoing outside before I shut the door.

My mom would swear up and down that she was a good cook, but after last Thanksgiving, I beg to differ. That year, we had pizza for Thanksgiving, so I think that pretty much explained itself.

I couldn't help but laugh, then instantly checked to make sure none of my neighbors were out and saw me laughing by myself. I continued munching on my last piece of bacon before I made my way down the sidewalk, the chilly air stinging my cheeks, and toward the subway, not knowing what exactly would be in store for me when I got there.

If you enjoyed this sample, look for
The Subway
on Amazon.

ACKNOWLEDGEMENTS

This story would not have been possible without help from some very important people.

To the real life Shawn and Luna, thank you for putting up with the endless hours I've spent lost in this story. Thank you for listening to me rant when the characters decided to tell the story differently than I had planned, and for your input when a scene was not working out.

To other friends and family who have encouraged me to keep going even when it felt like I was going nowhere, thank you.

And to the many Wattpad readers who have shown me nothing but love and support through this entire journey, you all have restored my faith in humanity. Never stop being the kind of people you are, the people I have enjoyed talking with and getting to know.

So much love to you all.

ABOUT THE AUTHOR

I am a thirty something mother to one amazing daughter, who continually challenges me to be better at everything I do. Our family lives in the north east part of the US, but we love to travel and see new things.

I have had a life-long love affair with books, but didn't work up the courage to try writing until about three years ago. After stumbling upon Wattpad, my addiction to creating these new little worlds grew. Hearing from my readers that one of my stories made them laugh, or cry, has become one of the highlights of my life. Reading can take you on an incredible journey, and if I can bring my readers even a small amount of happiness, then I consider my writing time well spent.

Made in the USA
Middletown, DE
11 December 2024

66671961R00203